DON'T
TRUST
HIM

BOOKS BY KAREN KING

Psychological Thrillers

The Stranger in My Bed

The Perfect Stepmother

The Mother-in-Law

The Family Reunion

The Retreat

Girl Next Door

Romantic Comedies

Snowy Nights at the Lonely Hearts Hotel

The Year of Starting Over

Single All the Way

DON'T TRUST HIM

KAREN KING

bookouture

Published by Bookouture in 2025

An imprint of Storyfire Ltd.
Carmelite House
50 Victoria Embankment
London EC4Y 0DZ

www.bookouture.com

The authorised representative in the EEA is Hachette Ireland
8 Castlecourt Centre
Dublin 15 D15 XTP3
Ireland
(email: info@hbgi.ie)

ISBN: 978-1-83618-363-1
eBook ISBN: 978-1-83618-362-4

PROLOGUE

SARAH

November
Then

The rain lashes down on the windscreen, making the visibility really poor. My hands are shaking as I clench the steering wheel and focus on the treacherous road ahead. It's bad enough having the darkness to contend with but this torrential rain makes it ten times worse. I grit my teeth, my knuckles white as I steer my Peugeot through the storm, my headlights on full beam so that I can negotiate the bends safely. Suddenly a streak of lightning zigzags across the black sky followed by a loud clap of thunder, startling me. The car swerves and I frantically right it again.

'Mum!' Liam screams from the back seat, his voice ragged with fear. 'I'm scared!'

Damn, Liam was fast asleep when I strapped him in and it takes a lot to wake him so I hoped he'd stay asleep for the entire journey. He's quite sensible for his seven years but like most young kids he hates storms. So do I, especially driving in one, but I had no choice. I couldn't risk even one more night at Charlie's. I had to get us away. Now I need to be strong, to focus, to keep us both safe.

'Close your eyes and go back to sleep, darling. We'll soon be there.'

Another streak of lightning. Another clap of thunder. Liam screams even louder. 'Mummy, I want to go back. I'm scared.'

Me too, son, me too. I take a deep breath to calm myself down and grip the steering wheel so tight that my knuckles hurt. 'It won't be long now,' I reassure him. How can I tell him that we can never go back to the house he's looked on as home for the past couple of months? That we've fled because our lives are in terrible danger?

The rain is stronger now, thrashing down onto the roof of the car. I have the wipers on full but can barely see through the windscreen. It's too dangerous to carry on. I need to find somewhere to pull up until the rain eases.

'Mummy! I want to sit in the front with you.' I can hear the raw fear in Liam's voice, then a click as he unbuckles his seatbelt.

'No, don't do that, Liam!' I look in the mirror and see that he's standing up. 'Sit down, Liam, and buckle up! Please!'

Lightning streaks across the sky again, illuminating a dark shadow in the road. It's a tree, the storm must have knocked it down. Thunder crashes as I hit my brakes but the car doesn't slow down. We're still heading towards the tree. Bile rising in my throat, I stamp on the brakes again and scream at Liam to fasten his seatbelt.

There's only one thing I can do. Frantically muttering prayers, I turn the steering wheel away from the tree towards the bush at the side of the road, hoping that Liam is now safely strapped in.

Then there's a bang and everything goes dark.

SEPTEMBER

1

SARAH

'Check out the hunk with his two little girls. I wouldn't kick him out of bed.' My best friend Tasha nudges me and signals to the left with her eyes as we stand outside the school gates, with her son, Ryan, and my son, Liam. It's the first day back after the summer holidays and both boys are messing around, reluctant to go into school. I know the feeling! I don't fancy going into work either.

I glance around and my eyes rest on a tall, fair-haired guy walking towards us, holding the hands of two adorable young girls, who are obviously his daughters. Both have blue eyes and blonde hair tied up in bunches and are wearing the same style of summery dresses, but the bigger girl's dress is red and the smaller one's is yellow. As they get closer, I see that the younger one has a softer, heart-shaped face and a button nose, whereas the older one has a square jaw and an upturned nose, like her dad.

My eyes swivel to the guy's white linen shirt, half tucked into dark blue shorts revealing suntanned, toned legs. The sleeves of the shirt are rolled up to his elbows and his thick hair is tousled as if he was so busy getting the kids ready he didn't have time to style it. The shirt has a V-neck, lace-up collar – very sexy. He glances over as if sensing me staring at him, and his gorgeous greeny-blue eyes hold mine for a moment as his lips curve into a small smile. Then the younger girl tugs at his hand and he turns away to talk to her.

Wow.

'He smiled at us,' Tasha says, preening. Actually I'm pretty sure it's me he was smiling at, not both of us, but I don't say so. I'm not interested in drooling over this hot dad, like the other women in the playground are. I vowed that I was finished with men three years ago and have stuck to it.

I've learnt the hard way not to be taken in by a handsome face.

Tasha can't keep her eyes off him though. 'I haven't seen him or the girls before,' she whispers. 'They must have just moved to the area. Maybe the mum has to leave for work earlier than him or they're sharing the school run?'

'Or maybe she's a high flier and he's a house husband,' I suggest.

Wykham Manor, in a leafy area of Solihull, a suburb in the middle of England, has a good reputation. Even the moneyed parents in the area send their kids here knowing they will get a good education.

Hot Dad is now almost at the gates. Lacey, dressed in her usual skintight leggings and vest top, clutches her six-year-old daughter Scarlett's hand and struts over to him, a big red lipsticked smile on her face, her heavily mascaraed eyes sparkling, her blonde hair extensions swaying over her shoulders.

Lacey and her Mum Gang live in the more affluent area of the village and always turn up for school with a full face of makeup and poured into designer sportswear. They head for the gym after taking their kids to school, then have a healthy lunch together. Lucky them. Me and Tasha have to work – me as a dental receptionist and Tasha in the big library in the town centre – so we dress in smart trousers or a skirt and blouse, and wear minimal makeup. Today my dark, wavy hair is swept up into a topknot bun, while Tasha's auburn, poker-straight hair is tied back into a sleek ponytail that swishes from side to side as she talks.

'It's refreshing to see a dad doing the school run,' I hear Lacey say. She holds out her hand. 'I'm Lacey. And this is Scarlett. Are you new here? I don't think I've seen your daughters before.' She looks around. 'Is their mother at work?'

Hot Dad looks a bit surprised at her directness but smiles back. 'We moved in during the summer holidays. I'm Charlie and this is Mia,' he says, nodding to indicate the older girl. 'And this is Daisy. Mia's a bit nervous about starting a new school, aren't you, love?' He catches Lacey's eye again. 'I'm a single parent.' His voice is rich and deep.

'Wowee, a single dad!' Tasha whispers. 'Well, that's a turn-up for the books.'

Lacey touches Charlie's arm sympathetically. 'Sorry to hear that. I know what it's like. I'm a single mum.' She bends down to talk to Mia, her pert, newly enhanced boobs peeping out of her top. 'Don't worry, darling. Scarlett will go in with you and show you the way. What class are you in?'

'Mrs Wilson's,' Charlie replies. 'And thank you for the offer but I have to take her in as it's her first day. I'd appreciate you looking out for Mia in the playground though, Scarlett.'

'Of course she will, won't you, pet?' Lacey asks Scarlett, who nods shyly.

'Thanks, Scarlett,' Charlie says again and hurries into the playground still holding both his daughters' hands. Lacey turns back to the watching group of mums and grins triumphantly.

'God help him if Lacey has her eye on him, she'll eat him up for breakfast and spit him out,' Tasha says, her ponytail swinging as she turns to watch Lacey totter off to join her clone-like best friend, Kelly. A group of other mums immediately crowd around Lacey and form a huddle. Lacey split from her partner a couple of years ago and has had a steady stream of boyfriends since, all suntanned, handsome and fit. I bet she's hoping Charlie will be her next conquest. Kelly is newly single now though and I'm sure she will give Lacey a run for her money.

'Geez, he's got the whole Mum Gang after him.' I roll my eyes.

'You have to admit that he's easy on the eye,' Tasha says dreamily.

'Not my type.' I shrug and watch as Liam and Ryan run off through the school gates then turn to wave at us. Liam is so like his dad with his olive skin, jet-black hair and slim build, though he has my hazel eyes. Ryan is smaller than Liam – they're in the same class and only a month apart in age – with auburn hair, like Tasha.

'Well, I'm off, I'll leave you all to drool.'

'Don't pretend you're not interested,' Tasha says with a grin. 'I know there's a libido beating in there somewhere.'

Tasha and me met at neonatal class and have been best friends ever since. She's a single mum, like me, and she's been my rock. She and Ryan's dad, Jay, split up just after me and Todd, Liam's dad, and she's always trying a new dating app although wining, dining and a bit of loving is all she says she wants, not a relationship.

'Nope, I'm officially closed for business,' I say, hopefully sounding more light-hearted than I feel.

'It's only a bit of fun, nothing serious. You should put yourself out there.' She gives me a quizzical look. 'You shouldn't keep beating yourself up about what happened on Arran. It was a mistake. Everyone makes mistakes.'

The memory I try to keep buried springs into my mind, and I shut it down. Tasha thinks she knows what happened but she doesn't. No one does.

2

Three Years Ago
Arran, Scotland

Liam was only three when me and Todd split up. I'd practically been a single mother before then anyway – Todd works on an oil rig in Dubai and was only home every other month, So most of the time I went to bed alone, woke up alone, and spent my days devoted to looking after Liam. Tasha was still with Jay then, so apart from sharing the occasional cup of coffee, or glass of wine, with her it was just me and Liam. I tried to tell Todd how lonely and isolated I felt but even when he was home he wasn't much company. Most days he either sat in front of the TV or went out with his mates. His excuse was that he'd worked four weeks solid and needed to relax.

We grew further and further apart, we weren't arguing, we were almost indifferent to each other, even so when Todd said he'd had enough and wanted to move permanently to Dubai, it was a shock. It meant that I was totally alone.

Tasha tried to support me but she was working and looking after Ryan, who was quite demanding. My mum FaceTimed every week and could see that I was struggling so invited us over to Arran to stay with her and my stepdad, Bill, they had a three-bedroom cottage in Brodick with a large garden.

I jumped at the offer. The stunning Isle of Arran seemed the ideal place to get away from it all, with its rocky coastline and heather moors in the north and sandy coves and soft rolling hills in the south. I imagined me and Liam going for long walks along the beach, enjoying the peace and fresh air.

It was so peaceful on Arran and we soon settled in. It was great to see Mum again, and have hands-on help with Liam from her and Bill. I got myself a job in a local store, made a few friends, and for the first few months we were happy.

Then I met Dylan. He walked into the shop one morning for a loaf of bread and bottle of milk and charmed his way into asking me out for a date. He was gorgeous, with tousled dark hair that swept over his deep brown eyes, a trim moustache and little goatee. He was casually dressed in ripped jeans and a black tee shirt bearing the slogan BE WILD and exuded confidence. He told me he and a few friends were over for the summer, making a documentary. They were renting a large house overlooking the beach. He seemed so self-assured and a bit edgy, like he'd lived a life a lot more interesting than mine. And here he was asking me out. I'd felt alone for so long, even when I was with Todd he hadn't shown much interest in me, that I was swept off my feet immediately. I agreed to meet him in the local pub that night, knowing that Mum and Bill would be only too happy to look after Liam. They were retired and adored having us around, doting on their little grandson. Liam already had a strong bond with them.

From then on, I saw Dylan regularly. Mum was happy that I was getting out and about and had made friends until she discovered who I was seeing. She told me that Dylan had a 'reputation' and I should stay clear of him and his crowd but I was having more fun than I'd had for a long time. I'd always been quiet and sensible but suddenly I threw caution to the winds. I wanted to live a little and do the things I'd never done in my teens and early twenties.

We went kayaking, abseiling, roaring around the island on Dylan's motorbike, drinking on the sandy beach with friends until the early hours of the morning. I still spent time with Liam, of course, but I knew that he was safe and happy with Mum and Bill, so I enjoyed my new-found freedom. The last four years I'd been pregnant then almost a single mum to Liam and there hadn't been much chance to let my hair down and now I was enjoying it while I could.

I was falling more and more for Dylan, and getting drawn into his freedom-loving gang of friends. I was having the time of my life.

Until it all went wrong.

3

Now

As a part-timer at the local dentist, I share the shift with Yvonne, the other receptionist. I do nine thirty until two thirty and Yvonne does two thirty until six thirty. It works out perfectly as it allows me to take Liam to school and pick him up, it's not a full-time wage but Todd pays a decent amount of maintenance so we cope. We've managed to keep our divorce amicable and Liam talks to his dad on FaceTime regularly. Todd flies over from Dubai to see Liam a couple of times a year, sometimes having him for a sleepover at the hotel he's staying in to 'give me a break'. Most of the time though it's just me and Liam, and that's the way I'm going to keep it.

When I go to collect Liam from school, I see Daisy clutching the hand of a tall, silver-haired woman who is elegantly dressed in tailored cotton slacks and a print blouse, standing away from the main cluster of mums.

Then Crystal, another mum, shouts, 'Alice!' and goes over to talk to the woman. They're so chatty and relaxed, it's obvious they know each other. Crystal really gets up my nose – her husband, Brandon, works in finance and is often away, while Crystal believes that mothers should always be there for their children so doesn't work. Lucky her to have the choice! And to be wealthy enough to have a live-in au pair! She fills her time volunteering: she's the chair of the PTA and very active in the WI – Women's Institute – and is unbelievably pushy and sanctimonious. I bet she's trying to talk Alice, whoever she is, into doing some fundraising.

Crystal's in full-charm mode, all smiles and head nodding as she talks in her clipped voice, clearly enunciating all the vowels. Her short fair hair frames her face perfectly and today she's dressed in a black linen suit and a white blouse that is obviously designer. I bet she wears designer to go to bed. Honestly, I can't stand her, she's so stuck up, but Alice seems to be hanging onto her every word.

A few minutes later, Mia comes running out of school with Liam. She sees the older woman and cries, 'Nanny!' Alice's face breaks into a big smile and she holds out her arms wide, Mia runs into them and she hugs her tight.

'Hello, darling.' Her voice is refined and cultured, not pseudo-posh like Crystal's.

She must be Hot Dad's mother, as I can see now that she has the same facial bone structure as Charlie, and her eyes are greeny-blue like his, but not as bright. She looks as if she's in her early seventies and is wearing light makeup. The girls clearly adore her. I wonder where their mother is. Charlie said he was a 'single parent' not a widower.

'See you tomorrow, Alice,' Crystal says as the woman walks off with the two little girls. A regular arrangement then.

Lucky Charlie to have a mum nearby who can help. Like I did once.

I push the thought from my mind and walk over to the car with Liam. The afternoon is taken up with preparing us a meal, homework, chores, all the usual stuff. I like to keep busy. But later that evening when Liam is in bed, I look at the ringed date on my calendar and a shiver of apprehension runs through me. Just over two weeks. I've been dreading this for three years. I lean back and close my eyes and I'm transported back to that terrible time.

4

Three Years Ago
Arran, Scotland

Mum kept warning me that Dylan was trouble but I ignored her. I was so smitten with him, with my new fun life. He constantly told me that he loved me, adored me, and I believed him. He knew I had a young son but I didn't introduce him to Liam, I didn't want to bring a new man into Liam's life, especially as Dylan and his group were only here for a few months, when the documentary was finished they'd be gone. This was just a carefree time that I intended to enjoy to the full. So I kept Dylan, and his friends, separate from my home life.

Dylan was charming, fun, attentive – and jealous. He hated it if another man showed me any attention. I should have seen that as a warning sign but I didn't. I was actually flattered, thinking it meant that he loved me. Can you believe that? The only way that I can explain it is that Todd had showed me so little attention that Dylan completely blew me away. It had been a long time since Todd had told me he loved me, and then he'd never said it the way Dylan did, cupping my face with his hands and looking soulfully into my eyes. I would snuggle into him, revelling in his adoration and trying to ignore the little prickle of unease that wormed in my belly when he held me tight and said he'd never let anyone take me away from him.

One night there was a party at their big house overlooking the beach. Lots of people were there, plenty of drink was flowing, music playing. I looked around at everyone and couldn't believe that I was included in this fantastic group of people. Mum and Bill were looking after Liam, who would be tucked up safely in bed now, and I felt so happy and free. Scott, the director, who I'd met a couple of times, started talking to me about the documentary they were making. He was really cool and interesting and I sat enthralled, sipping my lager as I listened to him. I guess I listened too long. Dylan came over, his dark eyes flashing sparks of fury, the lager sloshing around in his half full glass. 'I think you need to get your own girlfriend to impress, mate,' he barked at Scott. Then he grabbed my wrist and pulled me to my feet, dragging me away.

'Hey, hang on,' I protested but he merely tightened his grip and dragged me outside. He spun me around, his eyes glinting, jaw clenched, a vein pulsating in his forehead. 'How fucking dare you flirt with someone else right in front of my eyes?'

I backed away, my heart thumping. 'I wasn't flirting! Scott was telling me about the documentary. It sounds really interesting and he said he's looking for local people to star in it.'

'Offered you a part, has he, if you drop your knickers for him?' Dylan snarled.

I recoiled, swallowing down the lump of fear in my throat. I didn't recognise this vile, hostile Dylan. He had always been so kind and considerate to me. It was the drink, I told myself, he'd had too much lager. I needed to get home, leave him to sober up, and tomorrow he would regret it all and say he was sorry.

'Of course not, you're being ridiculous,' I told him, my voice wobbling with terror.

He stood threateningly, his face inches from mine. 'Being ridiculous, am I? I'll show you who's being fucking ridiculous.' He raised his hand and I instinctively cowered.

'I wouldn't do that, mate, if you know what's good for you.'

It was Scott. I recognised the voice but didn't dare turn around.

'And what's it to you?' Dylan snapped, his attention turned to the other man who must have been standing behind me.

I was shaking now, wondering what the hell had happened and how I could defuse this.

'Take yourself home and sober up,' Scott told him. 'Otherwise I'll be pulling your contract.'

Dylan turned back to me. 'You're not fucking worth it.' Then he spun around and stormed off.

I still didn't dare turn around. It was like I was frozen to the spot.

'Are you okay, Sarah?'

I finally turned. 'I'm okay.' I swallowed. 'He's not usually like that.'

'I think he's shown his true colours and you need to get him out of your life,' Scott said quietly. 'Let me call you a taxi home. You look pretty shook up.'

I was shaken to the core. I had never been threatened like that before and it had terrified me. Later when I was in the safety of my bedroom I looked at my wrist and saw a big bruise where Dylan had grasped it.

Scott was right. I needed to get Dylan out of my life.

5

Now

I watch with amusement over the next week as the Mum Gang pounce on Charlie as soon as he arrives at the school. Crystal always makes a beeline for him and they look very at ease together so my assumption that they're old friends seems valid.

Tasha pretends she isn't interested, but I can see by the way she flicks her ponytail and giggles that she fancies him. And as for Lacey and Kelly, their clothes get more revealing every day. I'm so determined not to join the Charlie fan club that I practically ignore him.

'Look at them, shall we make a bet who gets to go out with Charlie first?' Tasha suggests on Monday, her green eyes sparkling with amusement.

'Poor guy, he doesn't stand a chance with that lot,' I say sympathetically. 'Anyway I'm off to work. I'm late already.'

Suddenly a couple of children go running past and there's a cry as one trips and falls to the ground. I bend down to help her up and see that it's Daisy, Charlie's youngest. 'Are you all right, sweetie?' I ask softly.

'I've hurt my leg.' Daisy's bottom lip wobbles.

'Daisy, darling. I told you to stay by me.' Charlie has reached us now and scoops his young daughter into his arms. He's wearing light blue skinnies and a blue-and-white patterned short-sleeved shirt today. Smart casual seems to be his style, I like it. Todd was always in trackie bottoms and a tee shirt or hoodie whereas Dylan... I push the thought away. I'm not even going to give head space to that man.

'It's only a scrape but it must be sore,' I tell him.

'Let's get you home, love, and clean it,' he says. He smiles at me. 'Thanks for helping her.'

'No problem.' I meet his eyes then glance away, my heart racing a little. There's no denying that he's gorgeous.

We walk back to the car park together, and as I get into my car a text pings in from Tasha.

You are now the most hated mum in the playground. You should see the glares the Mum Gang gave you.

A horn beeps and I almost do a double take when I see Charlie pulling away in a silver Range Rover Evoque. I wish I'd at least given my black Peugeot 206 a clean, it looks quite shabby by comparison. Daisy is strapped in a car seat in the back, waving at me, and I watch them drive off.

When I arrive at work, I put on my overall, wash my hands and head for the kitchen to make a coffee for everyone, as I do every morning. I enjoy my job, it's only a small dental practice with a husband-and-wife team, Tom and Maddie, and me and Yvonne. We're like one big family.

'Morning, Sarah.' Tom pops his head around the door. 'How's things with you?'

I flash him a bright smile as I take three mugs off the mug

stand – we all have our own colour, navy for Tom, green for Maddie, purple for me – leaving Yvonne's red one still hanging. 'Good, thanks. How's Maddie today?' Maddie hadn't looked well on Friday, she thought she had a cold coming, so had left early.

'She dosed herself up with hot lemon and honey at the weekend and is feeling fine now,' he replies. 'Here, I'll take the coffees up with me.' He takes the two mugs of instant that I've just made and heads up the stairs to the surgery, and I take mine into reception and open the door. Halfway through the morning Charlie walks in with Daisy, who is holding a baby doll. We stare at each other in surprise for a moment, then he smiles and my stomach does a little flip. 'Hello again.' He glances at my name badge. 'I didn't realise you worked here, Sarah.'

'Hello.' I give him a welcoming smile and for a second he holds my gaze. I break away first and glance at the screen at the name of the next patient: Daisy Harris. I didn't know Charlie's surname so hadn't put two and two together.

Daisy stares at me with her big blue eyes and clutches her doll tightly. She really is a sweet girl. 'How's your knee, Daisy?' I ask her.

'Better,' she says quietly. She looks shy and a bit nervous.

'Daisy's here for a check-up. I like to get the girls used to regular dentist visits.' Charlie flashes me an easy, friendly smile that reveals nice, even, white teeth. Not glo-white, thank goodness, I hate the trend for teeth so white they dazzle you, it looks so false. Nothing about Charlie Harris looks false. You can't tell by appearances, I remind myself, anyone can put on a good act.

'Good idea. We wish more parents would do that.' I glance back at the screen and see that he registered and made the appointment last week when Yvonne was on duty. 'I see this is Daisy's first visit.'

'Yes. We recently moved to the area. Me, Mia and Daisy.'

He glances down at the little girl. 'Daisy is a bit nervous, aren't you, sweetheart?'

I wonder again what's happened to her mother. In my experience it's usually the guys who walk away, but here is Charlie caring for his daughters alone. 'Most kids are nervous but Mr and Mrs Preston, our two dentists, are brilliant with children.' I smile reassuringly at Daisy. 'All you have to do is open your mouth wide so the dentist can see what amazing teeth you have then you will get a sticker and a pretty new toothbrush. Does that sound okay to you?'

Daisy nods.

'I'd like to go in with her,' Charlie says. His eyes are holding mine, they're such a gorgeous colour, almost like the sea. And the way his sandy hair is parted down the middle and flops over his eyes makes me want to run my hands through it. I bet he won't stay a single dad for long.

'Of course. If you and Daisy take a seat, the dentist will be with you soon.'

Daisy is called up a few minutes later, and another couple of patients arrive so I'm preoccupied when Charlie and Daisy come down again. 'Look what I've got!' Daisy proudly shows me a sticker and a sparkly purple toothbrush. 'Purple is my favourite colour.'

'Mine too!' I show her my mug and she giggles. Then I glance at Charlie. 'No problems then?'

'None at all. Thanks for your help.'

'It's a pleasure.' He's staring at me with those gorgeous eyes and I get the feeling that he wants to say something more. My throat is suddenly dry and I turn to the little girl. 'Bye, Daisy.'

'Come on, Daisy, let's get you back to nursery,' he says to his daughter. Then he lingers for a moment and turns to me. 'See you tomorrow morning at the school gates.'

.   .   .

The day flies by. When I arrive at school to pick Liam up, Daisy is there with Alice and she shouts hello. I give her a finger wave.

Alice turns around in surprise and looks questioningly at me. Daisy says something to her then Alice nods at me before turning back around.

'Hey, why are Daisy and her nan so friendly with you?' Tasha asks as she joins me.

'Charlie brought Daisy into the dentist for a check-up. She was nervous and I helped settle her.'

'So now you're bessie mates with him? Get you!'

'No, I'm not, I told you I just helped settle Daisy at the dentist. It's my job.'

'Methinks the lady doth protest too much,' Tasha says and I roll my eyes.

When Daisy and Mia come along with their nan, Daisy waves again as they go past.

Tasha nudges me in the ribs with her elbow. 'Have you seen the looks Kelly and Lacey are giving you? I bet they make a voodoo doll of you when they're home and stick pins in it!'

'I've told you I'm not interested in Charlie,' I almost snap.

I'm lying. I am interested in him. And I have a feeling he's interested in me too. He seems a genuinely nice guy and from what I've seen he adores his daughters.

Dylan seemed a nice guy too, I remind myself. And look how that turned out.

Three Years Ago
Arran, Scotland

Dylan phoned me the next morning. He was so contrite, his voice soft and persuading, begging me to meet him.

'You behaved appallingly and you bruised my arm,' I told him.

'I'm so sorry, darling. I love you so much. I am so scared of losing you and when I saw that Scott fawning over you, I just saw red.'

'He wasn't fawning over me! He was talking to me. You completely overreacted. And you scared me,' I told him firmly.

'I really am sorry. Please come and meet me for a coffee,' he said. 'We can talk things over.'

I'm ashamed to admit that I was still taken in by his charm, that I really wasn't ready to give up my fun life. 'I can't come yet. Mum's out and I have Liam to look after.'

'Bring the wee lad with you. I'd love to meet him,' Dylan said.

So I did. I fastened Liam into his car seat and drove off to meet Dylan. He came to me arms outstretched, gave me a big hug, apologised, and scooped Liam into a hug too. He'd even bought him a toy fire engine, which Liam loved. We had a coffee and chatted, Liam had a milkshake and Dylan was charm personified. I found it hard to reconcile the man in front of me, the man I'd been going out with for the past couple of months, with the foul-mouthed, abusive man he'd been last night. So I excused it, reasoned he'd drunk too much, overreacted and hadn't meant to grab my arm so tight, and I agreed to give him another chance.

'I'll see you later then,' Dylan said, as he kissed me. 'Eight o'clock at the beach.'

I drove to the supermarket to get a few things, I was buzzing. So happy that Dylan was back to normal and it had all been because he'd drunk too much. Although I knew that was no excuse.

I put the shopping down by my car and opened the door to strap Liam in but my handbag slipped out of my hand. The guy about to get into the car next to me picked it up and handed it to me.

'Thanks so much,' I said with a smile as I took it off him.

'You look like you've got your hands full. Want me to put your shopping in the boot while you strap in the little one?' he asked.

'That's very kind of you,' I said. 'Thanks.'

I picked up Liam while the man opened my car boot then suddenly there was a loud roar of anger. 'What the fuck are you doing with my woman!' Dylan was marching across the car park towards us. His face was red with anger, his eyes bulging, his fists clenched by his side. Fear snaked through me.

Liam started shaking in my arms and I pressed him tighter to me to soothe him. What the hell was the matter with Dylan?

'Hey, steady on, mate. I'm just being a good Samaritan here,' the man said evenly.

'Stop it, Dylan, this man is helping me put the shopping away,' I shouted, my fingers trembling as I tried to strap Liam in the car, but Dylan had reached the man and thumped him in the face.

I stood in front of Liam, who was crying now, to try and block his view, and glanced over my shoulder. I was horrified at the violent attack that was taking place. The poor man was lying on the floor and Dylan was booting him hard.

'Stop it!' I yelled. Dylan didn't even look at me, he carried on booting the man, who was now curled up into the foetal position, trying to protect himself. There was no one else around to help. So I took out my phone and called the police, my voice shaking.

Within minutes a police car was speeding into the car park, lights flashing.

Dylan struggled as the police pulled him off the man, then he looked over at me, his eyes bulging, his mouth twisted into a snarl. 'You bitch! You'll pay for this!'

Now

We get up late the next morning and it's a mad dash to get ready. When we finally pile into my car parked outside on the drive, it won't start.

'Just what I need!' I groan as I turn the ignition for the umpteenth time. Nothing happens.

'Am I going to be late?'

I can hear the anxiety in Liam's voice, he hates being late for school, hates anything that draws attention to him. 'Not if we walk fast,' I say. Good job I'm wearing my work trousers and flats.

Fortunately, it's only a ten-minute walk, and it's quite mild still with only a slight breeze. Autumn is coming though, and soon the pavement will be scattered with the leaves from the trees lining the streets. I love living in this quiet suburban part of town, it's pretty, and although we don't see much of the neighbours they're always friendly when we bump into them. 'We need to go a bit faster,' I urge Liam, who is trudging behind me.

'My legs ache,' he protests, still dawdling.

Most of the other kids have already gone in when we arrive.

'I knew I'd be late! I told you!' Liam shouts and he runs ahead without even stopping to wave at me.

I feel so guilty, I hate for him to go into school upset. And now I've got to get the bus to work, we will have to walk home this afternoon, and somehow I have to find time to get the car sorted.

'Hi, Sarah!'

I spin around in surprise at the sound of Charlie's voice. He's flocked by a group of mums who are hanging onto his every word, and looks drop-dead gorgeous in straight-legged black jeans, a white collarless shirt with the sleeves rolled up and black trainers. He walks away from the group and heads over to me. It seems like he wants to chat about something.

'Hi,' I say hesitantly. I'm flattered but I can't stop, I really need to get to work and the bus is due soon.

'I wanted to thank you again for being so good with Daisy yesterday. She was terrified about going to the dentist and you really calmed her down.'

'Anytime.' I smile at him. I can sense the curious looks from the other mums and have to admit that it does feel good that Charlie has gone out of his way to talk to me. I wish I had time to milk this moment. 'Sorry I have to dash. I'm due into work at nine thirty and I have to get the bus as my car refused to start.'

'Oh, please let me give you a lift, I'm going into town anyway,' he offers.

I hesitate. I can already feel an attraction to Charlie and want to keep my distance, I'm not getting involved with anyone again. I really do need to get to work though so it would be stupid to refuse a lift. 'That would be great, thank you.' I can feel the daggers as I walk over with Charlie to his car.

He opens the passenger door to reveal cream leather seats – cream! With two young daughters! My old Peugeot has dark grey seats and they get messy enough. I slide onto the passenger seat and fasten my seatbelt. Charlie gets in beside me and I can't resist looking out of the window and finger-waving to the Mum Gang, who are all agog, mouths practically touching the floor.

'I'm sorry, I seem to have made you the subject of a bit of gossip. I hope you haven't got a jealous husband or partner that might take this the wrong way,' Charlie says as he switches on the engine, his rich voice a mixture of concern and amusement.

He doesn't know the terrible memory that remark brings back but I reply lightly, 'Nope, I got divorced years ago. It's just me and Liam now.'

Charlie indicates and pulls out. 'It's hard when a marriage doesn't work out, isn't it? Does Liam see his dad?'

'Now and again. Todd works in Dubai on an oil rig, which was part of the problem. He FaceTimes or calls Liam when he can and visits a couple of times a year.'

'That's good, I know that it isn't a lot and most of the care is obviously falling on you but it's so important for a child to have contact with both parents.' He glances in the mirror, indicates and takes the right turn into town. 'My wife, Lynn, walked out eighteen months ago and hasn't bothered to see the girls since. Daisy rarely asks about her now, I think she's forgotten her, but Mia is old enough to remember and still misses her.'

'You mean you never even hear from her at all? She doesn't see the girls?' Then I realise how nosy I sound. 'Sorry, I don't mean to pry. I just can't imagine any mother walking out on her kids and never seeing them again.' I shake my head in bewilderment.

He keeps his eyes firmly on the road but there's an edge to his voice. 'Lynn left a note saying she loved someone else and was going to live with him and for me to take care of the girls.' He pulls into the car park now, brings the car to a halt and turns to me. 'It was just before our seventh wedding anniversary and it was so sudden. Mia was nearly five and Daisy barely two.'

I can see the anger and pain in his eyes and my heart goes out to him, and to Mia and Daisy. What Lynn did to them was so cruel. Unthinkable.

How could any mother just walk out and disappear? Never come back to see her young daughters or have anything to do with them again?

Then I think of my mum and how I will never see her again.

Three Years Ago
Arran, Scotland

Arran is a small island and news travels fast. It didn't take long for what Dylan had done to reach Mum and she was fuming when I returned home.

'I warned you about that man but you wouldn't listen. All you cared about was having fun.' Her face was pinched, her words sharp, like daggers. 'And look at the state of that wee lad! How could you take him with you and let him see such violence?'

I held Liam closer. He was shaking, his head buried in my shoulder.

Then Mum's eyes widened as they rested on my arm. I looked down and saw that my sleeve had ridden up, revealing the deep bruises around my wrist.

'Did that monster do that?' she demanded.

It was pointless denying it. I nodded my head wordlessly.

'And that wasn't done today, not to bruise like that. Yet still you met up with him today. And you took Liam with you!' Her lip curled up in scorn, her eyes narrowed in contempt.

'Now, let's give the lass a chance to get her words out,' Bill said gently. 'And we don't want to be upsetting the wee lad any further.'

'Can you take Liam out in the garden to see the birds, please? Me and Sarah need to talk,' Mum said, her tone eerily flat.

'Aye.' Bill rose from his chair and took Liam out of my arms. 'Come on, son, let's have a natter to the birds.'

As soon as the back door shut behind them, Mum started. Hands on hips, she let rip. How I was an unfit mother. How she'd warned me time and time again about Dylan.

'How could you put Liam in danger like that? That monster is unhinged! He could have killed that man. What if he had hit you? Or Liam? Not to mention the mental scars that poor lad will be left with after witnessing someone having a beating like that.'

'He didn't see it, I stood in front of him and blocked his view,' I protested.

Mum wasn't to be abated. 'He saw enough. He looks traumatised. I can't believe you went to meet that brute after he did that to you.' She pointed to my wrist.

'I was going to finish with him. Then he said it was an accident. He hadn't meant it. He was so sorry and—'

'And you were so desperate to carry on pretending you were single and carefree again you were prepared to continue seeing him. And couldn't even wait for me to come home so took your little son with you – knowing what that animal was capable of. You're not fit to be a mother!'

I gasped at her cruel words. 'I've finished with him! I was the one who called the police as soon as Dylan started attacking that man!'

'What do you want for that, a medal? It's time you started

putting Liam first. And if you can't do that, if you want to carry on like you don't have a child, then maybe I should call social services and arrange for me to have custody of Liam. Then you can go off and do whatever you want with whoever you want!' She gave me a contemptuous look then spun on her heels and went to join Bill and Liam out in the garden.

Her words had cut me to the quick. I'll never forgive her for this, I vowed.

Now

'Thanks so much for the lift,' I say, conscious I need to go into work but not quite ready to get out of the car yet.

'You're welcome.' Charlie hesitates. 'Look, have you booked your car into a garage yet? If not, I can take a look, if you want? I'm a trained mechanic, although I now teach basic literacy at the local college.'

'That's really kind of you...' My eyes flick to his white shirt.

'It's really not a problem. How about I come back to your home after work? Mum picks the girls up from school and gives them their tea so I have time. And don't worry, I have overalls, I won't mess up my clothes,' he adds as though reading my mind.

He looks at me hesitantly, as if wondering if he's being too pushy. It's nice of him to offer to help when we hardly know each other. I feel like I should say that I don't want to trouble him and will take the car into the garage, but to be honest I'm a bit short this month and could do without expensive bills. And he looks like he genuinely wants to help so it would be churlish to refuse, wouldn't it?

'Thank you, I really appreciate it. I'm lost without my car.'

'I would be too. Give me your address and I should be there about four thirty.'

'That's brilliant. Thanks so much! Shall I text it to you?'

Charlie takes his phone out of his pocket. 'Sure. Let's exchange numbers then I can message you if anything comes up and I'm a bit late.'

I swipe my screen and show him my number. He keys it in and a second later a text zaps in from him with a wave emoji. My heart does a little flip as I save it to my contacts list then reply with my address and a smiley emoji.

'Thanks again. See you later!' I cross the road and head down the street. It's only a couple of minutes' walk to the surgery from here, but before I can reach it, my phone rings.

It's Tasha. I accept the call, knowing she will only keep ringing until I do. 'Hi, Tasha, what's up? I'm due in work in five mins,' I remind her.

'I jet off early one morning and you're the talk of the playground. Apparently, you and Mr Hottie went off together.'

It didn't take long for that to get around, did it? 'My car's broken down so Charlie gave me a lift. Look, Tash, I've got to go.' I'm standing outside the practice now. 'I'll catch up with you later.' I end the call and go in, a little flustered.

I find it hard to concentrate all morning, Charlie is on my mind. It's nice of him to try to fix my car but I can't help feeling a bit awkward about him coming to my small two-bed terrace. I've checked Charlie's address on our records and realise he lives in the posh area of town, the one where the houses are all huge, detached and set back from the road. I really don't want to invite him in but I'll have to offer him a coffee, and what if he wants to use the bathroom?

He's doing me a favour and won't care what my house is like. Besides, I've put a home together from nothing in three years, I remind myself. I should get him a thank you gift though,

something to show my appreciation. Maybe a bottle of whisky –
Bill always said that's the equivalent of a bunch of flowers for
a man.

I'm in the supermarket in my lunch break getting a large
bottle when Tasha phones again. 'How about I collect Liam
from school and drop him back home? I'd pick you up from
work but I don't have time.'

Great! That will give me time to have a quick tidy around
before Charlie arrives. 'Thanks, that would be fab,' I tell her.

Maddie lets me leave work a bit earlier so I can catch the
bus and I manage to get home by three. I groan as I open the
door and see the shoes cluttered in the hall, the coats half
hanging off the coat rack and the old newspapers still piled up
on the bottom of the stairs.

Rushing around, I put the shoes on the rack, hang the coats
up, put the papers in the green bin then head into the lounge.
Thankfully the navy cord sofa is still quite decent-looking so I
plump up the fluffy grey scatter cushions then go through to the
kitchen to tidy up and load the dishwasher. I head up the stairs
to clean the bathroom next. I pick up Liam's Pokémon pyjamas
from the floor, dropping them in the washing basket, and am
cleaning toothpaste from the sink when there's a knock at the
door. That'll be Tasha with Liam.

I open the door and Tasha is in before I can stop her,
heading straight for the kitchen. She clearly wants a coffee and
a chat, but Charlie will be here in less than an hour and I want
to put the vacuum around. Tasha is already filling the kettle and
switching it on though, we're such good friends that we're
completely at ease in each other's houses. Ryan and Liam head
straight upstairs to play, which thankfully means that downstairs will stay tidy.

I didn't think this through when Tasha offered to pick Liam
up from school, I should have known that she'd come in for a
bit. The question is, do I tell her I don't have time to chat and

why – in which case she will definitely hang about? Or should I just hope she's gone by the time Charlie arrives?

'Hey, wake up, dreamy.' Tasha snaps her fingers in front of my face.

I blink. 'Sorry.' I have to tell her, she's my best friend. Besides she's bound to find out. 'Charlie's offered to pop around after work and take a look at my car. I was just wondering if I had time to vac around.'

'It's lucky I can't stay long then. I've got to get back, so I'll have a lot of milk in mine please.' She winks and grins. 'I've got a date tonight. I signed up to a new dating app and have had loads of matches. One of them, Caleb, sounds great. We've been messaging each other for a few days now, he lives not too far away. We're meeting at the Centurian for a meal, Mum's having Ryan overnight.' She's taking two mugs out of my cupboard and passes them to me just as the kettle boils. 'You should try the app, it would do you good to get out a bit, and you might meet someone you like.'

I spoon coffee into the mugs and pour hot water on top, adding a good dollop of milk to hers, then hand it to her. 'I've told you I'm not interested in having another relationship. And even if I was, I wouldn't want to hook up with a stranger. It makes me nervous.' I meet her eye. 'Be careful, Tash.'

She pulls a face. 'You're as bad as my mum!'

My mum tried to warn me too, I remember. Why didn't I listen to her?

Three Years Ago
Arran, Scotland

I called Tasha that night. I knew that she and Jay had separated a couple of months ago, and she'd kept asking me to come back to the Midlands. She said she missed her best friend. Her house was only small but she said we could have Ryan's room and Ryan could go in with her. So I packed mine and Liam's things and booked us onto the early ferry the next morning.

I didn't tell Mum we were leaving. I sneaked out with Liam before she and Bill got up, leaving a note on the kitchen table to say that I'd gone back to England and would never forgive her for what she said so she wasn't to contact me. She never did.

We stayed with Tasha for a while, then I found a house not too far from her and we settled down. I confided in Tasha one night about what had happened, leaving out the part about Dylan beating up that man and being sent to prison, I was too ashamed to mention that, to tell Tasha exactly what sort of man I'd dated and exposed Liam to. She was very sympathetic.

'You were lonely and vulnerable and just wanted to have a bit of fun,' she said. 'Your mum should be supporting you not criticising you.'

'Liam means the world to me and Mum knows that. It was all a terrible mistake and I'm ashamed of myself. But I'm a good mother. I am. And I'll never forgive Mum for saying that I'm not fit to be a mother and she would take custody of Liam.'

I knew that I had taken my eye off the ball though. Liam should have been my priority and I vowed he would be from then on. I tried to put Dylan out of my mind. I learnt later that he'd already got a previous conviction for GBH so was sentenced to four years in prison, with a stipulation that he had to serve three. I was safe. For now.

11

Charlie arrives about ten minutes after Tasha leaves. I've been watching for him out of the window and see his Range Rover pull up on the kerb. I open the door and go down the path to him as he gets out. 'Hi, thanks for this.'

'No problem.' He grabs a pair of overalls from the passenger seat. 'Mind if I just put these on? Then I'll get cracking.'

He puts one jean-clad leg then the other into the overalls and sexily wriggles into them right there on the drive, pulling them over his hips then slipping his arms into them. I have to stop myself from reaching out to help him do the buttons up.

'Would you like a coffee before you start? Or I can bring one out to you?' I offer.

'Thanks but I'd better get straight on. If you need new parts, I might be able to get them tonight if I'm quick.'

'I really appreciate this,' I say as I hand him my car keys.

'No problem at all.' He takes a toolbox out of the boot of his car, then goes over to mine, which is parked on the drive. He turns the key and the engine turns over but doesn't kick in. He tries again but still has the same response so he gets out, lifts up the bonnet and starts looking under it. I leave him to it and go inside to check on Liam.

His math's homework is laid out on the table in the kitchen and he's frowning as he chews the end of his pencil. 'I can't do it!'

I pull out the chair beside him. 'Let's take a look.'

We're both preoccupied with the maths when we hear my car engine running. Liam's face lights up. 'Charlie's fixed it!'

Already! I go outside, Liam right behind me. 'That's brilliant, what was wrong with it?'

Charlie is wiping his hands on a grubby cloth which he must have had in his car. 'A dirty spark plug. I've cleaned it and put it back in for you. It should be fine now but if you have any other problems let me know.'

'You're a lifesaver.' I look at the dirty cloth. 'Would you like to come in and wash your hands properly? And maybe have a coffee now?'

'I'd love to – and a coffee will be very welcome.'

He follows me into the kitchen and washes his hands in the sink while I put the kettle on. Liam stands by Charlie, watching him.

'You're clever to fix our car,' he says admiringly.

'Not really. My job used to be fixing cars,' Charlie replies, reaching for the hand towel Liam offers him.

Liam looks impressed. 'My dad works on an oil rig,' he says importantly.

Charlie nods. 'Now that is clever.'

Liam beams. Then he turns to me. 'I'm hungry. Can I have a cheese toastie?'

'Sure.' I'll fix myself something later. I glance at Charlie, wondering if he's hungry, although I'm pretty sure he's used to fancier food than cheese toasties. 'You're welcome to one if you want.'

'I'm good, thanks, Mum will have dinner ready for when I get home.'

'Does she live with you?' I ask.

'No, she lives nearby but she prefers to look after the girls in their own home. It's less disruptive for them.'

'I can understand that.' I get the sandwich toaster out while Liam fetches the bread, cheese and tomato ketchup. Liam would have tomato ketchup on his cereal if I let him.

Charlie sips his coffee and watches as we make the toastie and Liam pours himself a glass of drinkable yoghurt. 'You've got him well trained.'

'I'm a single mum, we need to be a team,' I reply. 'I'm sure you must be the same with your girls.'

'I would be but... well, Mum helps a lot and to be honest she mollycoddles them a bit.' His eyes meet mine and I wonder if his mother takes over. Like mine did.

As if sensing my thoughts, Charlie asks softly, 'How about you? Are you close to your mum?'

'She lives on Arran, we don't see her much,' I say. I don't tell him about the big argument we had. The one that made me run away from Arran, the one that's kept me from her for years. But Mum's words are seared in my heart: *You're not fit to be a mother!*

12

Charlie finishes his coffee and gets to his feet. 'I'll be off now then. See you at the school gates in the morning. He puts a hand on Liam's head and ruffles his hair. 'You're a good kid to help your mum.'

Liam's face lights with pleasure. 'Me and Mum look after each other,' he says.

'That's great, that's the way it should be,' Charlie replies.

'Before you go...' I take the bottle of whisky I bought earlier out of the cupboard and hand it to him. 'A small thank you for fixing my car. My stepdad always said that all men love a good whisky.'

Charlie's eyes twinkle. 'We certainly do. Thank you.' He leans forward and kisses me on the cheek. A featherlight kiss but I jolt as if I've been burnt, my eyes shooting to his gorgeous turquoise ones where I'm sure I can see shock registered there too. My heart stills as our eyes meet and lock. Charlie breaks the gaze first and holds up the bottle of whisky. 'Thank you so much for this. I'd better be off now.'

I see him to the door, feeling awkward. Why the hell did I react like that? Because it's been such a long time since a guy kissed me, even if it was only on the cheek, I remind myself. And he looked startled too when his lips touched my skin.

I turn back to Liam, who is stuffing the last of his toastie into his mouth. 'Shall we find a film to watch together before you go to bed?'

He shoots out of his seat. 'Can I choose?'

'Of course.'

He chooses *Minions*, which we've seen countless times before, but I don't mind watching it again. I love this time of the day, when it's just me and my son, indoors, safe from the rest of the world. I wish I could freeze time and keep Liam like this forever but of course I can't. Every day he's growing up and I can't stop that, so I'm determined to make the most of the time we have now.

When I arrive with Liam at school the next morning, Alice and Daisy are standing at the gate, shouting goodbye to Mia as she runs into school. I wonder if Charlie has had to go into work early, or if he's avoiding me after that strange moment that passed between us yesterday. Daisy sees me, shouts and waves, then Alice turns and nods.

'Sarah!' Tasha waves to me and comes hurrying over. 'How did it go with Charlie yesterday?'

'What? You're seeing Charlie? Well, you didn't waste your time getting your hooks into him, did you?'

I swivel around to see Lacey, arms crossed over her tight pink vest and wearing equally tight black leggings, glaring at me. She's standing with her Mum Gang, who are now all gaping at me and whispering. Lacey flicks back her bottle-blonde tresses. 'You've only known him five minutes.'

'Calm down, ladies, he was only fixing Sarah's car,' Tasha says.

'Clever trick, playing damsel in distress,' Kelly sneers. She's standing beside Lacey, her sleek dark hair draped over her shoulders, and clad in equally skintight vest and leggings. They're like a pair of Barbie dolls those two.

'There is nothing going on between me and Charlie,' I tell her adamantly. I could kill Tasha for shouting that out.

'Down, girls. Charlie was just doing a good deed.' Tasha is beside me now. 'Did he find out what was wrong with your car?'

'It was a dirty spark plug.'

As soon as I say the words, a jeer goes up. 'That old trick!' Lacey scoffs.

'Oh, grow up,' I tell her. Honestly, they're all acting more like the Mean Girls than grown women! Out of the corner of my eye, I notice that Alice is looking at me curiously. How embarrassing for her to hear all this. I don't want her to think that I'm after her son like the rest of the Mum Gang.

'Take no notice of them,' I say to Alice, 'Charlie was helping me out, that's all.'

'I know, dear. He told me that he fixed your car for you, he used to be a mechanic. I hope it's running okay this morning. It's so frustrating to be without transport, isn't it?' Her tone is cool but I appreciate her letting them all know that Charlie had worked as a mechanic, and was simply doing me a favour.

'It really is. I'm very grateful for his help.'

With that well-timed confirmation from Alice, the Mum Gang disperse, though I'm sure I haven't heard the last of it from them. 'Sorry,' Tasha says, linking her arm through mine. 'I should have thought. I didn't mean to set the jungle drums going.'

'It's okay.' I walk back to the car park with Tasha, taking one last look behind me at Alice, now deep in conversation with Crystal. 'How did your date go?'

'Fab. We really got on. We're seeing each other again,' she tells me.

'How about you pop around for a coffee after school and

you can tell me more,' I suggest. I'm happy for Tasha – she says she's only having a bit of fun, but I know she hates being on her own with Ryan and his dad is rarely on the scene.

The day passes quickly at work, and when I go to collect Liam from school I see Crystal talking to Alice again.

'Charlie is too busy but I'd be very interested in joining the PTA, if I'm allowed,' I hear Alice say.

'Of course, that would be wonderful. When would be a convenient time to talk further about it? Perhaps Charlie should be present too, he may want to contribute or help out with one of our fundraisers.'

'Why don't you come around this evening, about eight?' Alice suggests. 'We'll both be home then.'

Crystal saunters off, looking delighted, and Alice walks off as well, both young girls clutching her hands and chattering happily.

It shouldn't bother me that Crystal is going around to Charlie's house tonight but it does. 'They look chummy,' I remark to Tasha.

'Yeah, Crystal, Alice and Charlie go way back, apparently. Charlie's father worked at the same firm as Crystal's dad,' Tasha tells me. I don't ask her how she knows this, Tasha seems to know everything that's going on. We both belong to the school WhatsApp group but I tend to mute it, the notifications drive me nuts. Tasha probably chats to some of the mums in the evening when Ryan is in bed, but I prefer to relax watching a box set, or doing a wordsearch. I like to keep my head down and my circle small. I find it difficult to trust anyone except Tasha.

Tasha comes back with me for a coffee and the boys immediately disappear upstairs to play. Tasha tells me all about her date and shows me a photo of her and Caleb: he looks like an average, normal guy and it sounds like they're a good match.

She's mid-sentence when a text pings in, from Charlie.

Tasha leans forward to look at my phone. 'You have each other's number.' Her tone is loaded.

'Yes, we swapped numbers yesterday so I could give him my address and he could message me when he was on his way to fix my car,' I reply, unsure why I feel such a strong need to justify it.

She nods at the still unopened message. 'Well, aren't you going to read it?'

I would have preferred to read it without Tasha looking over my shoulder but I know she won't let up so I open it.

Hi, how's the car doing? Thanks so much for the whisky, it's one of my favourite brands. I'll be having a tot later. Charlie

He's included a smiley emoji for good measure.

'You bought him a bottle of whisky?' Tash is giving me *that* look.

'Yes, to say thank you for fixing my car.'

Tasha folds her arms and cocks her head to one side. 'It's clear that you and Charlie have the hots for each other. It's a good job I've met Caleb or I'd be jealous.'

'Don't be daft, we're just friends,' I retort. 'Charlie doesn't fancy me and I don't fancy him.'

If I don't fancy him, though, then why am I so bothered about Crystal going around his house tonight? And why am I hoping that he doesn't offer her some of the whisky I bought him?

Even if Charlie is attracted to me, it won't go any further. I daren't risk getting involved with anyone ever again.

Later, when Liam is tucked up in bed, I go into the kitchen to pour myself a small glass of wine. My eyes dart to the circled date on the calendar on the wall. My hand shakes a little as I pour the wine, my mind going back to that night on Arran when

Dylan had been arrested. A few weeks ago I read online that he's been granted parole.

I turn back to look at the ringed date again. The date Dylan will be paroled.

Will he keep his threat to make me pay for reporting him to the police?

13

ALICE

Charlie doesn't look too pleased when I tell him that Crystal is coming around tonight to talk to us about the PTA. 'I've got a load of marking to do,' he protests. 'Why couldn't you meet her alone at your place, Mum?'

'It will only be an hour of your time, and you're the girls' father so should be involved. I'll do most of it, of course, but you need to show an interest, dear.'

I didn't think he would like it, but it's for his own good. He needs to make a good impression after all that trouble with Lynn. Not that it was Charlie's fault but it won't hurt to show everyone how upstanding and respectable he is.

Everything I do is for Charlie, always has been. And now I have the girls' interests to look after too. They need a secure home life, and I intend to make sure that they get it.

I've seen how all the women are circling my son at the school gates, but it's not the obvious ones I'm worried about. My Charlie would never go for one of those false, heavily made up, Botoxed women flaunting their bodies in tight vests and leggings. He prefers women who are quieter, more refined. Like Lynn. I warned him about her, could see that it was all an act and she wasn't the right one for him and now look what's happened.

And this Sarah, she's the same. Clever enough not to hang around him, salivating like the others, acts like she's not interested, but she's soon wormed her way in with Daisy, and got Charlie fixing her car.

Well, I know her game and I'll put a stop to her.

14

SARAH

Sunday's so mild that I really feel like getting outside in the fresh air. It's been hard to take my mind off Dylan's imminent release. I keep reminding myself that he doesn't know where I live. No one on Arran does. And that he made his threat in anger. He'll have cooled down, probably regrets everything, after a stint in prison.

Or be even angrier.

I've got to stop torturing myself like this. I need to get out. 'Shall we go and feed the ducks?' I ask Liam. There's a little duck pond about ten minutes' walk away, and a playpark with swings and a slide right by it. Liam loves to go there.

He looks up from his iPad. 'Yeah. Can I just finish this game? I'm nearly up to the next level.'

'Sure.' I leave him to finish and go into the kitchen to get the bag of birdseed I always keep for the ducks, then put a bag of crisps and a bottle of flavoured water into my bag too. Liam's bound to want a snack after he's had a play at the park.

A few minutes later he comes in, pulling on his coat. 'Ready!'

He chatters happily to me as we set off along the leafy path through the wood and come out into the clearing where the pond is. There is no one else feeding the few ducks swimming around there so I give Liam the bag of birdseed and he runs over. 'Don't go too near the water!' I warn him.

'I won't!'

I join him as he stands a few feet away from the edge, scoops a handful of seed in his hand and throws it in the water. The ducks quack loudly and swim over to it. A couple of cheeky ones waddle out of the pond and quack hopefully at Liam.

'Liam!' We both turn to see Mia running towards us. Charlie is a little behind her, holding Daisy's hand.

'Great minds think alike!' Charlie grins.

I'm surprised to see them over in my neck of the woods. 'Do you often come here?' I ask.

'Now and again. I had to grab a few things from the DIY store so promised the girls if they behaved we'd go to the park.' He glances at the bag of birdseed in my hand. 'I'm afraid that I didn't come prepared to feed the ducks though.'

'Mia and Daisy can share my birdseed,' Liam offers.

The two girls hold out their hands eagerly as Liam pours some birdseed into Mia's palm, then Daisy's, and they giggle as they throw it in the water, the ducks swarming.

Me and Charlie watch them. The pond isn't very deep but I keep my eye on Liam, ready to rescue him if he falls in.

'How's the car?' Charlie asks.

'Great thanks,' I reply, my gaze still firmly fixed on Liam until I can't help quickly glancing at Charlie. 'Thanks so much again.'

His eyes are on the girls but his lips curve into a smile. 'A pleasure.'

When the kids have finished feeding the ducks, Mia and Liam run on ahead to the park and jump on a swing each, but Daisy stays by her dad, holding his hand. Charlie helps her into the swing, tells her to hold on tight then gently pushes her. I watch him as he interacts with her. He's so good with his girls.

Liam and Mia jump off and run over to the slide, and after a while, Daisy wants to join in. I watch proudly as Liam stands back and lets Daisy go up the slide before him.

The kids play happily for a while, with me and Charlie chatting as we watch them, until Mia asks to go to McDonald's.

'Can we go too?' Liam asks excitedly, bouncing up and down.

'I haven't got the car, remember,' I remind him.

'You can come with us, I'll drop you back home afterwards,' Charlie offers.

'Can we, please, Mum?' Liam begs.

It's been such a fantastic afternoon I don't want to go home either. I've really enjoyed Charlie's company, and Liam and the girls have played so well. 'I have to admit, that sounds great,' I agree.

We all pile into Charlie's car and head off for the McDonald's in town. The kids have a Happy Meal each while me and Charlie both have a chicken burger and coffee. The kids chat happily as they eat, comparing the free toys from their meals.

'Do you often come to McDonald's for lunch on a Sunday?' I ask Charlie.

He shakes his head. 'Mum usually cooks a dinner for us all but now and again I want a day just for us. I don't get to spend much time with the girls what with school and work so I try to make sure we have an "us day" at least once a month. I had to grab some stuff from the DIY and remembered this park so thought we'd drop off here.' He takes a bite of his burger then asks, 'How about you?'

I don't tell him that I have a chicken in the fridge ready to cook us a dinner when we came back from the park. I merely shrug my shoulders and say, 'It's usually a Saturday thing but it's good to do something different now and again.'

'Have you lived in the area long?' he asks me.

'Just over three years.' I don't tell him about Arran, I don't want to talk about it. 'What made you swap being a mechanic for a literacy skills tutor?' I ask, changing the subject.

He looks thoughtful. 'Does it sound trite to say that I wanted to do something useful with my life?' He scratches behind his ear. 'I sort of drifted into being a mechanic. When I was a teenager I got a part-time job with one of Dad's friends who owned a garage, then I went on to train as a mechanic, and when the garage came for sale Dad helped me buy it. My heart wasn't really in it. So I sold the garage and retrained.'

I wonder what his parents thought of that. And Lynn. I don't ask though. I don't want to pry, and the more I ask about him, the more he will ask about me.

Daisy tugs Charlie's sleeve then and tells him that she has a headache. He places his hand on her forehead. 'She doesn't seem to have a temperature but I guess I'd better get her home.'

'We're ready to go too,' I say, and we head back out to the car.

'Thanks for a lovely day,' Charlie says as he drops us off. 'I've really enjoyed it. Let's do it again sometime.'

'I'd like that,' I reply. I put my arm around Liam's shoulder and watch Charlie drive off. I feel so at ease with him, and Liam got on really well with the two girls.

'Charlie's nice,' Liam says as we walk back into the house.

'Yes, he is,' I agree. 'And you enjoyed playing with Mia and Daisy, didn't you?'

He nods. 'Can I play with my iPad for a bit now?'

'Twenty minutes,' I tell him.

He goes off to get it and I sit down with a magazine, my mind mulling over the afternoon. Funny how I keep bumping into Charlie out of school: him coming to the dentist, rescuing me when my car was broken down and now seeing him at the duck pond. It's almost as if fate keeps pushing us together. I wonder what made him go to the shop by us when there is a big retail unit and a park over his way. Whatever it was, I'm pleased. We'd never have bumped into him otherwise and it has been such a nice day. I'm really warming to Charlie, and I'm pretty sure he feels the same. I'm wary, of course I am, but Charlie isn't Dylan. He's kind, caring and brilliant with his girls. I can trust him.

Can't I?

15

When we arrive at school the next morning we pass Tasha about to get in her car. 'I'm in a rush today, Ryan's carried on in,' she shouts.

'Am I late?' Liam frets as we hurry to the playground.

'No, we're fine.' He's such a worrier. I think he gets that off me, although I've not always been that way. I glance around but there's no sign of Charlie and his girls. Maybe he's already gone, too. Liam kisses me goodbye and runs off through the open gates.

The Mum Gang are all clustered around Crystal, who's spouting off about the fabulous evening she had at Charlie's last week, how he and his mother are going to help out with the PTA. 'Of course, we're old friends,' she says. 'Charlie and I go back a long way.'

I edge a bit closer, wanting to hear more.

'What's his house like?' Lacey asks all wide-eyed.

'Gorgeous, and he and Alice always make me feel so welcome. We all had a little nightcap together.' Crystal's voice drifts over to me as I'm sure it was meant to. I wonder if that nightcap was the whisky I bought Charlie, and that she knows it was my gift. I fix my attention on Liam, who has turned to wave to me, and pretend that I'm not listening. Alice was the one who organised the meeting, I remind myself. And what Charlie does in his spare time is nothing to do with me. I'm tempted to tell them about bumping into Charlie yesterday and going to McDonald's together but I don't want our burgeoning friendship to become a subject of gossip.

I blow Liam a kiss and head back to my car, I'm about to open the door when Charlie pulls up.

'Morning. You're cutting it fine,' I say as he gets out and opens the back door for Mia. Daisy is still strapped in her car seat, looking very flushed. And now I can see that Charlie looks stressed. 'Is everything okay?'

'Daisy is ill, I think she's picked up a bug from nursery. I've had to book the morning off work to take her to the doctor's. Mum offered to take her but I don't want her to catch anything, some of these viruses can be really nasty.'

'She said she had a headache yesterday,' I remember. Poor Daisy looks so miserable and Charlie so flustered that I instinctively want to help. 'Look, how about I take Mia into school, save you leaving Daisy in the car alone?'

He runs his hand through his gorgeous floppy hair. 'Thank you, that would be great.' He crouches down so that he's face level with Mia. 'You go with Sarah, darling, and either me or Nanny will pick you up later. Okay?'

Mia nods. 'Bye, Daddy. Bye, Daisy.'

Daisy gives a feeble little wave from the back seat. I hold my hand out tentatively, wondering if Mia would prefer to walk beside me. 'Shall we go?'

She slips her hand in mine and we walk over to the playground.

'My head hurts too,' she says as we reach the gates.

I look anxiously at her. Is it my imagination or does she look a bit pale? 'Did you tell Daddy?'

She shakes her head. 'It's only just started.'

'If you don't feel better soon, let your teacher know,' I tell her.

'I will,' she promises. She lets go of my hand and runs into the playground. Crystal and the Mum Gang are still huddled in the corner, gossiping. I can feel their eyes on me and refuse to look their way until Crystal calls me.

'Why are you taking Mia into school? Is everything all right with Charlie?'

'Daisy is ill so he's taking her to the doctor's. I bumped into them in the car park and offered to take Mia in,' I answer.

'Oh dear, I must phone him and see if he needs any help. We're old friends, you know.'

Of course I know, she's told everyone in the playground this morning. 'I'm sure he'll reach out if he needs help. He has my number, and I expect he has yours too.'

'He has your number?' Crystal repeats, her brow puckered. She leaves the group and sidles over to me. 'I hope that you're not reading too much into Charlie's friendliness with you. He's that kind of guy, happy to help anyone out. I wouldn't want you getting the wrong impression,' she whispers.

'Seriously, Crystal, I'm just helping out in return as he's a friend,' I tell her. 'You'll have to excuse me, I've got to go to work.'

I head off back to my car, Crystal's words stinging in my ears. I do like Charlie, but maybe I should keep my distance from him a bit. I hope it doesn't look like I'm chasing him, like the rest of the Mum Gang.

Or like Tasha – I know she likes him even though she's now dating someone else. I don't want to step on her toes. She's a good friend but if you rub her up the wrong way you know it, and I don't want to fall out with her.

Especially given what she knows about me.

16

I've only been in work a couple of hours when the secretary phones me to say that Liam has come out in spots and they think it's chickenpox. 'It's going around the school, several children are off with it,' she says.

Oh great, just what I need! That means I'm going to have to take time off work. I tell her I'll come and collect him as soon as I can, then check with Yvonne to see if she can cover for me.

'No problem, you go and look after Liam,' she says.

Maddie is really understanding too. 'Take as much time as you need,' she tells me, and I'm so grateful for how considerate they are. I'm anxious to get to Liam. I can't help feeling guilty too as he said he didn't feel well this morning but I thought he was trying to pull a fast one. It's hard being a single mum!

As I head to the car park I get a message from Charlie.

Daisy has chickenpox and the school have called to say they think Mia has it too. I'm on my way to collect her. I hope Liam doesn't get it.

Too late. The school have phoned me too, I'm on my way to pick him up. I hope Mia and Daisy aren't very ill with it.

Charlie is about to get in his car as I pull up, and I can see Daisy and Mia sitting in the back. He turns to me as I open my car door. 'This is a nightmare. I can't leave the girls with Mum, she had a bad attack of shingles a couple of years ago and I can't risk her getting it again – not at her age,' he adds. 'I'll have to book some time off work. I could do without this at the beginning of a new term.' He looks so agitated, I feel sorry for him.

'You can leave them both with me,' I offer impulsively. The words pop out before I even think what I'm saying. 'My boss has given me time off for Liam, so they can all keep each other company. And don't worry, I'm DBS checked. I went on trips with Liam's nursery so had to get one and have kept it up to date.'

I can see the relief in Charlie's eyes. 'Really? Are you sure? That would be amazing but it's a lot for you to handle.'

I can't take the offer back now, and I don't want to. I know how tough it is being a single parent, and Charlie and his girls have been through enough with their mother walking out. I want to help. 'It's no trouble. Liam will be much happier with company than at home bored on his own.'

'Sarah, you're a lifesaver.' Charlie beams. 'I could hug you.'

'I'm happy to help,' I tell him, careful not to let the effect of his words come through in my voice.

'Then please, come and look after all the kids at my house. We've got plenty of room and I don't want them all messing up your home,' he insists. 'Plus the girls have all their things there so it will be easier for you.' He gives me a steady look. 'And you must let me pay you.'

'Absolutely not,' I tell him, not sure whether I should be offended by his offer. He's right, though, it would be a bit of a squash to have three children cooped up in my small house, as he knows, he's seen it, which is probably what's made him offer. 'It does makes sense to come around to yours so the girls can be in their own home, though. Liam can bring a few of his things with him.'

'You're a lifesaver, Sarah. I'm so grateful.' He reaches out and touches my arm and there goes that jolt of electricity again. This time Charlie lets his hand linger for a few seconds, as if he's enjoying the connection as much as I am. When he removes it I shiver involuntarily. 'I'd better text you my address,' he says, taking out his phone and tapping at the keys. A few seconds later the text pings into my phone.

'That's settled then. Shall we come around for eight thirty tomorrow morning? Would that be okay?' I ask, marvelling at how steady my voice is when I'm like jelly inside. Am I mad to offer to spend the rest of the week at this man's house when he has this effect on me? He'll be at work all day, I can go as soon as he comes home, I tell myself.

'Perfect. And don't worry about bringing any food with you, I've got plenty in,' he tells me.

'How about I make us all a meal in the evening, then me and Liam can go home afterwards,' I suggest. 'I don't mind as I'll need to cook for us but I'd better tell you that I'm only a basic cook. You won't be getting cordon bleu.' Alice is so elegant, and so 'proper', I imagine that she is a very skilled cook. She probably hosted lots of dinner parties when Charlie's dad was alive.

'That would be great, if you're sure, and basic is good for me. I'm more than happy to put a meal together and do most of the cooking at the weekend but Mum always insists on having a meal ready when I come home, she likes to be useful. She's so upset that she can't be with them now when they're ill.'

I think of how the little girls run to Alice and hug her, how pleased she always is to see them. She must be devasted that she can't help now when Charlie needs it so much. I'm glad that I offered and pleased that I can step in and repay Charlie for coming to my rescue.

Tasha phones me later for an update and can't believe it when I tell her that I'm going to look after all the kids at Charlie's house. 'I knew you two fancied each other!' Is that resentment I hear in her voice?

'I don't fancy Charlie. I'm merely helping him out, like he did for me.'

'Yeah, right! And I thought you'd vowed to never get involved again.' This from the woman who's been trying to persuade me to sign up to a dating app for the past couple of months.

'I am not getting involved! We're friends. Besides, it makes sense for me to look after Charlie's girls too. I've already been given the time off work.'

'Chill, I'm only kidding you.' Tasha lightens her tone. Phew! She is the last person I want to upset – I don't know what I'd have done without her over the past few years. 'When Liam is better we must fix something up for you to meet Caleb, you'll love him.'

'Going that well, is it?' I tease.

'Really well. In fact, he's coming around tonight. I'll message you tomorrow and tell you all about it. Enjoy yourself at Charlie's. You're going to be the talk of the playground, you know.'

I sigh. 'We're simply friends, Tash.'

'Yeah, yeah,' she chuckles as she ends the call.

I think how lucky she is to have her mum nearby, always ready to help out with Ryan. Charlie too.

I had that once. Me and my mum were so close, especially after the divorce. I loved Dad, but I could see why they split up: Dad was a drifter, popping in and out of our lives, gambling his wages, running up debts. Poor Mum held down two jobs to pay the bills and keep a roof over our heads. She was on her own for years after the divorce, then she went on holiday to the Isle of Arran, met Bill and they've been together ever since.

They were both so welcoming when I went to stay, and I was grateful for their support. It was good to be able to relax, and to have help with Liam. Until it all went wrong.

Now I wonder if I'll ever see them again. I know Liam misses them, but I can't forgive Mum for what she said to me. And I don't think she'll ever forgive me for what I did.

'Wow, Mum!' Liam exclaims, his eyes wide with wonder as I pull up in front of some huge metal gates the next morning. 'Lucky Mia and Daisy living here!'

I can hardly believe it either. I knew that Charlie lived in the posh quarter but I didn't expect this. There is a sign that reads 'The Gables' on the brick pillar of the right gate, and through the bars I can make out a huge bricked house like the ones you see for sale in the top price range at the estate agents. A wide path winds through expansive, expertly mowed lawns, leading to a paved driveway, big enough to park at least a dozen cars. 'Wow' is definitely the right word.

'How do we get in?' Liam asks.

'There's a bell on the pillar, I'll ring that.' I am about to get out when the gates start to open. Charlie must have been looking out for us. I close the car door again and drive in, gazing in awe at the large lawn, beautiful flower beds and spectacular double-fronted detached house. I can count six windows on the front so goodness knows how many rooms there are, and there's a separate twin garage with white doors on the left side. This has got to be worth well over a million pounds.

I wonder what Charlie thought of our tiny two-bed terrace. I reckon his front garden is bigger than my entire house and back garden together. And it isn't even mine, I rent it.

'You found us okay then.' Charlie has opened the front door and is standing on the doorstep.

'Yes, the satnav did its job,' I say, trying to act as if I'm not blown away by his magnificent home.

Charlie opens the door wide. 'Go right in. The girls are waiting for you. Straight down the hall and second door on the left is the playroom,' he tells Liam. Liam doesn't need telling twice and is off before I even step into the wide, white-and-black diamond-tiled hallway with dark oak doors lining each side, and a wooden, twisty staircase in the middle. I catch my breath, it's like something out of a film.

'I can't tell you how grateful I am to you for doing this.' Charlie closes the heavy wooden door behind me. 'It really is kind of you.'

I shrug in an effort to be nonchalant as I follow him down the hall, past a couple of closed doors on both sides. 'I might as well look after three kids as one. How are the girls? Liam is more or less his normal self – if it wasn't for the spots, you wouldn't think he was ill.'

'Yes, Mia is the same but Daisy is a bit fretful.' Charlie turns right into a huge kitchen with fitted teak cupboards on every wall, and a polished wooden table with six chairs on the far side. There's a long window across the sink where I can see the lawned garden, with flower borders. 'I've explained that you're looking after them while I work. If it gets too much for you, or if any of the kids take a turn for the worse, please phone me right away and I'll come straight home,' Charlie continues.

'I will,' I promise. 'But I'm sure I'll cope and the girls will be fine.'

Charlie gives me a quick tour: first, the kitchen – with quick instructions on how to use the splendid-looking coffee machine and the gleaming range – which leads into the kids' playroom, where Liam is now happily bouncing on an indoor trampoline while Daisy is building bricks and Mia is drawing on a blackboard. Huge French doors lead out into the garden, where an area has been fenced off for the girls to play in with a slide, swings, a Wendy house and a rabbit hutch. Liam will love that, he adores animals.

'That's Thumper. I bought him for the girls after Lynn left, hoping it would help keep their mind off things,' Charlie offers ruefully. 'You don't have to worry about looking after him. I'll do that. Best not to let the kids touch him until they're all better though.'

Opposite the kitchen is the family room with two comfy soft leather sofas, a few chairs, a TV and wall unit and patio windows. The room before the kitchen is the dining room, then a large lounge at the front of the house with a posher sofa, bigger TV and a couple of glass cabinets full of figurines, which I can see are a well-known brand. 'We only use this room when we're entertaining, the girls never come in here,' Charlie tells me.

'So this is out of bounds. Any other rooms the kids shouldn't go in?' I ask.

'Mia and Daisy know the rules and I'm sure Liam won't wander.' There's something about the way he says this that makes me shoot a look at him but he's turned away now and is crossing the hall. The room opposite is Charlie's study – which he doesn't open and I gather is also out of bounds.

'I'll make sure that Liam keeps to the back of the house,' I reassure him as we continue the tour, passing a downstairs bathroom and separate loo then going upstairs where there are six bedrooms. Six!

'This is Mia's room.' Charlie opens the door of the first one and I inwardly gasp at how beautiful it is, with a big double bed draped in a rainbow-coloured net canopy. The duvet cover has a rainbow on it too. There are lots of plush toys including a big rocking horse, a dressing table, toybox and a reading corner with a rainbow-coloured beanbag by a full bookcase.

'And this is Daisy's room.' Charlie leads us to the next room, which is purple and white – purple is Daisy's favourite colour, I remember. There's a heart-shaped photo frame with several photos in it on the wall of each bedroom. Both rooms look like something out of a magazine.

'They're gorgeous!' I exclaim. My mind flashes to Liam's tiny bedroom with his combined cabin bunk bed, wardrobe and desk, and Pokémon duvet cover and curtains. There's barely enough room for him to sit on the floor and play with his toys. I'm surprised that the girls don't share a room though, Daisy is so young.

As if reading my mind, Charlie says, 'Most nights they snuggle up together, taking it in turns to sleep in each other's bed, but I think it's important that they have their own space if they want it.

'This is my room,' he says, indicating a closed door next to Daisy's, 'and these are three guest rooms and a family bathroom.' He doesn't open the doors to them but turns back and heads for the stairs.

Tour ended and subtle message received, I'm only to go into the girls' bedrooms. Fair enough. I wouldn't want anyone to wander around my house poking into things either.

'Help yourself to anything you need, I want you and Liam to feel at home,' Charlie says as we go down the winding staircase. 'What would you like the girls to call you? I've just realised that I don't know your last name.' We're walking towards the playroom now.

'It's Foster, they can call me Sarah.'

Charlie opens the door of the playroom, where all three kids are still playing happily. Hardly surprising as the girls have everything they could possibly want in here: a TV, an iPad each, cupboards of toys, a desk with crayons and colouring books on it, a dolls' house and a wooden rocking horse. There's even a child's train set laid out on a table with miniature people lining up at the station. Liam and Mia are playing with it but Daisy is sitting down at the desk, colouring.

'I have to go to work now, girls, remember that Auntie Sarah and Liam will be here until I get home. Are you both okay with that?' I'm a bit taken aback by the 'Auntie Sarah', it makes us sound closer than we are but I guess Charlie wants the girls to feel safe with me. He squats down to eye level as he speaks to them and they nod. He really is good with them.

'Thanks again, Sarah.' He touches my arm lightly. 'I'm teaching most of the day so won't be able to answer any messages right away but if you need anything urgently, call Mum.' He sends me a text. 'That's her number.' He hugs and kisses the girls, gives Liam a high five and leaves.

I go through to the kitchen to make myself a cup of coffee – I've been dying to try out the state-of-the-art coffee machine. I ponder for a minute or two on what coffee to go for then plump for a latte and take it over to the table, where I can sit and sip it while keeping an eye on the kids. Daisy's face is puckered into a little frown as she concentrates on her colouring, and Mia and Liam are laughing as they put the tiny figures in the train and watch them go around the track.

The girls are so sweet and it's clear that Charlie idolises them. How could their mother desert them? Simply walk out and never come back? I shake my head. The thought of a life without Liam would be horrible. I could never leave him. Never.

A tight lump of emotion forms in my throat as I remember the danger I put him in. And that Dylan is due to be released tomorrow.

18

'My head hurts, Auntie Sarah.' Daisy tugs on my jeans, her voice quivering.

'Does it?' I place the back of my hand on her forehead. It feels hot. 'Come into the kitchen and let me take your temperature.'

Her little soft hand in mine, we go into the kitchen. I put my mug on the worktop and sit Daisy down on the chair, then reach up to the top corner cupboard where Charlie told me he keeps his first-aid kit. Her temperature is a bit high but not enough to worry about. I glance at the clock. Charlie said she last had Calpol at seven so she could have some more now. 'I'll give you some more medicine, darling, then maybe you'd like to lie down on the sofa for a bit.'

Daisy nods, her big blue eyes following me as I go to the fridge for the medicine. She takes it readily, then holds my hand as we walk into the family lounge and lies down on the sofa, snuggling up on a pillow as I put a thin blanket over her. Her eyes close and she is soon asleep. I sit watching her for a while, she looks so young and vulnerable.

Does her mother ever think about her? Surely she misses

her. Relationships break up, but to walk away and never see your kids again is unforgivable.

I stand up and look around the lounge. There are several family photos on the wall but they're all of Charlie and the girls, or the girls with their grandmother. None of their mother.

I cast my mind back to what Charlie said her name is. Lynn, that's it. Maybe there's a photo of her in the wall frames in the girls' rooms. Liam has a photo of him and Todd by his bed, and a little photo album of them both together which he likes to look through.

'We're hungry,' Liam announces as he and Mia walk in. They're covered in even more spots now, but they seem fine otherwise.

'Is Daisy okay?' Mia asks, frowning as she sees her younger sister asleep on the sofa.

'She has a headache so I gave her some more medicine. How are you both feeling? Do you have a headache?'

'No, but I'm itchy,' Liam complains, scratching at his arm.

'Me too,' Mia agrees.

'Try not to scratch.' I take both their temperatures. Both are very slightly up but that is normal with chickenpox, so I give them both some medicine and put more ointment on their spots. 'That should help you be more comfortable,' I say. 'Now how about I do you a milkshake each and some biscuits to tide you over until lunchtime?'

They nod eagerly and follow me into the kitchen for their snack, sitting at the table to eat. I check on Daisy, who is still sleeping peacefully, then go back to the kitchen where I can hear Liam and Mia chatting away.

'You're lucky to have a mum,' Mia says to Liam.

'Why doesn't your mum live with you?' Liam replies, licking the cream out of the middle of his biscuit.

I pause at the doorway. They haven't noticed me yet and I don't want to interrupt.

Mia shrugs. 'She doesn't want to. She left just before my birthday when I was five and she hasn't come back.' Her voice wobbles a bit. 'She didn't even say goodbye.'

What sort of mother leaves just before her daughter's birthday, and doesn't say goodbye to them? I stand still, waiting to hear what else Mia tells Liam.

Liam takes a bite out of the biscuit. 'Did she send you a present?'

Mia shakes her head sadly, her bottom lip quivering. 'No. She doesn't send us cards or presents. Never. Nan said she's forgotten all about us and got a new life.'

That's harsh of Alice. Even if she, understandably, doesn't like Lynn after what she did, she should think of the poor children's feelings. They're very young for her to be so brutal.

Liam seems to consider this a bit. 'My dad's got a new life too, but he still remembers me. He sends me presents and talks to me on FaceTime and comes to see me sometimes.'

'You're lucky.' Mia takes a swig of her strawberry milkshake then wipes her mouth with the back of her hand. 'I wish I could see my mum. Daisy doesn't remember her but I do. She was lots of fun. She used to make cakes with me, and play dolls' house, and read me bedtimes stories. And she was always cuddling Daisy and singing her to sleep.'

I can hear the tremble in her voice and want to go and hug her but I'm not sure she'd want me to have heard. So I decide to stop the conversation before Mia gets too upset and walk in saying in a loud, bright voice, 'How are you getting on with that milk and biscuits?'

'Almost finished,' Liam replies but Mia keeps her gaze fixed on her glass of milkshake and doesn't say anything.

Poor kid. She obviously misses her mum, and it sounds like Lynn was very loving to the two little girls. So why has she completely disappeared from their lives? It doesn't make sense.

19

I can't believe how incredible Charlie's house is, even the front lounge where the children aren't allowed – it's very old fashioned with dated wood furniture and thick velvet drapes at the window, not the sort of room I'd imagine Charlie choosing. I wonder how Charlie can afford a house like this as a skills tutor, then remember he sold his own garage.

Alice FaceTimes a few times to check on the girls, Charlie has obviously given her my number. She always asks me how I am, and asks after Liam too, which is cordial of her, though I think it is her way of keeping an eye on me and making sure I am looking after her granddaughters. I guess that after their mother deserted them, it's only natural she's a bit overprotective. Probably she's lonely too and misses them.

I wonder if Alice ever oversteps the mark and Charlie bites his tongue because he needs her so much. Grandmothers can be more protective of their grandchildren than their own children, I think, remembering my own mother. I know that Liam misses his nan, and I feel guilty about that, but what could I do after what happened? She had no right to threaten to take Liam from me.

A lump forms in my throat and I swallow it down. It takes two to break and rebuild a relationship and Mum has never apologised or tried to get back in touch. Neither have I, I acknowledge, I can't bring myself to. Anyway, I think that the fewer people who know where I am now the better. I can't take the risk of Dylan being able to track me down. A clean break is best for everyone.

I'm just taking a casserole out of the oven when Charlie comes home carrying a chocolate trifle. 'I couldn't resist it. Daisy and Mia love trifle – does Liam?'

Before I can answer, Liam comes running in. 'Chocolate trifle. Fab!'

When the meal is finished and the kids have gone into the dayroom to watch a film, we're still sitting drinking coffee.

'How have they been?' Charlie asks.

'Okay – itchy and a bit irritable now and again but mostly they've been playing nicely. They all fell asleep this afternoon, cuddled up together watching a film.' It was so sweet to see the three of them all side by side on the sofa, fast asleep under a shared throw.

'That's great.' He cocks his head to one side. 'I hope Mum hasn't been too much of a nuisance? I meant to tell you that she asked for your number so she could check on the girls. She didn't phone every hour, did she?'

I shake my head. 'Not quite.'

Charlie groans and puts his hands over his face. 'So sorry!'

'Don't worry, it's understandable that she's concerned, she barely knows me. I'm sure she feels really bad that she can't come and look after them herself.'

'Yeah, she fusses a bit but her heart's in the right place. I don't know what I'd have done without her when Lynn left.'

'That must have been hard for you,' I say. 'Did you move here so you could be closer to your mum?'

Charlie sips his coffee thoughtfully. 'It was Mum's idea, but it made sense. This is my family home, I was brought up here and I'm the only child. It's too big for Mum since Dad died so she passed it over to me a couple of months ago and moved into a modern apartment on a nearby retirement complex.'

Wow! Fancy being gifted a house like this! 'I'm sorry to hear about your dad. That must have been tough for your mum.'

'It was a few years ago, but yeah, they'd been married a long time. And Mum felt too lonely here by herself, and she wanted me to be nearby so she could help with the girls. They spent a lot of time here anyway, so it made sense. Plus it was a new start for us all.' His face clouds over. 'The girls, especially Mia, kept waiting for their mum to come back. There were too many memories of Lynn in that house, I was glad to leave it.'

Do you keep waiting for her to come back? I want to ask but I stop myself. We're not close enough for me to ask that sort of question. 'It must have been a difficult time for you,' I say again.

'It was, but I'm over Lynn, if that's what you're wondering. I want her to come back for the girls, I want her to have a relationship with them. They need their mum.' His face darkens and a muscle tightens in his jaw. 'I'll never forgive her for walking out on them like this.'

I don't blame him. It's a terrible thing for a parent to do.

He runs a hand through his hair. 'Sorry for boring you with my problems. How about you? You said that Liam's father works on an oil rig but is still in Liam's life. Do you have family nearby?'

I shake my head. 'My parents are divorced, my mum lives on the Isle of Arran and my dad lives in Thailand, both with new partners. My older brother, Leo, works in Manchester as an events manager. We're not particularly close.'

'You certainly seem to manage well, and you and Liam have

a fantastic relationship. It's really good of you to look after the girls, are you sure you can cope for the rest of the week? And that you won't allow me to pay you?'

I take that as my cue to go so I stand up. 'Absolutely, they've been no trouble at all and Liam has enjoyed playing here, it's taken his mind off his itchy spots.' I grab my handbag from the chair. 'We'll be back for eight thirty tomorrow, and no I definitely won't accept payment, don't be silly.'

'I can't thank you enough,' Charlie says softly. He's gazing at me with those gorgeous greeny-blue eyes of his and I can't tear myself away from them, I'm sinking into them. I pull myself together and hope he hasn't noticed the flush I can feel heating up my cheeks.

'It's no problem. It makes no sense for us both to have time off work.'

Charlie reaches out and touches my arm. 'I'll see you tomorrow then.'

I'm wearing a soft cotton long-sleeved shirt but the feel of his fingers sends a shiver up my arm. I turn away, scared that my eyes will give away the sudden surge of longing that shoots through me. 'Liam,' I shout. 'We need to go home, love.'

Liam comes out from the playroom looking downcast. 'I wish we didn't have to go home. It's fun here. Our house is so tiny,' he grumbles.

Charlie puts his hand on Liam's shoulder. 'Your home is lovely and cosy. And your things are there, that's what matters, not what size it is,' he says. 'Lots of people haven't got a home.' He sounds like he means it, not like he's simply spouting it out.

Liam looks a bit guilty. 'I guess,' he mumbles.

'Anyway, we'll be back tomorrow,' I add. 'Bye, Charlie.'

Liam is so tired when we get home that he goes straight to bed, crashing out almost instantly. He's had a busy day and enjoyed playing with the girls, and as I stand and watch him sleep, I find myself wishing that he had a brother or sister. It must be lonely for him, only the two of us.

I've just settled down with a mug of cocoa and my word-search book when Tasha rings to tell me how things are going with Caleb. 'I can't believe how at ease I feel with him, and he's so gorgeous. He's a keeper, Sarah.'

'So Charlie is out of the frame then?' I ask lightly, crossing my fingers as I wait for her answer.

'Yep and a good job too or I'd be scratching your eyes out!' Tasha chuckles. 'Were your ears burning today? The Mum Gang are fuming that you're over at Charlie's looking after his girls.'

I can imagine them talking and I can't help smiling to myself that out of all the mums that were after Charlie, I'm the one who's got close to him.

Then words of warning shoot into my mind: *Careful, don't get too close.*

20

ALICE

I'm devastated that I can't be there to look after my precious granddaughters when Charlie needs me. I'm willing to risk catching shingles again but Charlie won't hear of it. He is so protective of me. 'Sarah is going to look after the girls,' he told me over the phone. 'Her son Liam has chickenpox too so the kids can all be together.'

I tried to talk him out of it, he hardly knows the woman, but he was adamant. 'I've already lost my dad, I don't want to lose my mum too.'

I know that he wants to keep me safe but I can't bear the thought of a whole week without seeing my beloved son and granddaughters. Today has dragged so much, without my usual trip to the school to pick up the girls. I make myself a cup of chamomile tea to calm my nerves and take it over to the window seat, looking out at the immaculately landscaped gardens surrounding the apartment block I now live in.

I don't like this Sarah. She's taking advantage of Charlie, worming herself in. I've no doubt she's looking after the girls, it will all be part of her ploy to hook Charlie. I bet she's mooching though, poking around to see what she can find. I don't trust her at all.

It's a pity Crystal's daughter, Phoebe, has chickenpox too and they've gone to spend the week with Crystal's parents. Otherwise Charlie would have asked her to look after Mia and Daisy, and I'd have felt much more comfortable with that.

Charlie worries too much about me. He's always been a sweet boy. He loved to sit by me on the sofa and cuddle up while I read him a story, and followed me everywhere like a shadow. I was lucky that I didn't have to work – Kenneth's salary as an investment banker was more than enough to keep the three of us. We were both so happy to finally have a baby of our own, we'd been trying for years, and we wanted to spend as much time as we could with our son. Especially me, Charlie is my world. And he and the girls have become even more dear to me since my Kenneth died.

Charlie was so shaken up after what happened with Lynn, it was all he could do to keep it together and look after those darling girls. So of course I stepped in to help, what mother wouldn't?

And now this Sarah has got her hooks into him. I knew as soon as I saw her that she was a threat but I didn't expect things to move so fast. She only met Charlie a couple of weeks ago and already she and her son are in his house and she's looking after *my* granddaughters. She saw her opportunity and seized it.

She's clever. She acts like she's the doting mother, not interested in men, but she doesn't fool me – she was quick enough to get Charlie fixing her car, and to offer to look after Daisy and Mia.

Well, everyone has their secrets, and I'm going to find out Sarah's.

21

SARAH

I'm on edge this morning, a wave of nausea flowing over me. Dylan will be released today. I take a few deep breaths to calm myself down. He doesn't know where I live. And he won't risk it, he's on parole. He expressed his regret for what happened and kept his nose clean so got released early. Surely he won't mess that up to come after me? I can't help glancing around as we go out the front door and climb into the car though.

I study my reflection in the rearview mirror: I usually wear a light-coloured lipstick but today I've gone for one with plum tones and have added a light layer of dark brown mascara to bring out the hazel flecks in my eyes. If Tasha saw me, she'd accuse me of making an extra effort just for Charlie, and she'd be right.

Liam's face and body are covered in red spots but he's cheerful enough and fidgeting in the back seat. I can see he's eager to go to Charlie's again. He's not the only one.

Charlie must have been looking out for us again because the gates open as soon as I pull up.

Daisy and Mia are both tucking into breakfast and still dressed in their pyjamas. 'I'm running a bit late, sorry. Daisy had a disturbed night.' Charlie grabs his jacket and briefcase. 'Leave them in their pjs all day if it's easier, I don't mind.'

'I'll see how they go. Has Daisy got a temperature?' I feel her forehead, it's a bit warm.

'She did have and I gave her some Calpol. I've written the time down on the memo board. It's dropped a bit now.' He looks at Daisy anxiously. 'Maybe I should stay home. It's not fair to leave you to cope. And she might need me.'

'I'm sure she'll be fine. You're okay with Auntie Sarah, aren't you, poppet?' I ask, kneeling down by Daisy. She nods.

Charlie still looks hesitant. 'You'll phone me if she gets any worse?'

I pick up Daisy and she snuggles into my shoulder, sucking her thumb. 'I promise you I'll take care of them both and send you regular updates.'

The anxiety doesn't leave his eyes but his body relaxes a little. 'I can't thank you enough.' He leans over and kisses Daisy. 'Bye, darling. I'll be back as soon as I can.'

As he straightens up his eyes meet mine and for a moment our gazes are locked and I think he's going to kiss me too. My heart is thudding in my chest so loud I'm sure he must be able to hear it, and I can't tear my eyes away from his. I'm sinking into the big black pools of his pupils. Then I hear him catch his breath and I feel dazed as he turns away to say goodbye to Mia.

Charlie hasn't been gone long when Alice FaceTimes. The girls sit down on the sofa, with the iPad standing on the coffee table, to talk to her. Liam hovers in the background and Alice waves to him too. After a while the kids get bored, say goodbye and go off to play but Alice stays on the screen. 'It's very good of you to look after Mia and Daisy,' she says.

'It's no trouble.' I sit down so that I can see her better. 'And it makes sense as Liam has chickenpox too.'

'I wish I could help. I'm sure Liam's nan feels the same, you always want to look after your grandchildren.'

That hits home. 'My mum lives in Scotland.' I change the subject. 'They'll all be better soon then you can see them again.'

'I know. And at least I can keep in touch this way. I'll call again soon.'

I have no doubt that she will.

Daisy comes back rubbing her eyes. 'I'm tired,' she says as she climbs onto the sofa and rests her head on the cushion.

'Have a little rest then,' I say, pulling the throw from the back and tucking it over her. I turn the TV to the kids' channel and sit down beside her. She smiles up at me and her eyes start to close.

When she's fast asleep I go and check on Liam and Mia. They're both playing happily. It was a good idea to offer to look after Charlie's girls – Liam would have been fed up and miserable cooped up at home so this suits us all.

Daisy perks up after her sleep and we all have a drink and a snack then play a few games of Sleeping Dinosaurs, which is great fun. We're all roaring with laughter as we race each other around the board trying to get past the dinosaurs without waking them.

The next time Alice FaceTimes, the girls fidget as they talk to her, wanting to get back to the game. She looks a bit put out. 'I can see that you're having fun so I'll talk to you again later,' she says.

I know that she's missing the girls but surely once a day is enough to call them. I wonder if it's the girls she's checking up on or me.

After playing a couple more games we have lunch and the children all snuggle up on the sofa to sleep.

I message Charlie to let him know that Daisy's temperature

has dropped, she's eaten lunch and we've had a fun morning playing games, then I go into the kitchen and check the well-stocked fridge and freezer, wondering what to cook for tea. Alice phones. Again.

I don't want to wake the girls so I ignore her call and carry on looking through the freezer. I find a family-size shepherd's pie which looks homemade so I'm guessing Alice made it. That should do us all. Then my phone rings. I groan, wondering if it's Alice again, but when I check the screen I see that it's Charlie so I answer immediately.

'Is everything all right? Mum said she phoned and you didn't answer.' I can hear the anxiety in his voice.

'It's all fine, the kids are all asleep on the sofa.' I can't believe that Alice has phoned him at work and worried him like this. 'I was checking the freezer to see what to have for dinner and must have missed your mum's call. She's already phoned twice,' I add. God, the woman is a bit suffocating.

'Sorry, she does fuss sometimes.' There's a pause. 'I have a meeting after work so might be a bit late. Is that a problem?'

'Not at all. We have no set time to get home.'

Charlie doesn't arrive home until half past six, and by the time we've eaten, exchanging our news for the day, it's gone eight and the kids are all yawning.

Mia and Daisy want me to read them a bedtime story so Liam comes up too and sits on the edge of Daisy's big bed, listening and joining in. I look up from the book and realise that all three kids have fallen asleep.

The bedroom door opens and Charlie creeps in. His expression softens as he sees the three sleeping children. 'I'm so sorry to keep you so late,' he says. 'And now you have to drive home too.'

'Don't worry, Liam will fall asleep again as soon as we get

home,' I reply although Liam looks so peaceful I wish I didn't have to wake him.

Charlie looks at me hesitantly, as if he wants to say something and isn't sure how I'll take it.

'What's the matter?' I ask, wondering if he's annoyed that I've let Liam lie on Daisy's bed. 'Liam wanted to listen to the story too,' I explain hastily. 'I didn't expect him to fall asleep.'

'They're all so tired.' He rubs his cheek with his hand. 'Look, I hope I'm not out of line here but I'm wondering if it would be easier if you and Liam stayed over here for the next couple of nights? It's a lot for him to be taken out into the cold to come over here every morning then back again every night, when he's not well.'

Stay here in Charlie's house? I hesitate, remembering the growing attraction between us and wonder exactly what he's suggesting.

'We've got plenty of spare rooms,' he adds, as if he's guessed what I'm thinking. 'You could leave Liam here while you go and get some clothes and anything else you both need and I'll sort out your bedrooms.'

All above board then. And it does make sense. Plus, I won't have to worry about Dylan for the next few days. I look at Liam's sleepy face: it seems a shame to disturb him and I'd have to carry him from the car into the house. 'Thank you, that will make things easier. I'll go home and grab us some things. I won't be long.' With a last look at Liam sleeping so peacefully, I go downstairs, grab my coat and car keys, and set off.

Tasha phones as I pull up at my house. I ignore the call. She'll want a long chat and I don't have time. I glance around nervously: it's dark now and I can't help wondering if Dylan could be lurking in the shadows. I just want to get in, get our clothes and get back to the safety of Charlie's house.

22

Liam is still fast asleep with Mia and Daisy when I get back to Charlie's.

'I've made up the two guest rooms, they're next door to each other,' Charlie tells me as he shows me both rooms which are at the end of the hall. 'Mum's room is the one nearest to the girls.'

Suddenly Daisy wakes and starts crying, which wakes Liam and Mia too. Liam stumbles out of her bedroom rubbing his eyes. 'I'm tired.'

'I know, darling. We're staying at Charlie's tonight so you can get straight into bed. You have this room, look, next to mine.'

I take his hand and lead him to his bedroom. His eyes open wide. 'Wow! I'm sleeping here?'

'Yes, just until the weekend. It saves us travelling back and forth. I've got a few of your things in here.' I hold up the backpack containing his pyjamas, a couple of trackie bottoms and tops, iPad, joke book and the plush blue dinosaur he had off my mum and Bill when we stayed over there. Liam loves it and always sleeps with it.

'Can I go to bed now?' he asks.

'Of course. Have a wash, brush your teeth and get changed

into your pjs first. The bathroom is here.' I open the door Charlie indicated was the family bathroom and take a step back in awe. It is huge, three times the size of our poky bathroom. We both gawp at the large, white-and-grey-tiled step-in shower, freestanding claw-footed bath, huge grey fluffy rug in the middle of the floor, double washbasin with dual mirrors and wide bay window with slate-grey blinds.

'Wowee, Mum!' Liam's eyes are as wide as saucers.

Wowee, indeed! I am almost afraid to let Liam loose in here, although there's nothing he can break and it looks easy to keep clean.

'Get yourself ready for bed and I'll go and get you a drink,' I tell him. I'll get one for Mia and Daisy too, the chickenpox makes them so thirsty.

When I return, Charlie is just coming out of Mia's bedroom. He spots the drinks on the tray, thanks me and takes them to the girls. I go back to Liam, who is now happily tucked into bed, lying on two pillows, and place the glass of water on the bedside cabinet nearest to him.

'Are you going to be all right in here? I'm only next door if you need me.'

'Mum, this bed is like sleeping on a cloud!' He looks wonderstruck at the grandeur of it all. I am too.

'Night, darling. Call if you need me,' I say then realise that when I'm downstairs I won't hear him call in this huge house. His eyes are already closing though so I leave the bedroom door ajar and go down to join Charlie, who's in the kitchen making a hot chocolate. He glances over his shoulder at me as I walk in.

'I'm making myself a comfort drink. Fancy one?'

'I'd love one. Thanks.'

'Let's take them into the lounge,' he says, picking up both mugs and carrying them through to the family lounge. I follow him, wondering where to sit, then I see that Charlie's put both mugs down on the coffee table and has sat down in the corner of the nearest sofa, leaving plenty of room for me to sit by him. So I join him, keeping a reasonable space between us. He switches on the TV and selects a light comedy. 'Shall we watch this?' he asks.

'Sure,' I agree, feeling myself relax as I sip the hot drink.

We don't watch the programme, we sit and chat about his day at college and my day with the kids. It feels so right to be here, in Charlie's house, talking to him, I don't want to go to bed. I want to sit here and chat forever. Charlie doesn't seem in a rush either.

Eventually we both go upstairs, saying goodnight together on the landing before going to our separate bedrooms. I check on Liam, he's fast asleep and looks so cosy. Then I wash, change into my pyjamas and get into bed. Liam's right, it is like sleeping on a cloud. I sleep like a log all night.

The next two days pass so quickly. Apart from the spots being itchy, which affects Daisy more than the other two, the chickenpox doesn't really bother the children. Mia is quite independent, happy to go into the playroom with Liam and play with the many games or watch a cartoon on the TV, but Daisy is more clingy. She really seems to have taken to me and loves to sit on my lap for a cuddle. She wants me to read her a story and tuck her into bed the next evening, and Mia and Liam join us too. Charlie doesn't seem to mind. I guess that Alice probably reads to the girls before they go to bed, and that Daisy is missing her nan. Poor little mite. She's so sweet and always gives me a kiss on the cheek before she settles down to sleep. I've become really fond of the girls this week, and wonder more and more how their mother could have walked away from them.

And I've become much too fond of Charlie. I'm going to miss him and the girls. This last week we've become like a family unit and it has felt so right. I'm falling for him and I wonder if he's falling for me too.

'I'm so grateful for your help this week, Sarah. How about I treat you to dinner next weekend to thank you for all you've done for us?' Charlie asks when he comes home.

'There's no need,' I assure him. 'I'm glad to help.'

'I'd really like to. I'll miss you. Unless...' He hesitates. 'I feel like we've grown close this week but maybe I've imagined the connection?'

So he feels it too! Does he have the same tingling in his stomach that I get whenever we see each other? Does he wake up with the same eagerness to face the day as I do?

Does he lie in bed at night longing to go and join me, as I do with him?

I smile at him. 'I'll miss you too and I'd love to go for a meal with you. I can ask Tasha if she'll babysit for me.' I haven't told Tasha that we've stopped over at Charlie's the last two nights. Charlie hasn't told Alice either – I guess that neither of us wants the gossip, even though it has all been perfectly innocent.

Charlie looks delighted. 'Great. And Mum will stay over and look after the girls. She'll love that, she's missed them so much.'

'Let's arrange time and place in the week,' I say. 'I'd better get home now, I don't want to get back late.' I'm nervous about going back to the empty house and wish I could ask Charlie to come with me.

'Look, why don't you stay one more night? I'll order us all a takeaway and when the kids have gone to bed we can relax and open a bottle of wine.'

'Can we, Mum?' Liam begs, walking in and overhearing the end of the conversation. 'I don't want to go back to our little house. I want to stay in this big one with all the toys, and Daisy and Mia to play with.'

'I actually don't fancy going home in the dark to a cold house so if you're sure, yes please.'

'Positive.' Charlie kisses me on the cheek and my pulse races.

He's a really nice guy and he has two daughters he adores. I can trust him. I'm sure I can but I'll keep my wits about me. No one is going to put my son at risk again.

23

We end up staying at Charlie's for lunch the next day but I insist on us leaving then. I want to get home before it's dark. My heart is in my stomach as I pull up in my drive but all looks well. Mrs Stanton, our next-door neighbour, is tidying up the garden and greets me with a cheery hello. I open the door to find a few letters on the doormat – bills – and everything exactly as I left it. I breathe a sigh of relief. I have to stop being such a worrier. Dylan is in the past. I've always felt safe in this house, and I'm not going to let bad memories spoil it for me.

A text pings in from Charlie saying he misses me already and a warm glow fills me. We had a lovely evening last night, chatting and watching a box set, and we kissed goodnight before we went to bed. A proper kiss. I had the feeling he wanted to take it further but held back. It wasn't the right time, not with the kids in the house. But maybe soon. The thought brings a smile to my lips.

The weekend goes quickly and Liam settles down happily despite his protests that he wanted to stay at Charlie's. Home's home, no matter how big it is. He obviously wants more company though, so I resolve to arrange with Tasha for the boys to have more sleepovers.

Liam's blisters have all scabbed over by Monday so he can go back to school. Thank goodness, I'm anxious to get back to work and have something else to think about other than Charlie. He messaged me to say he has to go into work early and his mum is taking the girls to school, and how glad she is to be able to see them again. I'm sure she is, but I feel a bit flat now that things are back to normal. Last week was so special and I really miss Charlie and the girls.

When Mia and Daisy see me at the gates, they wave to me. 'Hello, Auntie Sarah,' they call. I blow a kiss to them and Alice inclines her head briefly.

The Mum Gang are out in force, arms folded, glancing over their shoulders at me, then turning back into a huddle to talk. There's no sign of Crystal today, so I wonder if Phoebe hasn't got over her chickenpox yet.

Daisy wriggles her hand free from Alice and runs over to us. 'I miss you, Auntie Sarah,' she says.

'I miss you too, darling.' I squat down to give her a cuddle. 'Are you going to nursery today?'

Daisy nods. 'I don't want to go.' Her bottom lip wobbles.

'That's because you've been poorly and missed a few days. You'll enjoy it when you get there and play with your friends again,' I tell her.

'Hello, Sarah. We've never actually been introduced, have we? Although I feel we know each other very well after all the FaceTime conversations last week.' Alice has walked over to follow Daisy. 'Thank you for looking after my granddaughters.'

'It's a pleasure. They were no trouble at all.'

'They are very well behaved.' Alice gently pats Daisy on the head. 'It was good of you to step in and save the day. Thankfully, they're better now and I can take over again.'

'Will you come back and live with us again soon?' Daisy asks. 'I want you to read me a bedtime story.'

Alice's breath comes out in a loud hiss and her lips purse together into a tight line. 'You stayed over?' she demanded.

'Only a couple of nights. In the guest bedrooms, of course. It made things easier for Charlie.' I keep my tone low, not wanting the Mum Gang to hear this. I'll never hear the last of it.

'Well, I'm sure you will be relieved to get back to your normal routine.' She takes Daisy's hand firmly. 'Come on, darling, let's get you to playschool and not bother Liam's mummy any further. I'm sure she has lots to do.'

As I watch Alice walk off with Daisy, I get the feeling that I've been dismissed.

'Well, how was your time at Charlie's?' Tasha asks as we walk to the car park together. She arrived too late to hear Daisy's outburst, thank goodness.

I smile at the memory. 'Wonderful, he's so easy to get on with and the girls are delightful. And he's taking me out for dinner this weekend to thank me.'

'So are you two dating now?'

I'm sure I can hear an edge to her voice and glance swiftly at her, but she's smiling. 'No, I told you we're just friends. How are things going with you and Caleb?' I ask.

Her eyes light up. 'Brilliant. In fact, we're going away for the weekend, Mum's having Ryan.'

Bang goes my plan of asking Tasha if Liam can stay over. 'That's fantastic. Where are you going?'

'Caleb's booked us into a hotel in Devon. He said that he wants us to have some "quality time" together.' She is holding her keys in her hands and presses the remote to open her car. 'See you later.'

I'm pleased for her, I really am, but I wish that Caleb hadn't decided to whisk her away the very same weekend that Charlie was going to take me for a meal. I've been really looking forward to it – I missed him this weekend.

I message Charlie later and explain about Tasha going away, and he replies almost immediately.

Shame, but let's have a meal with the kids then. We can do just the two of us another time. How about Sunday lunch?

My heart flips at his reply. He obviously really wants to see me. I message back:

That sounds great.

His next message pings in a few seconds later.

Mum's doing both school runs this week as I have to be in work early but I'll see you at pickup on Friday. Shall we hold hands and get them all talking?

I smile at this as I message back.

Better not. Tasha already thinks they're making voodoo dolls of me!

I'll protect you.

He then sends a GIF of a knight in armour fighting a dragon. I giggle, the silly exchange lifting my spirits.

Liam comes down looking glum. 'I wish we were still at Charlie's house. It's much nicer than ours,' he says.

I pat the cushion and he sits down by me. I put an arm

around his shoulders and hug him to me. 'I know that Charlie's house is bigger and posher than ours but this is our home and we love it, don't we?' I bend down to look at his face. Surely he isn't this upset just because of our small house. 'There will always be people with bigger houses, bigger cars, more money than us, but there are people who have less than us too, darling. People who don't even have a home.'

He nods. 'I know but...'

I tilt his chin up and look at his tear-filled eyes. 'What is it?'

'I wish I had brothers or sisters.' He gulps. 'And a nan. I miss my nan. I wish I could see her again.'

Liam asked after Mum and Bill when we first returned to England but gradually as the weeks passed and our lives got busy with nursery then school, work and friends he stopped mentioning them. Staying at Charlie's has brought it all back to him. I'm wondering now if I did the right thing offering to look after Mia and Daisy, especially staying over. It's unsettled Liam so much.

'Oh, darling.' I hold him tight and kiss his forehead. 'We will one day,' I say even though I don't see how we can, not after everything. 'I miss Nanny and Grandad too.'

'I know they live far away but why can't I speak to them on FaceTime, like I do my dad?' he asks.

For a moment I'm stumped for a reply. Then it comes to me. 'They don't have the internet, love,' I say. My heart is breaking to see him so upset. I wish I could turn back the clock and erase the events of that awful night. It will haunt me forever.

24

ALICE

I'm seething all the way home but I smile and chat to the girls. I cherish them too much to show them my anger. Besides I need to find out more about this woman so that I know what I'm dealing with.

When we get in I make them their favourite milkshake and give them both one of the butterfly cakes I made this afternoon, then I sit down beside them.

'I'm so glad you're both better. I really missed you last week. But I bet it was fun to have Liam and his mummy staying over.'

Mia nods as she takes off one of the butterfly wings and nibbles it. 'It was the best. Auntie Sarah is very kind and Liam is fun.'

Daisy dips her finger in the cream then licks it off before adding, 'Auntie Sarah gave me lots of cuddles which made me feel better and she read us a story every night.'

'That sounds wonderful,' I say. I'm inwardly fuming although I keep my tone light. 'I expect Daddy was glad of the company too.'

Mia nods. 'We all missed you though, Nanny. We're glad you can come and visit us again.'

'So am I.' I lean over and squeeze both their hands. 'I missed my girls.' I sit back up, my mind busy working out how I can ask the important question. Where did Sarah sleep? I need to know just how far she's got her claws into my Charlie.

'It was very good of Liam's mummy to sleep here so that she could help Daddy look after you in the night too. It's a good job I wasn't here so that she could have my room.'

Mia demolishes the other butterfly wing and licks the cream. Then she raises her eyes to mine. 'She didn't sleep in your room, Nanny.'

I gasp. I knew it. The scheming little tramp.

'Daddy said that room was for you so Liam and his mummy slept in the other rooms,' Mia adds.

I almost faint with relief. I should have known my Charlie, he wouldn't sleep with someone else when his daughters were in the next rooms.

'It's a good job Daddy has a lot of rooms, isn't it?' I say with a smile. 'Now shall we have a game of Snap?'

'Yes!' both girls chorus.

'Finish your cakes then wash your hands and I'll get the cards,' I tell them.

When Charlie comes home we're playing happily. 'Good to have you back, Mum,' he says, kissing me on the cheek.

'Good to be back, son,' I tell him. I don't mention Sarah to him. I've found out all I need to know.

And I've already worked out a plan to make sure she doesn't have the chance to get close to him again.

OCTOBER

25

SARAH

The week passes by quickly, which is good, as I'm eagerly counting the days until I see Charlie again. I've been so preoccupied with thoughts of him that it's pushed away my worry of Dylan turning up. As each day passes I feel more confident that he won't. After all, he said he regretted his actions and wanted to make a new start. I wish I could talk to Tasha about it but she doesn't know about Dylan's violent attack on that man, or about him going to prison. I've only told her about him being abusive towards me. I can't bear for anyone to know just how stupid I was, and how much danger I put my son in.

To my relief Charlie is there, with Daisy, to collect Mia on Friday. His face lights up when he sees me and he wraps me in a hug and kisses me on the cheek. Lacey and Kelly stare, their jaws dropping so much I expect to hear a clang as they hit the floor.

'I've missed you this week. Want to come back for a coffee before you go home?' I ask him.

He smiles. 'I'd love to.'

Charlie parks up behind me. I try not to think about how small my house is compared to his, how cheap the furniture is.

We're friends and friends accept each other as they are. I wait until Charlie and the girls get out of the car, then we all walk up the path.

I put the key in the lock and hesitate: something feels wrong. I can't put my finger on it but I can sense it.

'What's up?' Charlie asks.

I pull myself together and unlock the door. Liam and the girls run straight into the lounge. 'Put a film on for you all to watch, Liam!' I shout as me and Charlie walk on to the kitchen. The kitchen window is wide open and the blinds are flapping in the wind.

I frown in disbelief. I can't believe that I left that open. I always check the windows, the doors, the taps, the oven, everything before I leave the house.

Is it Dylan? Has he broken in and is waiting for me? I'm so glad that Charlie is with me, I'd be freaking out otherwise. I pull myself together and am about to walk over to close the window when Charlie grabs my arm and pulls me back.

'Stop!'

'What?' I turn to him, confused.

He points down to the floor. It's swimming in water.

A huge drop of water plops down to the floor. Then another. And another.

We both look up to the ceiling. I gasp, my hand flying to my mouth as my eyes rest on the big wet patch and the chunk of plasterboard hanging off, revealing the underside of the floor-boards. I can't tear my eyes from the big drops of water pouring through it into the pool spreading over the floor.

'Oh my God. It's coming from the bathroom. A pipe must have burst!' I turn around to race up the stairs to check but Charlie pulls me back.

'Careful – that's a lot of water. It might have weakened the floorboards. Best to turn your water off from the stopcock first so that no further damage is done. Where is it?'

'Under the sink,' I tell him.

Charlie kicks off his trainers and socks, rolls up his jeans then wades through the water over to the sink.

My mind races back to this morning when we left in a hurry. I checked the bathroom taps, I'm sure I did. I'm always so careful. Then the blind blows again and I look over at the open window. I remember now that I opened it to let a wasp out. I must have forgotten to close it. I take a deep breath as I feel panic rising in me. I could have been burgled, come home to no furniture, no TV.

'Done.'

Charlie stands up, wipes his hands on his jeans, then reaches over to close the window and turns back around, his eyes meeting mine. 'Don't beat yourself up. We all forget things when we're in a rush.'

'Mum?'

I spin around to see Liam standing in the doorway, eyes wide as saucers.

'Don't come in!' I yell at him.

He backs away. Mia and Daisy must have heard my shout because they come out of the lounge and join Liam. The three of them are standing in the doorway staring at the now completely water-covered kitchen floor.

'What's happened?' Mia asks.

'There's been a leak but we'll fix it. You three please go back into the lounge and watch TV while we sort this out,' Charlie says.

I race up the stairs, Charlie hot on my heels.

The bathroom door is closed and water is seeping under it onto the landing, the carpet will be ruined. I cautiously open the door and water spills out.

I groan when I see that the plug is in the sink, a flannel is draped over the base of the taps, blocking the overflow hole and water is pouring down over the washbasin. It wasn't a burst pipe then.

Charlie squeezes my shoulder. 'It's easily done.'

'Liam must have gone in after me to wash his hands and forgot to turn the tap off. I always go around and check that everything's switched off and secure though.'

'You said you were in a hurry.'

'Even so. I should have been more careful.' I take my phone out of my pocket. 'I'm going to have to tell my landlord. .'

I dial my landlord and there's no reply, so I leave a message telling him it is urgent.

Charlie's forehead creases into a frown. 'I don't think it's safe for you to stay here until this is fixed, Sarah. There's a lot of water in that bathroom. The ceiling could fall through at any time.'

He's right. I chew my lip. 'I'll ask Tasha if I can stay with her. Liam can bunk up with Ryan and I can sleep on the sofa. She won't mind, she's a good friend.'

'She's away, isn't she?' Charlie reminds me.

Damn. I'd forgotten she was going away with Caleb.

'I'll find a B&B.'

'There's no need.' Charlie touches my arm lightly, which sends a little quiver through me. 'You can stay at mine for the weekend.'

I relax my shoulders. It would be the perfect solution. 'If you're sure...'

'Positive. Grab a case and pack what you need for the weekend and we'll be off.'

I am so grateful for his help. I would much prefer to stay in Charlie's lovely home than a B&B and I'm sure Liam will be delighted.

'Thank you so much.'

I take photos of the kitchen and bathroom to send to my landlord, and let him know that we've turned off the water.

Charlie goes down to check on the kids while I grab a suit-case and throw in a change of clothes for me and Liam, my makeup and toiletries, and a few of Liam's favourite toys.

Charlie comes up, now with his trainers back on, takes the suitcases off me and carries them down. Liam, Daisy and Mia are all excited when we explain what's happening. We're about to go out the front door when there's a loud crash from the kitchen.

'What's happened now?' I run back through the lounge, Charlie right behind me.

I clasp my hand over my mouth in horror as I see that a chunk of plasterboard has fallen from the ceiling, bringing an avalanche of water with it. If we had been in there... I can't stop shaking at the thought of what could have happened.

Charlie puts his arm around me and pulls me close. 'It's all right, Sarah.'

It isn't all right though. What if that had landed on Liam? Or he'd gone into the bathroom and fallen through the floor? My young son could have been killed.

26

'I think we could both do with a drink, it's been an eventful evening,' Charlie says when all the kids are tucked up in bed and asleep. He goes over to the drinks cabinet and takes out the unopened bottle of whisky I bought him. So he didn't share it with Crystal. It's ridiculous how pleased that makes me.

'Do you fancy a shot?'

Why not? I could do with unwinding after the evening I've had and I'm partial to a drop of whisky. 'Please.'

'Ice?' Charlie asks.

I nod. He goes into the kitchen with the two small glasses, and when he returns there's an ice cube in each glass. He half fills the glasses with whisky and hands one to me. 'Cheers.'

I hold my glass out and chink it with his. 'Cheers.'

I'm halfway through my whisky when my landlord texts back to say he's got a contractor coming to look at the house in the morning and will get back to me then. Great. It should all be sorted soon. I read the text out to Charlie. 'Thank goodness we got home when we did, it could have been a lot worse,' I say.

'Yes, any longer and it could have brought the whole ceiling down. Anyway, let's look on the bright side: we're together for another evening, so let's enjoy it.' Charlie puts on a film and we have another glass of whisky. He puts his arm around my shoulders and I rest back against him, enjoying the closeness, the feel of his body against mine, a warm glow from the whisky seeping through my body. I let out a deep sigh and relax.

'I've missed you so much this week,' he murmurs, leaning over and kissing me on the nose, then his lips move down to mine. Maybe it's the whisky that makes me wrap my arm around his neck and pull him closer. The kiss gets deeper. More urgent. His body presses closer to mine, his hands are caressing my body and a low moan escapes my lips.

Charlie lifts his head and looks at me, his eyes hooded with desire. 'Want to go upstairs?' he asks softly.

I tell myself that I shouldn't, that I swore I'd never get involved with anyone again but I can't fight my attraction to Charlie any longer. I nod. As we link fingers and walk up the stairs together, I think how lucky I am to have Charlie by my side right now. The events of today have really shaken me up.

Charlie squeezes my hand reassuringly and smiles at me as he opens the door to his bedroom. I follow him in.

I don't want the kids to come in and find us in bed together, so I sneak out of bed early in the morning while Charlie is still asleep and go into the guest room I slept in before. I lie there going back over the events of the night before, it felt so right to be in Charlie's arms and make love to him. Did he feel the same? If not, where does that leave us?

I must have drifted off because I wake up to a tap on the door. 'Sarah.' It's Charlie.

'Come in!' I shout.

'I've brought you a cup of tea,' he says as he enters, bare-chested, pyjama bottoms slung low on his hips, holding a red-and-white striped mug. 'I wanted to check that you sneaked out of my bed in the middle of the night because you were worried about the kids finding us together, not because it was so awful you couldn't wait to get away.'

I sit up and grin as he plonks himself on the side of the bed and hands me the cup. 'Definitely the first.'

'That's a relief!' He kisses me on the nose. 'So how do you feel about us continuing to see each other?'

'I'd like that.' Actually I'd absolutely love it but I don't want to sound too eager.

'Me too.' He takes the cup off me, puts it down on the bedside table and kisses me. I respond enthusiastically.

'Are you Mum's boyfriend now?'

Liam! He's standing in the doorway grinning at us.

Charlie turns around to face him. 'Hello, Liam.' He looks at me and raises an eyebrow. 'I guess I am?' There's a question in his voice.

I touch his cheek and smile at Liam. 'Are you okay with that?'

'You bet!' he exclaims in delight and runs out to tell Mia and Daisy.

'Well, now the kids know it will soon be all around the school.'

I think how jealous Lacey, Kelly and the other mums will be and can't help smiling. 'You'll have to tell your mum before the gossip reaches her.'

A strange expression comes over his face, then it's gone. I almost feel as if I imagined it. 'I'll tell her later. Now how about I cook us all a nice breakfast then we can enjoy the day together?'

'That sounds perfect. I'll grab a quick shower and be down.'

It's a mild day so after breakfast the kids all play out in the garden. Liam is delighted to be able to hold Thumper at last –

he is so tame and lies calmly in Liam's arms as he strokes him. 'I wish I had a rabbit,' he says.

'You can share Thumper,' Mia tells him. She turns to her little sister. 'Can't he, Daisy?'

Daisy nods solemnly.

'Can I really?' Liam's eyes widen.

'Of course you can. But remember to fasten the pen properly when you put him back. Thumper is really clever and can push it open with his nose,' Mia warns him.

Liam nods firmly. 'I will.'

I watch him cuddling the rabbit and it looks so cute that I'd love to take a photo, but I've left my phone in the kitchen. After a while, Liam puts Thumper back into the hutch and carefully locks it. He's such a cautious boy. It's not like him to leave the tap running, although we had been in a rush yesterday morning.

Later that evening the landlord calls me and I put the speaker on so that Charlie can hear, in case he's trying to pull a fast one and charge me for the damage. He should have insurance for that. I listen in dismay as the landlord tells me that he's had a plasterer out and that it will take a month to do all the repairs because the carpet on the landing will have to be replaced too, and some of the kitchen cupboards.

'A month?' I gasp. 'Where am I supposed to stay for a month?'

His reply is curt: the flooding was my fault so that's my problem. Then he drops the bombshell. My contract is up next month and he won't be renewing it. He's going to get the ceiling repaired and sell up.

Me and my young son are homeless.

I fight back the tears as I end the phone call. Our home may be small and plain but it has been our sanctuary since we came back from Arran. I know Tasha won't see us on the streets, but Liam bunking up with Ryan and me dossing on the sofa isn't the same as having our own home. Even if I can find one to rent right away – which is highly unlikely as there's at least a dozen people after every rental in these parts – it will take a couple of weeks to do all the paperwork minimum.

Charlie immediately puts his arm around my shoulder. 'That's horrible of him but don't worry – you and Liam can stay with us until you find something else.'

'Thank you, that's really kind of you, but Tasha will put us up.' I don't want to be dependent on Charlie for a roof over our heads. I really like him and he's made it clear he likes me but it's too early in our relationship for us to be living together, even on a temporary basis.

'Does she have enough room?' he asks. 'And hasn't she got a new boyfriend?'

I bite my lip. 'It will be a bit crowded but Tasha won't mind.'

'Look, please stay here.' Charlie gives me a comforting hug. 'We've got plenty of room and we all get on well.'

'It's so generous of you...' My legs feel weak so I reach for the chair and sink down into it. I can't believe this has happened. Me and Liam need somewhere to live but it's too big a step to move in with Charlie, even if we are seeing each other and he seems really nice. I barely know him. And I swore I'd never get involved with someone again. What if he isn't what he seems? If it all goes wrong, like it did with Dylan.

'What's the matter, Mum?' Liam and the girls have come in from the playroom in time to catch Charlie's words and he's looking at me worriedly.

Charlie walks over to him, crouching down to look him in the eye.

'You can't go back to your old house because it needs to be repaired so I've suggested that you and your mum live here for a while, until she can find another home for you. Would you like that?'

I wish he hadn't done that. Now a big grin spreads over Liam's face. He jumps up and punches his fist in the air. 'Yes!'

Mia grins too. 'Liam's going to be like our brother!' she tells Daisy.

She and Liam high-five each other and Daisy dances around excitedly.

Charlie turns to me. 'Well, the kids think it's a good idea.'

I feel that my hand has been forced and am still not sure that it's the right thing to do. Though I have to admit that we'll be more comfortable here than at Tasha's.

'Sarah? Are you okay with this? Have I overstepped the mark?' Charlie asks.

He looks genuinely concerned and I feel myself relax. I'm worrying over nothing. If it doesn't work out at Charlie's I can leave and go to Tasha's.

'Only if you're absolutely sure? We could be here for a few weeks.'

'Not a problem at all. Stay as long as you need,' Charlie reassures me.

'Then thank you. I've very grateful.'

Charlie wraps me in a hug. 'It's a pleasure.'

I'll get onto all the local letting agents on Monday, I decide, and start the ball rolling finding us another home. I don't want to exploit Charlie's hospitality.

'Are you sad about having to leave your old house?' I hear Mia ask Liam as they make their way to the playroom.

'No, it's much nicer here,' Liam says.

A tiny suspicion sneaks into my mind as I hear his words and it lodges there. When we returned home last week Liam was very grumpy, complaining about how much better Charlie's house was.

Did he leave the tap running with the sink plugged on

purpose so we could stay here? I shake my head. No, Liam wouldn't do that. It must have been an accident.

And anyway, what about the open kitchen window? Did I really forget to close it?

Then another, more terrifying thought hits me.

Could Dylan be responsible? A warning of what's to come?

27

There's no sign of the landlord or any workmen when I arrive at our house on Sunday to pick up a few more things for the week ahead. I'll collect some more later this week and move our furniture into storage, and I'm grateful this will only be a quick trip. As I step inside the hall, memories come flooding back. Tasha had put us up when we came back from Arran and had wanted us all to get a bigger house together, but I desperately wanted our own home, and was delighted when this one came up. I fell in love with it right away, it was bright and cheerful, located in a quiet suburban street. It felt safe.

I turn into the lounge, looking at the familiar sofa me and Liam chose, the fluffy beige rug he used to sit on and play with his toys, and sometimes lay on to watch TV. Our photos on the wall. This has been our home for three years. Feeling overwhelmed, I sink down onto the sofa. I really like Charlie, and his house is amazing, but it isn't home. This is home.

Was home.

I swallow back the tears, pull myself together and go upstairs, taking the two suitcases off the top of the wardrobe and filling them with our clothes. Then I pick up Liam's rucksack and put a couple of his games in it, some books and the other things on his list.

The bathroom door is closed with a 'Keep Out' sign on it. I hesitate: the urge to open it and take a look is so strong. I leave the cases outside Liam's bedroom door and walk over to the bathroom, gingerly opening the door.

The vinyl has been taken up, exposing the bare, wet floor-boards. They look so fragile, as if one step on them would plunge you down to the kitchen below.

I shiver as I think of the lucky escape we had. Then I step back, pick up the cases and carry them downstairs and out of the front door.

As I wheel them down the drive to my car, Mrs Stanton comes out with a bin bag. She smiles at me.

'Hello, dear, did your friend catch up with you?'

I turn to her in surprise. 'What friend?'

'The one who was knocking on your door on Friday morning? I saw them when I was on my way out. I told them you were at work and to come back later.'

'What did they look like?' I ask.

'I didn't get a good look, dear. I didn't have my glasses on and they were wearing one of those baseball caps. To be honest I don't know whether it was a man or a woman. They were about your height, dressed casual in sweatshirt , jeans and trainers.'

Her words send a chill through me.

Could it be?

Stop it. You can't keep thinking like this.

It could have been someone selling something, we occasion-ally get door-to-door salespeople.

'Did they speak to you?' I ask. Surely she could tell what sex my mysterious visitor was by the voice.

She shakes her head. 'Not really, just sort of mumbled. Anyway, one of the workmen told me about the leak so I'm guessing you have to move out for a while – do you have a forwarding address if they come back? They seemed quite anxious to see you, they even went around the back to make sure you weren't in the garden.'

'No, I'm staying with a friend.' Then her words hit home. 'They went into my back garden?'

'I'm not sure if they actually went into the garden but I saw them looking over the fence.'

The open kitchen window pops into my mind again. I was sure I'd closed it. Was it Dylan? Had he opened the back window and sneaked in, turned the tap on and put the plug in the sink?

A shudder runs through me as I remember the chunk of plaster that fell off the kitchen ceiling. If that had fallen on us...

I'm starting to suspect this wasn't a careless accident. Not at all.

28

ALICE

I stare incredulously at Charlie. I hadn't expected this news when I popped in to see how they all were. I'm inwardly furious but I'm careful to keep all disapproval out of my voice. I know my boy, he's stubborn. If I protest too much, he'll only dig his heels in.

'You mean Sarah and her son are living here now? Is that wise, darling? It's terrible that Sarah's house is damaged and she has to move out but you've only known her a few weeks. Surely, she has friends or family she can stay with?' Sarah told me herself that her mother lives in Scotland. She should go there for a while instead of imposing on my son. Then she'll be out of Charlie's life.

'Her friend doesn't have a spare room and her family live hundreds of miles away. I can't see Sarah and Liam struggle when there's plenty of room here. Besides, Sarah and I are seeing each other. We're in a relationship.'

He's clearly struck with the woman, and she's taken advantage of his good nature. She enjoyed staying in this beautiful house when the girls were ill and has used this opportunity to

try and move in permanently. I'm so angry I could scream but I
muster up a concerned expression and keep my voice calm.

'It's very generous of you, dear, but don't you think it would
be best to help Sarah get her own place? You've only been
together five minutes and this must all be very unsettling for the
girls,' I gently suggest.

'Stop stressing, Mum, I would never do anything to upset
the girls. They love Sarah. And she is looking for her own place,
but it will take a few weeks. You know what the rental market is
like.'

He's very defensive about Sarah. Just as I feared, he's in love
with her. He was the same with Lynn. Charlie is a sucker for a
damsel in distress. Especially one who is clever enough to
pretend that she wants to stand on her own two feet.

'I'm sure you're doing what you think is best, and of course
I'll help any way I can. I can pick up Sarah's son from school
when I collect the girls. She's often a bit late so I'm sure she'll be
glad of the help.' I'm worried that once again I'm going to be
pushed out, which would be so dreadfully unfair after how hard
I've worked to keep the family together.

'That's really kind of you, Mum, thank you. But you've
done so much for us over the last eighteen months since Lynn
left – well, since Daisy was born actually – and I want you to
have a bit of time for yourself now. I'm going to talk to Sarah
later about us both sharing the school runs. I can do the morning
one and Sarah can pick them up in the afternoon.'

So suddenly he doesn't need me in his life.

He was the same when Lynn came onto the scene.

'I enjoy spending time with the girls and picking them up
from school. It gets me out of my apartment, and I don't want to
lose touch with them. You all mean such a lot to me,' I say
gently.

He gives me a hug. 'You'll always be a big part of our lives,
Mum, we all adore you. Look, why don't you pop around for an

hour tomorrow evening? It would be good for you to meet Sarah and Liam properly as they'll be with us for a while.'

'All right, dear,' I say, relieved that he isn't pushing me away. Not yet, anyway.

I don't trust this Sarah, and I'll be watching her. There's something about her that doesn't add up, and I'm going to find out what it is. She might think she's clever and has Charlie wrapped around her little finger but she's no match for me. She won't be here for long, I'll make sure of that.

29

SARAH

The person who was lurking around my home is on my mind all afternoon. I'm petrified that it could be Dylan, but now I've calmed down I remind myself that he doesn't know where we live. No one from Arran does, not even my mother. Besides, I'm sure that it isn't his style. Dylan saw red and lashed out – I really can't see him sneaking in through an open window, putting the plug in the sink and turning on the bathroom tap. I've got to stop letting my imagination run away with me, accept that it was an accident and concentrate on finding another home. Meanwhile, I want to make myself as useful as I can to Charlie, he has been so good to us.

'Shall I do the school runs tomorrow?' I ask Charlie that evening. 'It's pointless us both going, and you have to be in work earlier than me.'

'That would be helpful but I don't expect you to take over all the childcare while you're here,' he says. 'You're working too.' He hugs me and kisses me on the cheek. 'How about I drop them off and you pick them up? Mum is willing to still pick the girls up, and Liam too, but I wanted to give her a bit of a rest. She's done so much for us.'

I want to keep things as normal as possible for Liam. This is a big change for him. He's happy to be living here at the moment but he's used to being an only child. It's been just the two of us for years. 'How about I take them all for a couple of days, so they get used to the new situation, and then you can take them and I'll pick them up?'

He nods. 'Good idea. Prepare yourself for the gossip at the school gates though.'

He's right. When I arrive at the school gates the next morning with all three kids in tow, Lacey's eyes almost pop out of her head. 'Stayed over, did you?'

'Actually, me and Liam are living with Charlie for a while. The bathroom flooded at my house so I've had to move out.'

Lacey's face is a picture as she folds her arms across her very buxom chest. 'Well, that didn't take you long, did it? No wonder you were so quick to offer to look after his girls when they were ill. That was a clever trick.'

'It's always the quiet ones you have to watch,' Kelly adds. 'First you worm your way in with Charlie by offering to look after his girls then you mysteriously have to move out of your house so he offers you a roof over your head.'

'You've got a bloody cheek!' I tell her angrily. 'It's been horrible for me and Liam to lose our home like this and I'm very grateful to Charlie for offering us a place to stay. Not that it's any of your business!' I add.

'What's this?' Crystal struts over. 'You're living with Charlie?' She looks stunned.

'Oh for God's sake, not you as well! Nice of you to all ask how me and Liam are after what's happened!' I glare at them all and walk away.

I wish Tasha was here to give me support but when I rang her last night to let her know what had happened, she told me that Ryan's gone down with chickenpox now. Mind you, she sounded put out when I told her about the leak and our new living arrangements. 'Why are you staying at Charlie's when you barely know him?' she asked, almost angrily. 'You should have come here. Why didn't you phone me and tell me?'

'I didn't want to put you out, you don't want us cluttering up the house and me sleeping on the sofa. We'd have been on top of each other,' I say. 'And Ryan is ill.'

'We'd have managed, and Liam has already had chickenpox so he isn't going to get it again,' she said. 'You know that I'm always here for you.'

'I know, and back at you, but this does seem the best solution. It won't be for long.'

I'm sick of everyone, even my best friend, having a go at me for accepting Charlie's generous offer of a temporary home. I'm sure they'd have all done the same in my circumstances.

It's a busy morning and before I know it Yvonne's arrived to take over from me. She whistles when I fill her in with what's happened over the last week, ending with the flooding at the house. 'Wow, your landlord is out of order. I'm sure he can't do that. You've paid rent until the end of the month, and then there's your deposit. And your furniture. He should be providing you with alternative accommodation, surely.' She frowns. 'Where are you going to live?'

'He said it's my fault and I've caused a lot of damage,' I tell her. 'Charlie offered us to stay there until I get somewhere else, so if you see a two-bed house to rent anywhere please let me know.'

'I will,' she promises. Then she winks. 'Mind you, you might decide you want to stay at Charlie's.'

'I prefer my own home,' I snap. Then instantly regret it. 'Sorry, I'm a bit stressed.'

'Of course you are. I was only teasing,' Yvonne says, looking guilty.

Is that what everyone believes, that I engineered the leak so I could wheedle my way into Charlie's house? I think crossly as I get my coat and leave. I check my phone as I head for my car and see a message from Charlie saying he forgot to tell me that Alice is joining us for dinner tonight. I groan. I could do without this, but it's Charlie's house and Alice is his mum. I stop off at the local supermarket to grab something for tea before heading for the nursery to pick Daisy up, then the school.

When I get home with the three kids I see that the coats and shoes in the hall have been tidied up – Charlie must have come home and had a quick tidy around as his mother is dropping by later. The children go straight upstairs to change out of their school clothes and I head for the kitchen to start on dinner. I'm surprised to see an array of newly washed clothes flapping about on the washing line in the garden and the breakfast things cleared away. He must have been busy! I can hear giggling from the playroom and look through the open door to see all three kids now changed and sprawled out on the carpet playing Jenga, laughing when the tower falls. Liam looks up as if sensing that I'm watching him, and smiles. I smile back. 'Anyone want a milkshake?' I ask.

'Me!' they all shout in unison.

I load the milkshakes and a bowl of assorted biscuits on a tray and walk out of the kitchen with them, looking around in surprise when I hear Daisy shout, 'Nanny!' and run down the hall to greet Alice, who has just come in the front door.

I wasn't expecting Alice for ages yet and I don't like it that she's let herself in. She obviously has a key and Charlie has been happy for her to come and go as she pleases but it feels a little disrespectful when she knows that I've moved in.

'Oh, hello,' I stammer awkwardly. 'I wasn't expecting you yet.'

'Hello, dear.' She closes the door behind her and I notice the shopping bag in her hand. 'I popped around a bit earlier to tidy up for you. I know how hard it is to keep on top of things when you're both working. Especially after the children being so ill. Then I went to do a bit of shopping. Now, how are my favourite girls?' She gives Daisy a big hug and the little girl squeals in delight, then Mia runs over for a hug too. Alice's face lights up as she wraps her arms around them.

I need to tread carefully here, she's Charlie's mum and this is his home. And I've only been here five minutes so I can't start laying down the law. Liam is standing back, he looks wistful. I feel a lump in my throat. Poor Liam, he's really missed out on having grandparents.

I'm about to go over and give him a hug myself when Alice takes three bags of chocolate buttons out of her shopping bag. 'I've got some sweets for you all.' She beckons to Liam. 'You too, Liam.'

Liam's face breaks into a huge smile. 'Thank you.'

'Now off you all go to play, and don't get chocolate everywhere!' Alice says.

The kids run off into the playroom and Alice turns to me. 'Right, now put the kettle on, dear, and I'll do the dinner,' she says, opening a drawer and taking an apron out. 'I've made a shepherd's pie for tea, and an apple crumble for afterwards. They're Charlie's favourites. They're in the fridge, they just need heating up.'

She's only trying to be helpful, I tell myself, but I feel sidelined. She's come in and taken over, even taking charge of my own child, and has prepared dinner when I was going to do that myself. It's as if she's reminding me that I'm a guest here, letting me know my place. Enforcing that this is only a temporary situation and that she'll always come first as Charlie's mum, and still clearly views this as her family home. It's as if she wants to push me out.

A thought nudges in my mind.
Did she push Lynn out, too?

30

When Charlie comes home, dinner is almost ready and Alice has taken the washing off the line and is ironing it, despite my efforts to stop her and do it myself.

'Best if I do it, dear, Charlie is very particular about how things are done,' she says with a knowing smile.

'I've found him very easy-going,' I say, puzzled at her remark. Is she suggesting that Charlie is controlling?

'Ah, that's because you're a guest. Charlie is very polite with guests. He's been brought up that way. But I know my boy and how to keep him happy,' she replies as she expertly irons Charlie's shirt.

'Hello, Mum, you look busy.' I'm surprised when Charlie appears in the kitchen doorway. I hadn't heard the front door open, but then this house is massive so maybe sound doesn't carry well.

'Hello, son. I thought I'd come a bit earlier and give Sarah a helping hand, she was exhausted,' Alice says. 'She's only used to looking after one child, not three!'

She says it as if I complained about looking after the girls and I see the concern on Charlie's face. Is she deliberately trying to cause trouble between us?'

'It's really no problem, I can manage fine,' I say quickly.

Alice unplugs the iron. 'Dinner's almost done. I'll just put these clothes away then serve it out.'

'Great. I'll go and say hello to the girls and then I'll be with you.' Charlie disappears into the playroom. I go to the doorway and see Mia and Daisy run over and hug him. Liam looks up from the puzzle he's doing and smiles shyly. Charlie goes over to him and tousles his hair.

I turn back to see Alice walking out with the basket of ironed clothes.

'You sit down, I'll put those away,' I say quickly.

'Best for me to do it, dear, you're a guest here. Besides, you don't know where everything goes, do you?' Her tone is friendly but there's an edge to it.

I feel uncomfortable as I see her go upstairs with the basket. They're Charlie's and the girls' clothes, and she's obviously used to ironing them and putting them away, but I'm more than a guest. I'm living here now and me and Charlie can do the chores between us. Alice needs to step back a bit. I'll have a word with Charlie later, I decide, he'll know what to say to her without upsetting her. Meanwhile, I'd better lay the table.

Charlie comes in as I'm setting out the plates. He kisses me on the back of my neck. 'Where's Mum?'

I turn around to face him and he wraps his arms around my waist. 'She's upstairs putting the clothes away – she cleaned up and put the washing out and was ironing before I could stop her. And I was doing spaghetti bolognaise and Eton mess for tea, I didn't know Alice had made food and put it in the fridge.' The words are pouring out because I do feel a bit put out: I'd wanted to cook the meal for us all.

Charlie's eyes are tender and his face concerned. 'That sounds great, but it will keep so we can have it tomorrow. Let's indulge Mum for a bit, she's only trying to help and she really misses the girls. She's looked after us all for so long that it's hard for her to stop.'

'It's fine,' I tell him as he wraps me in an embrace. 'This is your home.'

'I want you to look on it as yours too, while you're here,' he tells me. 'But we need to give Mum time to adjust to the new situation.' He kisses me on the forehead. 'To be honest I do find her a bit... too much sometimes, but I know it's only because she wants to take care of us. Hopefully she'll start to back off now that you're here.'

I hope she does because I feel like she's watching me, judging me, waiting for me to put a step wrong.

Just like my own mother did.

31

I phone the landlord about fast-tracking my deposit when I finish work the next day. I think he owes me that much as he's made me and Liam homeless. I can't believe it when he tells me that my deposit is being kept back to pay for the repairs to the house.

'You can't do that!' I gasp. 'It was an accident! Surely you have insurance?'

'You left a tap running all day in a plugged sink, even managing to block up the overflow hole, which ruined the ceiling, the kitchen and the carpets. It's going to cost me more than your deposit to put right,' he says curtly. 'And why should I claim off my insurance and shove my premium up for your carelessness?'

I'm shaking with shock. I've lost our home and my deposit. I wish that I'd got the house through an agency rather than a private landlord, I might have been able to appeal. How can I get a new home for me and Charlie now? Payday is three weeks away and it will take me months to save up another deposit. And I bet the landlord won't give me a reference, so how am I going to get anywhere to rent?

What the hell am I going to do? I can't stay with Charlie indefinitely.

I walk over to my car, my mind in a whirl. Could I get a loan? Would Tom and Maddie give me an advance on my wages? Should I ask Todd? I don't want to turn to him but he's Liam's dad after all.

I sit in the car and take a few deep breaths to calm myself down. I can't drive in this state. I'll sort something out, I tell myself. There isn't a problem that can't be resolved, my grandad used to say. Feeling calmer, I start the engine and drive to the nursery to pick up Daisy.

'Auntie Sarah!' Daisy runs and hugs me when she sees me. She really is a sweet girl, as is Mia.

She holds my hand tight as we walk to the car park, chatting about her day and showing me the painting she has done. 'We'll put it on the fridge when we get home,' I promise.

'Really?' She looks excited and I wonder if that's not something Charlie does. Come to think of it, I haven't noticed any of the girls' work pinned up anywhere. Maybe he has a special place for it. I'll ask him when he gets home.

I strap her into the car seat and we set off for the school. The traffic is bad and I'm running late so when Tasha phones as I pull up, I don't answer, deciding to call her back later.

When we get home I tape Daisy's painting to the fridge door and she beams with delight. then the kids change and go out to play in the garden. I keep an eye on them as I wash the breakfast dishes, we'd left in a rush this morning. Charlie comes in and wraps his arms around my waist and kisses me on the neck. 'How's your day been?'

I look over my shoulder and feel my eyes fill up. Damn! I don't want to cry. I want to be strong, independent.

'Babe, what is it?' He gently spins me round and holds me close. 'What's happened?'

I gulp and tell him about my conversation with the landlord.

'I can't believe he's withholding my deposit but I've looked online and apparently he can do that. So it's going to take me longer than I thought to get us another house. Don't worry though, Tasha will let me and Liam stay with her until we save enough money for the deposit. If you don't mind me staying here until Ryan has got over chickenpox, I'll talk to Tasha and see if we can move in next weekend.'

I really don't want to move in with Tasha, we lived there for a few weeks when I came back from Arran and I felt like I was treading on eggshells. Tasha likes things done her way. I don't see what choice I have though.

'There's no need for you to do that. I've told you, you can stay here for as long as you need. There's plenty of room and we love having you and Liam here.'

It's so kind of him but we've only just started seeing each other and it is too soon. I promised myself Liam would come first, and I wouldn't dive into another relationship again.

'Thank you but I can't possibly. We could be here for months. And it's too soon for us to...'

'To what? Live together?' He puts his finger under my chin. 'We can take things slow. Look, would it make you feel better if you stayed as a lodger? Then we can let our relationship develop at its own pace.'

It's tempting. It's such a fabulous house and location, we all get on so well and Liam enjoys being with Mia and Daisy. And if Dylan is looking for me I'm safe here with Charlie's locked gates, and secure house.

I need to keep my independence though, make sure I don't rush into anything, and this would certainly help. 'If you're sure, then yes please, but only if you agree to me paying rent.'

'Okay if it makes you happy. Only a small rent though, I want you to be able to save for a deposit for your own house.' He kisses me. 'And there's no pressure. Make sure you get the house you want.'

What a wonderful man. I'd be mad to turn that offer down. 'That sounds perfect. Thank you.' I snuggle my head on his shoulder as his arms wrap around me.

Tasha isn't very pleased when she phones later and I tell her that I'm staying at Charlie's for the foreseeable.

'I can't believe that you're doing this when I've told you that you can live with me!'

I'm a bit taken aback by her attitude although I know that it's only because she's worried, trying to protect me. 'I'm going to be a lodger, Tasha, we're not living together. And it's really lovely of you but I don't want to put you and Ryan out, it would be a bit crowded for you.' I don't add that I'm worried we won't get on, I don't want to upset her. I'm sure she doesn't realise how bossy she can be. We all have our faults, don't we.

'We could rent a bigger house together,' she replies.

She'd suggested that before, when I came back from Arran, but I soon realised it wouldn't work. I love Tasha, she's a brilliant friend, but we don't gel as housemates.

She's acting as though I've chosen Charlie over her. I guess I have in a way, only because it's easier for everyone for us to stay at Charlie's.

'I'm thinking of you too, Tasha. What if you want Caleb to stay over? Or the two of you spend a cosy evening in together?' I point out.

There's a silence on the other end of the phone. 'Okay, but if it all goes wrong, you'll come straight here. Promise?'

'I promise.'

It's good to know that I have somewhere to go if it doesn't work out with Charlie, though. I don't know what I'd have done without Tasha to go to after what had happened on Arran.

'How's it working out, living in a mansion?' Lacey asks me in a sneering tone as I drop Liam and Mia off at school the next morning.

'It's all working out perfectly, thank you,' I say politely. I hug Liam and Mia then they run into the playground. Now I only have to drop Daisy off at nursery then get to work. I hold the young girl's hand and she chatters to me as we walk over to my car.

'Sarah!'

I turn at the sound of Crystal's voice. She's running towards me. 'Would you remind Charlie that it's the Autumn Fayre next weekend? He promised to help out at the games stalls. And Alice is baking some cakes.'

'No problem,' I tell her. 'I can help out too, if you want,' I offer.

Her face breaks into a big, false smile. 'Thank you but we're covered now. Although, of course, you're very welcome to attend the fayre.'

That's very generous of her seeing as the fayre is open to the public, but I merely smile and say, 'Of course I'll be there.'

. . .

I've just got in from work, sent the kids off to play and made myself a coffee when Alice walks in. 'Afternoon, dear, I've brought a casserole for dinner, save you cooking.'

It's thoughtful of her but I wish she'd let me know she was coming, and at least ring the bell.

'Thank you, I was about to cook some pasta,' I tell her.

'Oh, this is far healthier. Charlie is a working man, he needs more than pasta. I'll put it in the fridge, shall I?'

I see her look at my mug of coffee and instinctively ask her if she wants one. 'Tea, please,' she replies, 'I'll be back in a tick.'

I've got a feeling she's waiting for an invite to dinner. I guess it's the least I can do when she's brought the meal with her but she makes me feel like an unwanted lodger.

'Perhaps you'd like to stay for dinner?' I finally ask, despite my better judgement.

'That would be wonderful, I do miss the girls,' she says.

So I make her a cup of tea and then the kids come running in.

'Can we go out and see Thumper?' Liam asks. He adores Thumper.

I open my mouth to reply but Alice is there before me. 'Of course. I've brought some cabbage leaves, you can give him those. Here, let me come with you.'

I watch out of the kitchen window as Alice opens the hutch, then passes cabbage leaves to all three children to give to the rabbit. I'm pleased to see that she's talking to Liam, including him.

She's lonely, that's why she keeps popping in, I tell myself. Her life has revolved around Charlie and the girls for the past few years, she's finding it difficult to let go.

I hear the front door open. Charlie's home.

His face breaks into a grin as he walks into the kitchen. 'It is so good to come home and find you here.' He kisses me tenderly then looks out of the window. 'I saw Mum's car in the drive. Did you invite her over?'

'No, she came to see the girls and bring a casserole for tea.'

Alice comes back in. 'The children want to play outside a bit, but don't worry, we've locked Thumper's hutch.'

She goes over to Charlie and gives him a kiss on the cheek. 'How's your day been?'

'Hectic. As usual.'

'Come and tell me all about it,' she says, leading the way out into the lounge.

I wanted to hear about Charlie's day too, but I guess we can catch up later when Alice has gone home.

The back door opens and the children dash in. Liam's eyes are shining.

'Mum! Thumper ate the cabbage out of my hand!'

My heart lifts to see him look so happy.

It's a pleasant meal. The kids are full of beans, chatting away, they gel together so nicely. Liam tells a joke and the girls giggle, me and Charlie chuckle too, catching each other's eye.

I turn to Alice and am startled to see that her dark eyes are narrowed as she looks at Liam. Then suddenly she turns to me and smiles. I blink, wondering if I imagined it. 'How's the house-hunting going, Sarah? I'm sure you can't wait to get your own place again.'

'I have to save a deposit first, but I've registered with a few estate agents,' I tell her.

Charlie puts his hand on mine. 'There's no rush, love. I enjoy you being here.'

Alice purses her lips but says nothing. Not until we're halfway through dessert, when she asks casually, 'Are you planning a visit to your parents soon, Sarah? I know they live in

Scotland, I bet they miss Liam. I thought perhaps they might be a good option for you too if you're needing somewhere to stay for a while?'

I glance quickly at Liam, relieved to see that he's chatting to Daisy and Mia and hasn't heard Alice. 'I don't want to stay with my mum and stepdad as it will mean taking Liam out of school.'

'That's a shame. Family is so important. What about the rest of your family? Are you an only child like Charlie?'

'I've got an older brother who lives in Manchester and my father lives in Thailand.' I'm anxious to change the subject before Liam tunes into the conversation so I push my plate back and stand up. 'Would anyone like a coffee?'

'I'd love a macchiato,' Charlie replies.

'A straight white for me, please, dear, I don't go for these fancy coffees,' Alice says. She stands up too and goes to clear the plates.

'We'll do this, Mum. You go into the lounge and put your feet up,' Charlie tells her.

Charlie clears the table and loads the dishwasher while I make us both a macchiato and a white coffee for Alice and take it into the lounge, where she's sitting reading a magazine. Damn, it looks like she's going to be here for the evening. Then I go back to help Charlie tidy up.

A few minutes later Liam rushes into the kitchen, looking panicked. 'I didn't do it,' he says.

I stoop down so that I'm level with him. His eyes are red-rimmed, and he sniffs. 'Didn't do what, sweetheart?'

'Daisy said he spilt water over her picture.' Alice walks in with a very upset-looking Daisy.

'He did it on purpose because he wanted to use the red paint and Daisy had it,' Mia informs us. She puts her hands on her hips and glares at Liam.

Liam shakes his head and clings onto my hand. 'It was an accident.'

'Accident or not, it was very careless of Liam,' Alice says firmly. 'I think you should apologise, Liam.'

They're all looking at Liam. He lifts his eyes to meet Alice's, and she slowly nods her head.

'Sorry,' he mumbles.

I catch my breath as I see the fear in his eyes.

33

There's quite a bit of traffic when I leave work the next day so I'm a bit late picking up Daisy from nursery, which has a knock-on effect, making me late to pick up Liam and Mia from school. I know that there is no way the school would let them out without me, even so I hate to keep the children or the teachers waiting.

'Come on, darling. We need to hurry to get Mia and Liam,' I say as I unbuckle Daisy from her seat, hold her hand and hurry over to the car park.

'Nanny!' Daisy shouts. I follow her gaze and see Alice standing by the school gates, talking to Crystal. She's holding Mia's hand and Liam is beside her looking anxious.

'Ah, there you are, Sarah. Crystal asked me to meet her here to discuss the Autumn Fayre, a good thing really as you're late.' The accusation in her words is clear.

Crystal turns to me. 'Perhaps it might be a good idea if Alice still collected the children from school seeing as you work and could get caught up in traffic. It's so worrying for them when you're not here in time.'

'I was thinking the same, Sarah. I'm happy to pick Liam up too, I can take them back home and get dinner ready for you and Charlie.'

'You're so kind,' Crystal gushes. 'I'd love a mother-in-law like you.'

Alice beams. 'Well, Sarah is only staying with Charlie on a temporary basis because she's suddenly become homeless.' Alice manages to make me sound like a charity case. 'So I'm hardly her mother-in-law but I'm happy to help.' She bids goodbye to Crystal then walks back to the car with me. 'I'll pop in for a quick cuppa, it will be nice to catch up with the girls.'

The last thing I want is for Alice to come back with me, but what can I say?

Mia and Daisy opt to go in the car with their nan, but Liam wants to go with me.

'Are you okay, Liam? How was school?' I ask him.

'It was okay,' he mumbles.

I glance in the mirror and see that he looks troubled. 'I'm sorry I was late. I'll try not to be again but the traffic was busy from Daisy's nursery.'

'I wish you didn't have to pick up Daisy, then you wouldn't be late,' he says. 'Mia's nanny said I had to go home with her and I didn't want to.'

She was actually going to take the children home? That really is overstepping the mark. Maybe it's a good thing that Alice is coming back for a coffee, it will give us a chance to have a chat without Charlie around, I don't want to push Alice out but I need to set a few ground rules now that I'm going to be living with Charlie for a while.

Alice has arrived home before me and the girls are getting out of the car as we pull up. I hate it that she has a key. I know me and Charlie agreed that I'd stay on a lodger basis but I'm his girlfriend too, and Alice seems determined to ignore this.

Liam runs over to join them as they all go into the house. I go around to the boot to take out the shopping I bought in my break and freeze.

Someone has written on the boot in big capital white letters:

TRAMP.

34

I gasp, my hand flying to my mouth as I stare at that awful word sprawled across my car boot. Finally I tear my eyes from it and look over at the front door. Liam has gone inside now, with Mia, Daisy and Alice.

Thank goodness he didn't see it. All the cars behind me on the way home did though, you couldn't miss it!

Who has done this... and why? It wasn't there when I left work or I would have noticed it.

I cast my mind back: did I go around to the back of the car after work? Open the boot at all? No, I went straight to pick Daisy up from nursery. I put Daisy in the car seat, placing her backpack on the seat beside her, and drove to the school. So whoever wrote this must have done it this afternoon at work, or outside the school.

I bet it was Kelly or Lacey. They've made no secret of the fact that they are jealous of me being with Charlie. Tasha's words flash into my mind: *I bet they've got a voodoo doll of you and they're sticking pins in it.* Or what about Crystal? She clearly hates the fact that I'm staying with Charlie. I shake my head. No, I'm sure it isn't her style.

I turn around as I hear the gates open, then see Charlie's silver Evoque drive through.

He parks the car and walks over to me. 'What's up?'

I point to the boot of the car. 'Someone has written this on my car.'

He glances over and his eyes darken. 'What the hell!' He strides over, squats down and studies the horrible word. 'It's been written in whiteboard marker, it will come off easily with an alcohol-based remover.' He stands up, his face grim. 'When was this done?'

'I've only just spotted it. I think it might be one of the mums at the school. You know how bitchy they are about me going out with you. And now I'm living here...'

He looks at me thoughtfully. 'It's a bit over the top for them to do this though. Don't you think it's more likely to be kids randomly targeting you? Some of them think this type of thing is funny.'

Maybe he's right, maybe I'm reading more into this than there is.

'It feels personal.' I can hear the tremble in my voice and Charlie must have too because he's beside me in seconds, wrapping me in a warm embrace.

'I'm sure it isn't, love, although it must have been a shock for you. Did Mum see it?'

I shake my head. 'No, she went straight in with the kids.'

'Let me get if off for you, I've got some remover in my bag. I use these markers all the time.'

He opens his bag and takes out a sponge and a small bottle of liquid then proceeds to rub at the letters. To my relief they start to fade until they've finally disappeared completely. Thank goodness Charlie had some remover with him. I couldn't bear for anyone else to see that horrible word.

'There you are.' He puts the top back on the bottle then places it back in the front compartment of his bag.

Relief surges through me. 'Thanks.' Then I frown. 'What if they do it again?'

Or something worse? Could it be Dylan? Had he been following me and wrote that as a warning? I push the thought away, reminding myself that there's no way Dylan could trace me.

Charlie scratches his cheek. 'Why would they? I'm sure it was just a kid. Maybe a gang of them spurring each other on. Your car is parked in a public car park at work, isn't it? They could have done it to a few cars.'

He has a point. And I hope he's right, I really do. 'Do you think I should have reported it then? It's vandalism, isn't it?'

'The police are too overstretched to bother about minor things like this now. Forget it, it's horrible but unfortunately it's pretty common nowadays.' He reaches out for my hand. 'Sorry that Mum is here again but I promise I'll get rid of her early and we can have a cosy night together.'

That sounds exactly what I need.

'Ah, there you are, Sarah,' Alice says as we walk into the kitchen together. 'And Charlie too.' She gets up from the table and crosses the room to kiss him on the cheek.

'The children are in the playroom. I've just got time for a cup of coffee and a quick catch-up, then I'll be off. Crystal has invited me over to her house for dinner. She's having a PTA meeting. I'll phone you later and let you know how it went.'

Her sharp green eyes rest on mine and I'm sure I can see a hint of triumph there. 'Crystal and I are still really close, especially as Brandon works away a lot, like my Kenneth used to, and they only live a few doors away. To think she and Charlie were once engaged!'

35

I'm stunned. I shoot a look at Charlie but he's talking to Alice as if he's not even aware of the bombshell she's dropped.

'Okay, Mum. Take care driving home from Crystal's later,' he says.

'Of course I will. I'll phone you as soon as I get back to let you know that I've arrived safely.'

As soon as Charlie returns from walking Alice out, I pounce. 'I didn't know that you were engaged to Crystal and that she lives so close to us.' I try to keep my tone light but it comes out accusing.

He shoots me a confused look. 'We haven't really had much chance to discuss our past relationships, have we?' he replies calmly. His eyes hold mine. 'Why? Is it a problem?'

I shake my head. 'No, of course not. I was surprised that you hadn't mentioned it, that's all.' *And that Alice is still so friendly with her*, I want to add but Charlie looks so surprised by my reaction that I don't want to come across as neurotic.

'It was years ago,' he says dismissively. 'Let's talk about it later, when the kids are in bed.'

'Okay,' I agree. I don't want to make a big deal out of this, although it would be nice to know the facts.

We dish up the dinner between us and the children, all chatting about their day. Liam is a bit quiet, I notice, but then the girls are very giggly and chatty so perhaps he feels overwhelmed. And maybe still upset about the episode with Daisy's painting. He's not used to arguments, or to being with other children so much. I'll talk to him later, when I tuck him up in bed, make sure he's okay.

Mia and Daisy want Charlie to read them a story tonight but Liam says he wants to go into his own bed. 'Can you read me my story, Mum?' he asks.

'Of course, I'll be up in a few minutes. You have a wash and brush your teeth and get into bed,' I tell him.

Liam's face breaks into a smile and he dashes up the stairs. Charlie has already taken the girls up. When I go up a few minutes later Liam is sitting up in bed, his favourite dinosaur storybook already open.

I sit on the bed beside him and read to him, making all the voices he loves, and he joins in, then I close the book and put my arm around his shoulders.

'Mum...' Liam chews his bottom lip.

'What is it, darling?'

'I'm still your favourite, aren't I?'

I can hear the wobble in his voice and cuddle him closer. 'Of course, you always will be.' I kiss him on the cheek.

'Are you Mia and Daisy's mummy now too?'

'No, we're just staying with them for a bit. But while we're here we're all a bit like a family. Is that okay?'

He shrugs. 'I guess, but Mum, I didn't spill the water on Daisy's painting. Honest I didn't.'

I look at him, his bottom lip is trembling. 'I believe you,' I tell him.

His face brightens and we hug. 'Love you,' I tell him.

'Love you too,' he says. Then he lies down and I wrap the duvet over him.

'Sweet dreams, darling.'

As I go down the stairs I feel troubled. It's been Liam and me for so long and now this new set-up is clearly disturbing him. I really haven't prepared my young son enough for this major move, I realise. But then it all happened so fast. If it hadn't been for the flood and the landlord not renewing my contract, I wouldn't have moved in with Charlie.

Liam will settle down. And I'll find us another place to rent as soon as I can. I'll talk to Todd, see if he can help with the deposit, then we can move into our own place.

Anyway, I'm feeling a bit unsettled here myself, what with Alice interfering and Charlie keeping it a secret from me about having been engaged to Crystal.

When I get downstairs, I find Charlie in the kitchen opening a bottle of wine. 'Fancy a glass?' he asks. 'I think we could both do with unwinding a little.'

'Please.'

I go over to pick up my glass but he reaches out for my hand. 'I'm sorry that I didn't tell you about Crystal. I guess it never occurred to me, it was years ago, and we haven't really known each other long, have we?' He holds out a glass of wine. 'Let's go into the lounge and talk about it.'

He's right, we've only known each other a few weeks, and everything's happened so fast. He could have casually mentioned at some point though that he and Crystal used to be engaged and she lives a few doors away. But maybe I'm making it more than it is.

We sit together on the sofa and Charlie puts his arm around my shoulder, kissing my forehead. 'It was about twelve years ago that Crystal and I got engaged. Crystal's dad worked at the same firm as my dad, they often came around to visit or we went to theirs, and both sets of parents really wanted us to marry, to cement their relationship, I guess. We started going out together because it was expected of us, that's how it seemed to me anyway. I like Crystal, always have done, but I don't know if I ever loved her. I think she was more like a sister to me. And then the family started talking about us settling down and before I could draw breath we were engaged and Crystal and Mum were organising our wedding. I soon realised how much like Mum Crystal was, how she wanted everything just so. We started arguing, drifting apart. I was trying to think of a way to break up and let her down gently when she did it for me. She said I obviously wasn't invested in the relationship as much as she was and she deserved better. A couple of years later she married Brandon, who is far better suited to her as he's a high achiever and can give her the lifestyle she wants. Then I met Lynn. Both sets of parents remained friends and Crystal remained close to Mum.'

'Is that why she lives a few doors away? To be close to your mum?' I ask.

'In a way but she's only been there a few years. When that house came empty, Mum tried to talk Lynn and I into buying it, even offered to help with the mortgage, but Lynn was dead against it.'

I bet she was! I wouldn't want to live a few doors away from Alice.

'Next thing we knew Crystal and Brandon had bought it and Crystal soon took to popping around to see Mum when Brandon was away working.'

'What about when you moved in?'

'She pops in now and again, yes, but Mum is – was – here a lot. They're like mother and daughter really. And as I said,

Crystal and I are more like brother and sister. There are absolutely no romantic feelings on either side.'

'So she's never made a pass at you since you split up?' I
don't know why I ask that but a crease forms between his
eyebrows and I can see him hesitate. So she has. 'Once, when
she'd had a bit too much to drink,' he admits. 'Of course nothing
happened, and the next day she apologised and we've never
mentioned it since.' He looks worriedly at me. 'I hope you don't
mention it either, please. It could jeopardise Crystal's marriage
and I wouldn't want to do that.' His eyes meet mine. 'I promise
that there is nothing between us and hasn't been for a long time.
And that I wasn't deliberately keeping this from you.'

I nod. 'I know. Thanks for telling me. I didn't mean to make
a big thing of it, I was taken by surprise, that's all.'

I can see that he's genuine. And what right do I have to
make a fuss about him not telling me about his past when I
haven't told him about mine?

Tasha messages me later that evening.

Ryan's been asking if Liam can have a sleepover tomorrow. He's not contagious anymore and is bored stiff. Would that be okay? You can drop him off after school.

That would be great! Liam's fast asleep now but I'll check with him in the morning and I'm sure he would love that.

Maybe you could stay over too. We haven't had a girly night for ages.

I'd love to but not this week. I really need some time alone with Charlie, we haven't had a minute this week. Alice has been here. We'll sort out something soon. I promise.

Make sure you do! I miss my bestie.

Liam is excited to be staying at Ryan's when I tell him the next morning and Charlie suggests asking his mum to pick the girls up from school and have them overnight too. 'She'll enjoy having them and we can go out for that meal we had to cancel,' he says.

The meal we were going to have before the flood in my home. It seems such a long time ago. 'That's a great idea,' I tell him.

His face breaks into a smile and he hugs me close. I nestle my head into his shoulder, basking in his warmth, the tangy smell of his aftershave. Our moment of serenity is interrupted by a shout from the playroom, it sounds like the kids are arguing. 'I'll go and see to them,' Charlie says, giving me a kiss.

I'm glad Tasha has asked for Liam to go over. We could all do with a bit of time apart. It's not always easy gelling together as a family unit.

I drop Liam off at Tasha's after school, hoping to have a quick coffee and go, but Tasha wants to chat.

'How's it going at Charlie's? I bet you're out of favour with the Mum Gang, they must be missing their morning drool over Hot Dad,' Tasha says with a grin as she puts a steaming mug of coffee in front of me. I'm relieved to see her in such a good mood, she'd seemed so off with me when I turned down her offer to stay with them. 'You'd better watch out for those voodoo dolls!'

That reminds me that I haven't told her about the word scrawled across my car boot. Discovering that Charlie and Crystal used to be engaged pushed it out of my mind. I tell her all about it now. 'Charlie thinks it was probably kids messing around, he reckons they probably vandalised a few cars in the car park.'

Tasha frowns. 'It sounds a bit more personal than that to me.'

'I thought so too. Do you think it was Kelly or Lacey?'

Tasha scratches her ear thoughtfully. 'Could be, you're not on their Christmas card list, are you? Or maybe Crystal? Or how about Alice, she always gives you this pursed lip look as if she's really looking down on you.'

So Tasha has noticed that too!

'I know she doesn't approve of me, but surely she wouldn't do something like that, it doesn't seem her style.' Alice seems far too refined to write rude words on someone's car.

'I guess so. Maybe Charlie is right and it's kids messing about.' She reaches out and touches my hand. 'I hope it hasn't upset you.'

'It did a bit. It feels like someone's really got it in for me.' I shrug. 'I guess I'm overreacting.'

'I'd feel the same,' Tasha says sympathetically. 'Look, why don't you both stop over next Friday evening? It would do Liam good to play with Ryan again and we haven't had a catch-up over a bottle of wine for ages.'

That sounds exactly what we both need. I've missed Tasha, and it will be so good to have a chat and relax for a while. 'I'd love to but aren't you seeing Caleb?'

'Not until the Saturday, Ryan's sleeping at Mum's overnight.' She grins. 'And I'm hoping Caleb will sleep at mine.'

'It's still going well then?'

Tasha flashes me a big grin. 'Really well. Maybe it's a good idea you didn't move in with us after all.'

'Wow, moved to that level already? You must be smitten.'

'We both are. I didn't think I'd ever meet anyone it felt so right with,' Tasha says dreamily. 'I guess it must be like that for you and Charlie.' She flicks me a quick look and I nod.

'Aren't we the lucky ones?' Tasha opens a packet of chocolate biscuits, takes one out and passes the packet to me.

We chat and have another coffee and it's two hours later when I get back. Charlie's car is in the drive but there's no sign of him.

I call out for him as I look in the kitchen, lounge, even out to the garden. Maybe he's in the study. He sometimes goes in there for a couple of hours in the evening to do some marking in peace, and although he's never actually told me not to go in, I sense that it's out of bounds so I never do.

I go upstairs, deciding to shower and change, and see Charlie's bedroom door open. He must be getting ready.

'Charlie?' I push open the door. 'What time are we—'

I gasp as my eyes rest on Crystal sitting on the bed.

37

'Oh hello, Sarah. We weren't expecting you home yet,' she says coyly.

Anger is surging through me and my fists instinctively clench at my sides. What the hell is she doing here? I'm about to explode when Charlie walks out of the closet at the far end of the bedroom, a fur coat draped over his arm. 'I thought it was here somewhere... Hello, darling!' His face breaks into a smile when he sees me and he comes over to give me a warm kiss.

Not the sort of kiss that a cheating boyfriend caught in the act would give, unless he's a very good actor.

'Crystal wanted to borrow a fur coat. This used to be Mum and Dad's bedroom and Mum left some of the clothes she hardly wears here as her apartment is pretty small. ' He turns back to Crystal. 'Give it back to Mum when you've finished with it.'

'Thanks so much. You're a sweetie to hunt it down for me.' She stands up, giving me a triumphant smile as she takes the coat. 'I'll see myself out. See you soon.'

I'm flustered, wondering if it's all as innocent as it looks.

Crystal's married, I remind myself, and she and Charlie are old friends.

'Sorry, love, I expected her to wait downstairs. I didn't know that she'd followed me up until I heard her talking to you.' He drops a kiss on my forehead. 'Did Liam settle at Tasha's okay?'

I'm pretty certain that Crystal followed Charlie upstairs knowing I'd be coming home soon. I wouldn't even be surprised if Alice deliberately offered to lend her the fur coat for this very reason. I bite back my suspicions though and answer pleasantly. 'Yes, he's really excited to be having a sleepover.'

'Great.' He gives my shoulders a squeeze. 'And I'm looking forward to finally having our first proper date. Fancy a shower together to start the evening off in the right mood?'

He threads his arms around my waist and starts kissing me. I return the kisses eagerly and they become deeper and deeper. We don't make it into the shower for another hour.

Charlie has booked us a table at a very upmarket restaurant and we have a wonderful romantic meal with a bottle of champagne. The waiter pours us both a glass and Charlie holds his up for a toast. 'To us,' he says.

'To us,' I echo.

Then Charlie leans forward and says softly, 'I know we haven't known each other very long but I think I'm falling in love with you.'

My eyes flash to his face and as they sink into the sea-green pool of his eyes, I know that I'm falling in love with him too. 'Me too,' I whisper.

A little later Charlie gets up to go to the loo, and I sit back sipping my wine, thinking what a perfect evening it's been. Then suddenly I feel a prickle at the back of my neck, as if someone is watching me. I turn my head and look around. The other guests are eating and chatting. I must have imagined it.

Then I see someone standing by the restaurant window, looking in. They're wearing a hoodie and I can't make out their face but I sense they're staring at me, watching me. I shudder.

Is it Dylan?

38

I'm unsettled for the rest of the night and the next morning when I go to pick up Liam from Tasha's I can't help looking around, checking out if anyone is following me. I can't afford to be complacent to the danger we both might be in.

Liam is pleased to see me and looks so upbeat. It was definitely a good idea to let him have a sleepover with Ryan.

'They've had a great time. Don't forget to come over next Friday, both of you,' Tasha reminds me.

'Let me check with Charlie and make sure he hasn't made any arrangements for us all,' I tell her, realising that I forgot to mention it yesterday.

Alice and the girls are in when we get back and she doesn't seem in a rush to leave. Before I have a chance to greet the girls, Todd FaceTimes Liam, whose face lights up when he sees who's calling. Todd waves hello to me then Liam takes his iPad into his bedroom to talk to his dad.

'Do you let him speak to his father alone?' Alice asks disapprovingly.

'Yes. It's nice for them to have some alone time. Liam

doesn't get to see his father often – working on the oil rigs means he's away a lot,' I reply although I don't really see why I should have to explain to her. I'm beginning to get really fed up with her being constantly here and wouldn't be surprised if she suddenly announced that she might as well sell her apartment and move in. I bet that is why she gave the house to Charlie, she was planning on guilt-tripping him into moving in all together. Then I came along and scuppered her plans.

'I think I'd want to supervise it all the same,' she replies.

I take a deep breath and decide to ignore her and go over to Charlie, who's busy cleaning out Thumper's hutch with the girls.

'Do you fancy going out for a drive? It's a lovely day,' I suggest.

'Sure, we can go to the pub by the canal and have a shandy, there's a playground there for the kids.' He glances at his watch. 'Shall we say half an hour?'

'Perfect.' I kiss him on the cheek and go back into the kitchen, where Alice is loading the dishwasher.

'We're off out in a little while, Alice. Can I offer you another drink before you go?' I ask.

She looks taken aback. 'Off out? Charlie didn't say. Where are you going?'

'For a drive, we thought we'd take the kids to the park.' I go over to the kettle. 'Tea or coffee?'

'Neither, thank you.' She goes out in the garden and walks over to Charlie. I'm about to go out too, thinking she might be trying to persuade Charlie to invite her along, but Liam comes in, holding his iPad. 'Dad wants to talk to you.'

'Okay.' Todd usually has a word with me after talking to Liam, checking that everything's all right. 'Can you go and get tidied up please? We're going out soon.'

Liam always looks happy when he's spoken to Todd and I'm

pleased that they still have contact with each other, unlike Lynn and the girls.

'Hi, how's it going?' I ask as Todd's face stares out of the screen at me. He looks well, he's grown a bit of a beard and his olive skin is now tanned dark.

'All good here.' He pauses. 'Liam seems a bit unsettled though. Is everything all right there? You have moved in very quick with this chap.'

'Yes, well, it was out of necessity when our house got flooded. Have you any idea what it's like getting rental property over here?' I say defensively. Me and Todd might get on but that doesn't give him the right to question my decisions.

He holds up his hands, palms out. 'Not judging.'

'I should hope not seeing as you've swanned off to make a new life for yourself and I'm quite sure aren't living the life of a monk,' I snap.

'I know, I know, guilty as charged. But I still care about you both and surely I'm allowed to be concerned about my son?'

He's right, I think a bit guiltily, it was quick and Liam is unsettled. 'It was upsetting for us to lose our home like that but we're happy here at Charlie's until we can get another house,' I tell him. Then I pause and take the plunge. 'I don't suppose you could help towards the deposit, could you?' Todd pays regular maintenance and if I need extra because the washing machine's broken or something he will help towards it if he can.

'Sorry but I've just moved into a new flat myself. I've got a new girlfriend actually,' he confesses. 'And we've got furniture and everything to buy.' His deep brown eyes meet mine on the screen. 'I might be able to give you some in another month or so. I'll try.'

I nod. 'Thanks.' I know that he will if he can. Todd does care about Liam, he just doesn't want the full-time commitment of being a dad. And now he's got a new home and girlfriend, his money is going to be stretched.

We say goodbye and end the call. When I look up I see Alice standing at the back door, staring at me. Has she been listening in?

I force a smile on my face. 'Are you off now, Alice? We'll no doubt see you in the week.'

The look she gives me would freeze hell over. 'I'll go and get my bag from the playroom.' And she walks out of the kitchen.

Charlie comes in for a drink, and I can see he looks a bit uncomfortable. My guess is that Alice was badgering him to come out with us. I'm so pleased he managed to put her off.

Suddenly we hear Alice shout from the playroom. We both look at each other and go running in. Someone has knocked over a glass of orange cordial and it's spilt all over her phone.

'Look at the state of it!' She wipes it furiously on her jumper. 'If the liquid gets inside it, I won't be able to use it! Oh, you are clumsy, Liam!'

'It was Mia, she knocked my arm,' Liam protests, his bottom lip wobbling.

'No, I didn't! You're lying!' Mia shouts, jabbing her finger at Liam.

Alice shoots Liam a disapproving look. 'I realise it was an accident but please don't make things worse by blaming Mia. All you have to do is apologise.'

Liam's eyes are on her face and he's gone very pale.

'Sorry,' he mumbles, dropping his gaze and scuffing the carpet with his toes.

I frown and glance at Alice, who nods briskly at him. 'Be more careful next time. You could have completely ruined my phone.'

She's right, but I wish she'd spoken less harshly to him. Liam is such a sensitive lad. I put my arm around his shoulders. 'I'm sure he will be, he's not usually so careless.'

'Really?' Alice raises an eyebrow but turns away without saying anything else. I think about Daisy's painting, and the

plug being left in the sink at our house, and remind myself that
Liam is in fact being a bit careless lately. I wonder if anything is
troubling him and resolve to speak to him later.

We have a wonderful afternoon out and Liam and Mia seem to
have forgotten all about their quarrel, thank goodness. I sit and
watch them all play while Charlie goes into the pub to get us
another soft drink. I'm still bothered about the look on Liam's
face when Alice told him off. It's not the first time I've noticed
him acting nervous around her.

'Penny for them?' Charlie asks, putting my glass of lemon
and lime on the table in front of me and sliding into the space
on the bench next to me. He glances over at the kids playing.
'They're all enjoying themselves.'

'They are... but I'm a bit worried about Liam,' I confess.

Charlie takes a slow sip of non-alcoholic beer before asking,
'Why?'

'All these things that are going wrong, the tap being left on
in the sink in our bathroom, him spilling water over Daisy's
painting, his drink over your mum's phone. It's not like him.'

'It's probably a bit strange for him living in such a busy
household, he's used to it only being the two of you. He'll settle
down, don't worry. Look how great they're playing now.'

I look over at them. Liam is pushing Daisy on the swing and
Mia is in the swing next to her, and they're laughing and
shouting as they go higher and higher.

Suddenly, a prickling sensation creeps up the back of my
neck, as if someone is watching me. I turn around slowly scanning the pub gardens.

A woman with mousey brown hair and wearing a beige
duffle coat is standing by the park. She has her back to me and
seems to be watching the kids play, then she strides away across
the car park. Unease prickles the back of my neck as I watch

her. It's the same feeling I had when I opened the door to our house the day it was flooded out. And the other night at the restaurant.

I always sense danger. It's a family trait with the women..

I didn't sense danger that night three years ago, though, did I?

39

Tasha phones me later. 'There's a house coming empty over the road from me. I met the woman who lives there today and her husband has been offered a job in Wales. They've just given notice. Want to take a look at it on Friday? If you fancy it, we can ask them to give the landlord your details.'

If they've only recently given notice, then the landlord might not have advertised it yet and I could be first in the queue. I don't know how I could get a deposit together in a month, but I might be able to work something out. It's definitely worth looking at, although I am a bit uneasy about living so close to Tasha. She is great fun and very supportive but she can be a bit suffocating. Mind you, she has Caleb now so won't want to be around mine all the time.

'That sounds great, thanks, Tasha.'

When Charlie comes home I mention about staying at Tasha's on Friday evening. 'You haven't got plans for us, have you?' I ask.

'Nope, nothing planned, not with the Autumn Fayre on Saturday.' Alice and Crystal have both been on the phone several times this week already about that. You'd think they were running it single-handed. 'I think it would be great for you both to have a bit of time with your friends. This has all been overwhelming, I know.' He kisses me tenderly.

'Yeah, I think Liam could do with some "best friend" time, he was much happier after staying over at Ryan's on Friday. You can have some quality time with the girls too.' I was thinking of not mentioning the house until I've seen it, then decide I should be upfront. 'Tasha said that there's a house coming available by her soon, so I want to take a look at that too,' I tell him.

Charlie looks taken aback. 'There's no rush, Sarah. You can stay here as long as you like. You're happy here, aren't you?'

'Yes, but I don't want us to overstay our welcome. It was only ever a temporary arrangement,' I remind him. 'Not that I've got the deposit together yet, but at least I can take a look.'

He wraps his arms around me and kisses me. 'Whatever you want, love. There's no rush on my part.' He eases his head back, his arms still linked around my waist. 'Will you be all right sorting out the furniture in your old house? I feel guilty that I can't come and help you, but I've got roped in now.'

I've arranged for a van to pick up the furniture and other things from my old house next Saturday morning and put them into storage. I'd made a few trips back to the house to collect some things, but I couldn't bring everything to Charlie's.

'I'll be fine. It's not like I'm going to be doing any heavy lifting. I'll come out to the Autumn Fayre afterwards.'

'Great. And don't worry about picking up the girls from school on Friday, Mum will be delighted to do that, she's missed going to the school. It gets her out of the house and makes her feel useful. She'll pop back to mine with the kids and probably have dinner cooking by the time I come home.'

I bet she'll be mooching too, I think, going through my things and seeing what she can find out about me. I wish I could say that I don't want her in the house when I'm not there, but how can I when it's Charlie's house and Alice is his mother?

I'll have to make sure I don't leave anything around for her to snoop at, I resolve. I don't trust her at all. The word 'TRAMP' on the boot of my car flashes back into my mind. Could it have been Alice? If she knew what had happened on Arran, then she might call me that, or worse.

But if she knew, she would probably tell Charlie I wasn't fit to be around the girls, wouldn't she?

And anyway, how could she have found out my secret?

The thought sneaks into my mind again that it could be Dylan. Maybe it could have been him watching me through the window at the restaurant the other night too? I have to keep my wits about me.

'You enjoy your night with Tasha.' Charlie kisses me. 'And on Saturday night we can have some quality time together. How does that sound?'

'Perfect,' I say happily, pushing all thoughts of Alice and Dylan out of my mind.

The next few days pass without incident, and the more time I spend at Charlie's, the more it's starting to feel like home. I feel so safe and comfortable here that I don't want to leave.

'Let me know when you're at Tasha's so I can relax about you both,' Charlie tells me as he gives me a hug on Friday then tousles Liam's hair. 'And you enjoy the sleepover with your mate. It must be good to have no girls around.'

Liam grins. 'Yeah, they're not too bad though,' he adds.

'I'll let you know when we're starting out tomorrow,' I promise. 'Phone you later.'

Alice is picking up the girls today and I'm collecting Ryan before we go straight over to Tasha's. She's standing at the school gates when I arrive and briefly nods then turns away to whisper something to Crystal. I frown, wondering what they're discussing, then Liam and Ryan come running out together and we set off. Just as I'm about to close the car door, Lacey walks over to me.

'Charlie had enough of you already?'

'Me and Charlie are good, thanks, but I'm staying at Tasha's tonight for a girly night in.'

'The question is, what will Charlie be doing tonight while you're away?' Lacey asks, one hand on her hip, head cocked to one side.

I know that she's only saying that to stir things, to make me doubt Charlie, and I'm determined not to let her get to me.

I can't shake off the niggle that Charlie seemed quite eager for me to go, though. And the memory of Crystal sitting on Charlie's bed.

40

I like the look of the house immediately: it's a two-bed terrace like our old house but the small front garden is surrounded by a low fence and the rooms are a bit bigger. There's a garage, plus a back garden.

'It's great, isn't it? And directly opposite me,' Tasha says. 'I think it's perfect. We can babysit for each other, have girly nights, go shopping together.'

We knock on the door but no one answers. Then a woman comes out from the house next door and says that the tenants have gone away for a few days, which is a bummer as I'd hoped to look around. I stop myself from peering through the windows.

'Shall I pass on your number and we can take a proper look when they come back?' Tasha says.

'Yes, please!' I turn to my son, who is fooling around with Ryan. 'What about you, Liam? Do you like it? Shall we see if we can rent it?'

'Yeah!' he says eagerly. 'Can we get some fish and chips now?' We'd promised them a chippy supper, it's our tradition, followed by a bottle of wine for me and Tasha once the boys are in bed.

So we make our way to the chippy and then set off back to Tasha's, where we sit around the coffee table and eat the fish and chips out of the paper.

Tasha's home is very minimalistic and arty, with only a few photos and ornaments on show, carefully spaced out. Red cushions are scattered on her smart grey sofa and a big crimson rug covers the wooden floorboards. The wall unit running across the back wall and the TV stand are both black. I know that she'll send the boys upstairs to play as soon as they've finished eating – she hates toys cluttering up the downstairs space, whereas I prefer Liam to play where I can see him. I'm constantly checking on him and the girls at Charlie's house.

'We must do this more often,' I say.

She nods, her mouth full of chips. Then she crooks her little finger and holds it out. 'Pinky promise never to let a man come between us.'

Feeling guilty, I remember we made that promise when I came back from Arran.

'Pinky promise,' I say.

Tasha raises her eyebrow. 'I hope you mean it this time.'

I feel my cheeks flush. 'I meant it before. It was just the bathroom flooding, we had to get out and...' My voice trails off.

'You could have come here.' Her eyes are boring into me. Then her face breaks into a smile. 'It's fine. I'm only jesting. I get it. I know you'll never let a man come between us. Neither will I, no matter how much I like Caleb. You're my bestie and nothing is going to change that.'

'I've missed our chats,' Tasha says later that evening as we make our way through our second bottle of wine. The boys are happily watching a film and eating popcorn in bed, and we've spent the last couple of hours catching up on all our gossip.

I am way behind – it seems that Tasha and Caleb are getting on so well she is spending next weekend with him. 'Mum's having Ryan for the weekend , you know how she loves to spoil him.'

Her words make me think of my own mother. Have I been right to deprive Liam of a relationship with his grandparents? What choice did I have though?

'Talking about grandmothers, how are you getting on with Alice? I didn't get the impression that she was very happy about you moving in with Charlie. Not judging,' she adds hastily, 'it must have been horrible to lose your home like that, and I don't blame you for plumping for Charlie's posh house over this small one.' She looks dismissively around the room. 'You're always welcome here though, if things don't work out at Charlie's and you want to get out before the house across the road is vacant.'

'I know and thank you.' I pat her hands, grateful for all the support she's given me over the years. 'I think that Alice disapproves of me and can't wait for me to go,' I say, hesitating.

Tasha's green eyes meet mine over her wine glass. 'Spill, I can see that something's bothering you.'

'The kids have started arguing a bit, and Liam's acting a bit out of character.' I tell her about all the things that have gone wrong. 'It's not like him to be so careless and I know that he's a bit anxious around people he doesn't know well...'

I take another sip of wine, feeling myself relax as the cool liquid slides down my throat. 'There's another thing. I've been wondering if the bathroom flood was deliberate.'

Tasha raises an eyebrow. 'You think Liam did it so he could move into Charlie's?' She finishes her wine and reaches for the bottle to top it up.

'No, no, of course not.' I hold out my glass and she refills it.

'So how was it deliberate?'

I look down into my glass. I feel stupid voicing my fears now.

'Sarah? You can tell me anything, you know that.'

I chew my lip and raise my eyes to meet hers. 'Mrs Stanton next door said that someone had been looking for me, they even went around the back. And the kitchen window was open, Tash. I'm sure I closed it that morning. I always check, you know I do.' When I lived with Tasha for that short time when we came back from Arran, she made a joke of how many times I checked that doors were locked, taps were off, windows closed. I couldn't help it, I had to make sure Liam was safe.

'True, but anyone can be forgetful when they're in a rush.' She takes another sip of her wine, taking her time to swallow.

'I know. I guess I've got an overactive imagination. Although there's what happened to my car and...' I'm just about to tell her about the uneasy feeling I've been getting that someone is following me when her phone rings. She picks it up and a big smile lights up her face. 'It's Caleb.' She gets to her feet. 'Won't be long,' she whispers.

I take the opportunity to phone Charlie and see how he's getting on. His mobile rings out for ages but finally he answers. 'Hi, Sarah, how's it going?'

'Good,' I tell him. 'How's everything with you and the girls?'

'They're fine, tucked up in bed fast asleep.'

I hear another voice in the background. Alice's. She's talking to someone but I can't make out who.

'Ah, sorry, it sounds like you have company. Shall I call back later?'

'Thanks, love. Crystal has popped around to discuss the fayre tomorrow. I'll give you a call when she's gone.'

He ends the call and I sit there, my mind in a whirl. Did he know that Crystal was coming round? Is that why he was so eager for me to stay over at Tasha's?

41

ALICE

'Was that Sarah, darling? Surely she isn't checking up on you? She's only been gone a few hours,' I say. What a cheek! The woman was quick enough to go off to her friend's and leave Charlie and the girls, after he'd put a roof over her and her son's head. Now she wants to make sure he really is alone.

I hope she heard Crystal's voice when I spoke to her, wanting Sarah to know she's here. Crystal is such a lovely woman, we get on so well, it was such a shame when she and Charlie broke off their engagement. Now she and Brandon have separated – although that's top secret at the moment because Crystal hasn't told Phoebe yet. The young girl thinks her father is working away again. Crystal told me, she has always confided in me, and of course I'm hoping she and Charlie will get together again. Crystal and I have far more in common than Sarah, who always wants to keep me away from my beloved son and grandchildren.

'It's fine. I'll call her back later.' Charlie turns to Crystal. 'I think we've almost finished, haven't we?'

'Yes, I just have two more things to cross off the list.' She looks down at the piece of paper in her hand. That's another thing I like about Crystal: she uses pen and paper, proper note-books, not like Sarah, who writes everything on her iPad. Her son's got an iPad too, he's on it all the time. It's bad for children, no wonder he's so hyperactive. I've mentioned it to Charlie, told him to watch out that she doesn't get the girls addicted too. Lazy parenting, that's all it is.

'Are you still okay to be in charge of the games stall, Charlie?' Crystal is asking. 'You're good with the kids, and I'm sure some of the other fathers will join in, but I need someone responsible to keep an eye on it all.'

'No problem at all,' Charlie says. 'The girls will be with me and they'll enjoy that.'

'And you said you'd cover the cake stall with Ruth, Alice?' Crystal taps the pen on her lips. 'We've quite a list of people saying they'll bring cakes.'

'I've made a Victoria sponge and some blueberry muffins,' I tell her. 'Did you say we're next to the refreshment stall?'

Crystal nods. 'A couple of people are bringing tables and fold up chairs so that people can sit down, which will encourage them to buy more tea and cakes.' She looks at us both and smiles. 'I think this is going to bring in a substantial amount of money. 'With a bit of luck it will be enough to buy a new computer for the library. I'm so grateful for all your help.'

'Think nothing of it,' Charlie tells her.

That's my boy, always willing to help.

'Sarah will help too,' Charlie adds. 'She has to go back to her former home and organise her furniture to go into storage but she should be finished in time to come to the fayre.'

'Oh, I see. So unfortunate that she got flooded out like that. She's very lucky that you were there to rescue her.' Crystal taps her cheek with her pen. 'It's very generous of you to house them here, Charlie. You've only known her a few weeks too. I was quite surprised! Most people would have moved in with one of their friends, or their family.'

'It's working out great, actually. We all have to help each other out, don't you think?' Charlie gets up from the chair. 'Are we all finished then? I'll be there at ten thirty tomorrow.'

'Why not drop the girls off with me?' I suggest. 'You don't want them in your way. I'll bring them over when I bring the cakes.'

'It would be easier for you to stay over here, surely?' Crystal looks surprised.

'I must admit I am a bit nervous going back in the dark but I don't like to intrude now that Sarah has moved in.'

'Of course you can stay, Mum. Your room is still there, Sarah and Liam have the other two rooms,' Charlie says.

'Thank you, darling.' I stand up. 'Now shall we all have a nice cup of coffee?'

'That would be most welcome. A long black please,' Crystal says. 'And how about a spot of whisky or brandy in it, seeing as you're staying over and I'm only three doors away.'

'I'll do it, Mum.' Charlie is about to stand up but I motion for him to sit back down. 'Let me. You and Crystal can chat about school stuff.'

I go into the kitchen and take my time making the coffees, putting a generous dose of brandy in both Crystal's and Charlie's cups. I put some crisps and snacks in a bowl, then place it all on a tray and go into the lounge.

When I walk in Charlie and Crystal are in conversation about the current curriculum. I know my Charlie when he gets started, they'll be talking for ages.

I glance at the clock. Almost eleven. I bet Sarah is waiting for him to phone back. I smile to myself as I put the tray down on the table.

Sarah might think that she's got a permanent home here but I have plans of my own. And I'll soon have her gone.

42

SARAH

It's almost midnight before Charlie texts me.

Sorry I didn't realise the time. Is it too late to talk?

I want to hear his voice so I phone him straight back. 'Hi, is everything okay?'

'Yes, we got chatting and lost track of time. Crystal's just left and Mum's gone to bed.'

I'm floored. Crystal and his mother were there for hours. *Don't be jealous, Alice is there too, nothing is going on,* I tell myself. Although Alice very clearly regrets that Crystal and Charlie broke up, Crystal is married to someone else and I'm sure Alice wouldn't encourage her to cheat on her husband. Then I remember what Charlie said about Alice having just gone up to bed. 'Is Alice staying over then?'

'Yes, I don't want her driving over this late and her room is there, with spare clothes in it.'

I can't really object to his elderly mother staying over, can I?

'I feel bad about not being able to help with your furniture tomorrow. Are you sure you'll be okay?' Charlie asks.

'Yes, of course, there will be two men loading it into the van and then it's going straight to the storage unit so there's nothing heavy for me to do. Shall I meet you at the school then? Do you want me to pick up the girls first?'

'No, Mum's baking cakes for the cake stall so she'll take the girls with her. Come over whenever you're ready. The fayre starts at one thirty.'

'Should I bring anything?'

'No, it's all sorted. Look, I've got to go, Daisy's woken up and is calling me. See you tomorrow. Love you.'

'Love you,' I say back but he's already ended the call.

'Are we still doing our Hallowe'en party for the kids this year?' Tasha asks as me and Liam get ready to leave for our old house the next day. 'We'll hold it at mine, if you want?'

I'd forgotten all about it. Me and Tasha always have a Hallowe'en party for Ryan and Liam. They love dressing up, watching scary movies – child-friendly, of course – and eating spooky treats.

'Oh yes, please, Mum!' Liam begs.

'You can bring Daisy and Mia,' Tasha adds. 'The more the merrier.'

'Let me see if Charlie has anything planned. I have to dash now but I'll message you about it over the weekend.'

When I pull up outside the terraced house that used to be our home, the front door is open and the landlord's car is outside, plus a decorator's van. The removal van will have to park on the kerb. We get out of the car and I put my arm around Liam's shoulders as we look at the house. We had some happy times there.

'Can you help me get the boxes out of the back of the car?' I ask Liam. I packed them in the boot last night, and I hope there's enough space to put our remaining things in them, but if not I have bin bags.

I open the boot and take out the boxes and bags, carrying them over to the front door. The smell of paint hits me as I step inside. The landlord has already started doing it up ready to sell, then. 'Hello!' I shout.

The landlord pops his head over the banister. 'I'm up here. Be careful where you're walking and watch the lad too, I don't want any more accidents.'

I go into the kitchen and see that the ceiling has been repaired and the whole kitchen repainted. Our table and chairs have been pushed to one side and covered with a dustsheet. I look up at the ceiling, and the memory of the chunk of plaster-board crashing down to the floor, bringing a deluge of water with it, shoots across my mind.

Liam slips his hand in mine. 'It wasn't me,' he says quietly.

I turn my head to look at him. 'What wasn't you?'

'I didn't leave the tap on. It wasn't my fault.'

Has he been carrying this guilt with him all this time? I put my hand around his shoulder and pull him to me. 'It doesn't matter now, Liam.' He's only seven, he probably didn't even realise that he'd left the tap on. Children are easily distracted.

Maybe Liam is right and it wasn't him. What about the open kitchen window? And the person my neighbour saw?

'It does, because if the bathroom hadn't flooded, we'd still be living here.'

I hear the wobble in Liam's voice and frown. Why is he saying that? I bend down so I can look him in the eyes, which fill with tears as he drops his gaze. Does he miss his home? He'd been so excited to move into Charlie's house at first but now... 'Do you wish we still lived here, love?' I ask.

He nods.

'Don't you like it at Charlie's?'

He shrugs.

'You can tell me anything,' I say reassuringly. 'I don't want you to be unhappy. Please tell me if something is wrong.'

He bites his lip. 'It's strange and it doesn't feel like home,' he mumbles.

I want to question him further but the removal van arrives then. This will have to wait.

The landlord comes down as the two men are carrying our furniture to the van, ready to put into storage.

'You're sorted, aren't you? You've got somewhere to stay?'

Now he asks! 'Yes, we're staying with my boyfriend for the time being.'

He nods. 'No hard feelings then? You can see the damage that was done, so surely realise I wasn't being unreasonable in keeping your deposit, although I accept it was an accident and will give you a reference for your next place.'

I guess that's something. 'Thanks.'

He reaches in his pocket and takes out a small clear plastic bag with a badge in it. 'I found this in the bathroom, it looks like it's come off a bag or a trainer. I bet you've been looking everywhere for it.'

I stare down at the plastic bag and take out the badge. It's a silver one with a popular logo on it, the sort that would fit on the front of a shoe. It's definitely not mine, I've never seen it before. What was it doing in my bathroom?

Nausea churns in my belly as a strong gut feeling of danger envelops me.

43

The fayre has already started by the time we get there. The school car park is full and crowds of families are milling around the stalls. Liam soon spots Daisy and Mia playing with a gang of children, and Mia sees us and calls him over to join them.

'Can I, Mum?' he asks eagerly.

'Yes, but make sure you don't go out of the school grounds,' I warn him.

'I won't.' He runs off and I'm pleased to see him look happy again.

I look around for Charlie and spot Alice serving on the cake stall with Crystal. Lacey and Kelly are helping too. I hadn't realised that. I wonder if they volunteered so they can get close to Charlie. They're still so obviously put out that I'm living with the hot single dad they all coveted, I'm pretty sure that any one of them would jump into my shoes given the chance. I'm also pretty sure that although Charlie is polite and friendly when he meets them, he is not the slightest bit interested in them in that way.

I'm not so sure about his feelings for Crystal though. But

surely he wouldn't have an affair with a married woman, not after what Lynn did to him.

'Sarah!' I turn as I hear his voice and scan the stalls. There he is, waving. Of course, he'd said he was on the games stall. There are already quite a few parents with their children hanging around, eager to play the games. He loops his arm around my waist when I join him, and kisses me on the cheek. 'How did it go? I'm so sorry I couldn't come with you.'

'It was okay, it didn't take long. The landlord had already boxed up most of our stuff. He said he'll give me a reference, so that's something.'

'Brilliant. So bye-bye old life and hello new one with Charlie,' he says with a grin. 'And how was the house near Tasha's? Did you check it out?'

'Only from the outside, unfortunately the tenants were out, but it looks great, so I've asked Tasha to give the landlord my number.'

He nods. 'Like I said, there's no rush...'

Just then the girls and Liam come running over. 'Can we play some games?' they ask.

'You sure can. And maybe you can all help me for a bit? I could do with someone to pick up the skittles and collect the balls.'

'I can do that!' Liam offers eagerly.

'Brilliant! If it's okay with your mum, of course.'

They all look at me questioningly. 'Go ahead. I'll pop over and see if Alice needs any help with the cake stall,' I reply, noticing that Crystal has now gone.

'Thanks. Save a piece of cake for us, we'll be over later,' Charlie says.

'Chocolate for me, please.' Liam picks up the bucket as some children pay for tickets.

'I'll see if I can bring them over with a drink when we're not too busy,' I promise.

There's a queue around Alice's stall and she looks a bit flustered. 'Want any help?'

'Thank you, dear, we are a bit busy.'

After half an hour or so Crystal returns. 'Charlie's stall is very popular. I think my idea of having a "throw the sponge" game was inspired.'

I guess she came up with that idea last night. 'I'll take him and the kids a snack now you're back.' I put some cakes on a tray, buy some drinks from the stall next door and carry them over to Charlie and the children. I laugh out loud, almost dropping the tray, when I see that Charlie is sitting in the 'docks' being soaked with wet sponges and is wringing wet.

He looks pleased to see me. 'Great, refreshments! I'm taking a break, everyone.' He picks up a towel from a nearby stool and dries his face.

There's a collective groan from the kids and their mums as he walks off, waving a hand and promising he'll be back later. Charlie in a wet tee shirt that clings to his muscular body is quite a sight so I can understand why his stall is such a big attraction. Is that what made Crystal think of it? I swear that woman has pound symbols for pupils! Or is it the sight of Charlie in a wet tee shirt that appealed to her?

Charlie pulls out a stool for me and sits on one himself, the kids sit on the grass, and we all tuck into our cakes and drinks.

'I have to admit that I didn't fancy this at all, and was quite annoyed that Mum had invited Crystal around last night, but actually it's been fun and we've raised a lot of money, haven't we, Liam?' Charlie says.

Liam nods. 'Jordan's mum threw a sponge right into Charlie's face.' His eyes are twinkling and he looks so different from the anxious boy at our old house just a few hours earlier.

Charlie ruffles his hair. 'Your turn next, eh?'

'Yes!' Mia and Daisy shout together.

Liam's eyes open wide and he shakes his head. 'Not me!'

Charlie laughs. 'I'm only teasing.'

Despite the lightness in the air, I get that prickly feeling in the back of my neck again. I turn around and see a woman staring at us all.

She has mousy, shoulder-length hair and glasses, dressed in jeans, a beige duffle coat and brown boots. The fayre is open to the public so not everyone here is a parent, but the way she is intensely looking at Mia and Daisy unsettles me.

Then she meets my gaze and as her eyes bore into mine a chill runs through my entire body. I can't move. It's like I'm frozen in ice. My breath catches in my throat and time seems to stand still as our eyes lock.

Her face is inscrutable, unflinching, and I feel like she's sucking the breath out of me. Then she turns away and walks off and I let out my breath, holding onto the stool for support. I'm sure it's the same woman I saw at the pub. A shiver of apprehension trickles down my spine as I remember the shadowy figure I saw staring in the restaurant window. Was that this woman too?

Who is she? Does she have anything to do with the flood at the house? The vile writing on my car?

Another thought flashes into my mind. Could that woman be Lynn?

44

'Are you all right, Sarah? You've gone really pale.'

Charlie's voice brings me out of my daze. I blink as his face comes into focus. He's standing in front of me, his eyebrows drawn together in a worried frown.

'Do you know that woman?' I ask. I can hear the shake in my voice.

'What woman?' He looks around swiftly then back at me. 'There's a lot of people here,' he points out.

'She was here a minute ago.' My eyes search the crowd but she's disappeared.

Charlie touches my arm. 'What's the matter? Did she say something to you?'

'No.' I take a deep breath. 'She was staring at Daisy and Mia. I wondered...' I hesitate, wondering how to say it. Then I blurt it out. 'I thought it might be Lynn. What if she's come back for them?'

His eyes widen. 'Why on earth would you think that?' There's an edge to his voice and a flash in his eyes.

'She was staring at them so intently. And the other week

when we went to the pub with the kids, I think she was there too.'

'You didn't mention her. Was she staring at Mia and Daisy then as well?' he asks sharply.

'I'm not sure. I sensed something so I turned around and a woman in the same coat seemed to be watching the kids in the park but then she walked away.' I lick my lips, feeling awkward as I know this must be uncomfortable for Charlie. 'What if it is Lynn? Maybe she regrets leaving the girls and has come back.'

'I think your imagination is running away with you, Sarah. Lynn is not coming back. And if she did, why would she turn up here? She doesn't even know that Mia attends this school.'

'Maybe she went to your old house and they told her you'd moved? Then she saw the fayre advertised, so came to see if you and the girls were here? Did you leave a forwarding address for her?'

It all makes sense to me. Who else would stare at the girls like that?

Something flits across his face. 'Lynn made it quite clear that she was starting a new life and we would never see her again.'

He sounds irritated, but before I can reply the kids crowd around him. 'Can we have one last go of the bouncy castle?' Mia begs. 'Please, Dad?'

'Go on then, but make it quick!' he agrees. He rarely refuses the girls anything, Alice is the one who disciplines them. I guess Charlie is trying to make up for them losing their mother.

They all run off to the bouncy castle and Charlie goes over to help Alice pack away her stall so there's no chance to speak any further.

But I can't get the woman out of my mind.

Why is Charlie so sure it wasn't Lynn? I totally understand that he's hurt about how she so callously ditched him and the girls for another man, but she must miss her daughters. I couldn't bear to be away from Liam. And what if she and her new man have split up? She might feel like she can't just turn up because Charlie might be – understandably – angry.

When the kids are all in bed I go down into the kitchen to grab a snack. Charlie is already in there, opening a bottle of wine. He turns to me and holds out his arms. 'I'm sorry.'

I walk into his hug, and he holds me tight and nuzzles my neck. 'I didn't mean to snap but the girls and I, we've moved on. When Lynn walked out, Daisy was too young to understand, she kept crying for her mummy. Mia was old enough though and she spent hours staring out of the window waiting for her mother to walk back in. Every morning she said that this might be the day that Mummy came back and every night she prayed that she would. It was heartbreaking.' I can hear the bitterness in his voice and feel so sad for them all. It was such a cruel thing for Lynn to do. No wonder he's convinced himself and the girls that Lynn is never coming back. They have to get on with their lives and draw a line under it, accept that she's gone.

What if he is wrong though, and she does come back? Our relationship is so new, are we strong enough? Anxiety forms a lump in my stomach as I think how fond I've become of Charlie and his daughters, how much I enjoy having them in my life.

Despite everything, what if Charlie still loves Lynn? Where does that leave me?

45

It's half term this week so the kids are all home. I already booked the week off when I sorted out my holidays for the year, and Charlie is off most of the week too but he has to go in for meetings on Wednesday and Friday afternoon.

We're all a bit late getting up on Monday morning and enjoying a leisurely breakfast. I'm feeling happy that we have a week to spend together without having to rush around. We're planning on taking the kids to the cinema this afternoon and they're all looking forward to it, and Wednesday is Hallowe'en so we're having a party..

When I mentioned to Charlie that me and Tasha always have a party for the boys and suggested I take Mia and Daisy to Tasha's too, he immediately told me to invite them all here instead. Tasha was delighted. She's been itching to see Charlie's posh house. So tomorrow we're going shopping for Hallowe'en costumes and Wednesday Tasha is coming over in the afternoon to help me prepare for the party.

'I fancy a cup of tea before we go to the cinema. How about you?' I fill up the kettle and switch it on.

Charlie shakes his head, he's not a big tea drinker. 'I'll have some orange juice, thanks.'

I open the fridge to get the milk and orange juice and notice some leftover spinach. 'I take the bag out and hold it up. Who wants to give this to Thumper?'

'Me!' Both Liam and Mia hold up their hands.

'You can both give him some,' I say, taking two plastic bowls out of the cupboard and sharing the spinach between them.

They run outside with the bowls of spinach and I watch from the window as Mia opens the rabbit run and steps inside. Thumper hops over to greet them, and Mia puts the bowl on top of the hutch, bends down and picks up Thumper, cradling him in her arms. Liam waits patiently until she passes the rabbit to him and then runs back into the house. I sip my tea and watch Liam for a while: he always looks so happy and relaxed when he's stroking Thumper and sometimes I catch him talking to the little rabbit, as if he's confiding in him. I resolve to get him a pet when we move into our new home.

I glance at my phone as a text pings in. It's from Tasha.

The people over the road are back now and are happy for you to look at the house Friday afternoon about two. Can you make it?

Charlie's in work Friday afternoon, let me find out what time he starts.

Obviously I'll take Liam with me but it will be a bit much to turn up with the girls too, especially as Tasha and Ryan will also be there.

Charlie's in the playroom with the girls so I go and check with him. 'That'll be fine, I don't have to leave here until one thirty – but I'll drop the girls over to Mum's. She'll enjoy seeing them. Then you won't have to dash back.'

It probably means that we'll be stuck with Alice all evening, but I nod because I know it's our only option.

He takes hold of both my hands, his eyes holding mine. 'Remember you can stay here as long as you want so don't take the house if you don't like it.'

'I won't,' I promise. Part of me doesn't want to leave here. I love being with Charlie and the girls, but I know it's best for me and Liam if we have our own home.

'Right, the film starts soon, we'd all better get ready,' Charlie says. 'Go and wash your hands, girls, and put your coats and shoes on.'

'I'll get Liam, he's still outside with Thumper.'

Liam is sitting inside the pen, Thumper on his lap. 'We have to go now, Liam, or we'll miss the start of the film.'

'Okay, Mum.' Liam puts Thumper down onto the grass. 'Bye, Thumper,' he says cheerily and comes out of the pen. I close the gate behind him and we go inside.

At the cinema, we treat the kids to popcorn and a drink as a special treat, and settle down to watch the film. We all enjoy it immensely and are still laughing about it as we pile into Charlie's Range Rover to go home, grabbing a McDonald's on the way. The children chatter happily all the way home and Charlie turns his head to smile at me when we stop at some traffic lights. It's been such a good day.

It's dark when we get in, it gets dark so early now. We put the clocks back this Sunday and it will be dark even earlier then. I put the lights on and close the kitchen blinds and the kids go into the playroom to burn off some energy while Charlie goes out in the garden to check on Thumper. He comes back in a few minutes later, his brow furrowed. 'Thumper's gone!'

'What? How? Has he nibbled through the wire fence?'

'The gate of the pen was unlatched.' Charlie reaches up and

flicks the light switch that illuminates the whole bottom end of the garden. He also picks up the torch he keeps on top of the fridge. 'Don't mention it to the kids yet, he might not have gone far. I'll see if I can find him.'

I hope he can find the little rabbit, the girls will be devastated. And Liam too. I bite my lip as I remember that I was the one who closed the gate.

'There's no sign of Thumper,' Charlie says when he returns. He pulls out his chair and puts his head in his hands. 'How am I going to break this to the girls?'

'I don't see how the gate could be open. I dropped the latch. I know I did,' I tell him.

He sighs. 'I know you thought you did. I accept it was an accident, Sarah, but the gate was wide open. If the latch hasn't clicked properly Thumper can nudge it with his nose and open it.'

'I'm so sorry,' I say, my voice wobbling. The guilt overwhelms me and I don't know how to deal with it. All the children adore Thumper. This will devastate them.

'I'm going to have to tell the girls. I can't let them find out when they go out to feed him in the morning,' Charlie says.

I nod, not trusting myself to speak. I can feel the tears welling in my eyes. Every time we have a nice day and I think things are settling down, something happens.

Charlie waits until the children come in from the playroom then he gently breaks the news that Thumper is missing.

Daisy immediately bursts into tears while Mia and Liam run outside, with Charlie right behind them. I go over and give Daisy a hug. 'Don't cry, darling, I'm sure we'll find him.'

'He's my bestest friend ever,' Daisy sobs. 'Now someone's taken him.'

'Nobody's taken him. He might still be hopping around the garden, if we leave the pen open he might come back and take himself to bed.'

'I want to see,' Daisy whimpers so I take her hand and we walk outside together.

Charlie has the floodlights on and we all scour the garden, the children shouting, 'Thumper!' It's dark and chilly so I go back inside and get the children's coats, they pause to slip them on, then we all continue our search. We look everywhere, among the bushes, under the hedge, behind the shed, calling Thumper's name, but there's no sign of him.

'He's lost forever.' Mia's voice catches on a sob. Daisy is crying too, and Liam looks very upset and worried.

Tears are streaming down Mia's face. 'You were with him last. You forgot to close the gate. It's your fault he's lost. I hate you!' she shouts, prodding Liam's chest with her finger.

I see the colour drain from Liam's face. 'It wasn't me,' he stammers.

'No, it wasn't. I called Liam in and closed the gate,' I admit. 'And I promise you that I did close it. I heard the latch click.'

Mia's eyes turn to me and I can see the anger and distress in them. 'Thumper's gone just like Mummy!' She chokes back a sob. 'What if a fox has eaten him?'

Daisy wails and I go to pick her up to comfort her, but Charlie is back from his search of the top of the garden and he scoops Daisy up, holding her tight.

'He can't have gone far, maybe he's in a neighbour's garden. Are you in a neighbourhood Facebook or WhatsApp group, Charlie?' I ask, suddenly realising how little I still know about him. 'You could put a message in there?'

'I will, but right now I think we all need to go inside. It's cold and it won't help Thumper if we all get ill, will it?'

Charlie is carrying Daisy inside, with Mia holding onto his arm. Me and Liam are following, Liam clutching my hand and crying softly. We were all so happy and now I've ruined it.

Yet I'm sure I clicked the latch.

.

46

A little while later we're all sitting in the family room, trying to comfort the kids, when the gate bell rings. Charlie glances at the camera and frowns. 'It's Crystal.' Then he jumps up. 'And she's got Thumper!'

'Hooray!' Mia and Daisy jump up in delight and Liam's face breaks into a big smile.

Charlie presses the button to open the gates, which automatically switches the floodlight on, and goes to the front door. The girls and Liam run after him. I hold back a bit.

'I couldn't believe my eyes when I saw him eating the lettuce in our garden. Cheeky little devil.' I hear Crystal's tinkling laugh and she steps in, holding Thumper. 'I was going to text you but then I thought I'd bring him round instead. I know the girls will be missing him dreadfully.'

I can't see the girls' faces but Liam's lights up like a Christmas tree when he sees the rabbit, and I'm sure Mia and Daisy have the same reaction.

'We came home to find him gone and the girls were devastated. Thank you so much, Crystal.'

Crystal hands him Thumper then stoops down to talk to Daisy and Mia. 'He must have smelt our lettuces!' she says.

'He ran away, we thought we lost him,' Daisy sniffs, rubbing her eyes.

'Did you forget to lock his rabbit pen?' Crystal asks gently.

'Auntie Sarah did,' Mia says.

Crystal stands up and looks down the hall, her eyes resting on me.

'That was very careless of you, Sarah.'

Charlie turns to me. 'Accidents happen,' he says. 'Now I know you'd all like to cuddle Thumper but I'm going to put him in his pen because he's had a very exciting day and probably needs to rest.' He looks over his shoulder at Crystal. 'Do you have time to stay for a drink? I'd like to thank you properly. Mia and Daisy wouldn't have slept tonight worrying about Thumper.'

'I'd love to.'

I can't help feeling resentful that it was Crystal who saved the day. Then I scold myself for being petty when I should be glad that the rabbit is safely home. All three children go outside with Charlie to witness Thumper being put safely back in his pen, leaving me alone in the kitchen with Crystal.

'It was lucky for you he stopped off in my garden for a snack,' Crystal says. 'I'm sure you didn't mean to leave the hutch unlatched but he could have been lost for good. Or killed.'

'I'm certain I locked the pen. I guess the latch must have not quite clicked and the wind blew it open,' I say. 'I'll make sure it doesn't happen again.'

'I'm sure you will.' Crystal folds her arms and tilts her head to one side. 'You and your son are a bit careless, aren't you? First you flood out your own house, then you move into Charlie's and things start to go wrong here too.'

I'm fuming! 'Seriously?' I put my hands on my hips. 'It was

very traumatic for us to lose our home,' I retort. 'And while I'm glad you found Thumper, I don't think that gives you the right to be so rude to me.'

The back door opens and Charlie comes in with the girls. 'I think this calls for a glass of wine to celebrate, and ice cream for you children,' he announces.

'Yes!' the three children all cheer as Charlie gets the ice cream out of the freezer.

'Actually I'd like ice cream as well as the wine, if I'm allowed,' Crystal says in a silly pseudo little girl voice. 'Phoebe is in her pjs watching a film with Sacha, our au pair, so won't miss me.'

Charlie grins over his shoulder at her. 'Anything for you. You're a lifesaver.'

Crystal throws me a smug look. I turn away and reach for the ice cream dishes.

Then a thought worms into my head.

Crystal lives three doors away. Isn't it a bit strange that Thumper was found in her garden and not any of the ones in between?

Mr Thomson next door has a massive vegetable patch that would keep a bunny happily eating all night.

Did Crystal sneak in and open the hutch while we were out and take Thumper back to hers? I shake my head. I'm getting paranoid. That would be such a crazy thing to do. Besides, the only way into the house is through the electric gates and you need the electronic key fob to open those.

Only me, Charlie and Alice have one of those.

47

The next day me and Charlie take the kids shopping for
Hallowe'en costumes. Mia chooses a bat costume consisting of
black leotard and tights, with huge black wings with a purple
lining, Daisy is a cute orange pumpkin and Liam picks a
skeleton so he can match Ryan.

'What about you and Tasha, are you two dressing up?'
Charlie asks.

'We're usually witches. I've still got my outfit but it's in
storage so I'd better buy a new one,' I reply. I buy a purple and
black outfit with a matching witch's hat and Charlie chooses a
gorgeous purple wizard's cloak with silver stars on it.

'You need a wand too,' Liam says, picking up a silver one
for him.

Charlie waves it over the three children. 'Now you'll all
have to be good or I'll turn you into toads!'

They all giggle.

'What about food?' Charlie asks.

'Tasha is making a Hallowe'en cake and I'm doing the spook
juice and some freaky biscuits – the kids can help me make

those tomorrow.' I'm really looking forward to this. Our first family party at Charlie's.

The next day the kids all enjoy rolling out the pastry and using the Hallowe'en cutters I bought to make ghost, witch and bat shapes. They help stir the icing too, and I put it in different bowls so they can add food colouring. Green for the witches' faces, black for bats, white for ghosts. They're all giggling and covered in icing when Charlie sets off for work.

'Don't be late home, Daddy,' Daisy says. She looks adorable with a blob of white icing on her nose.

'I won't,' he promises.

Mia beams, her eyes sparkling. 'This is going to be the best Hallowe'en party ever.'

Charlie wraps his arms around my waist and kisses me on the neck. 'This is so wonderful for them,' he says. 'I'll be back for five. Are you sure you're okay to cope on your own until then?'

'Of course, Tasha and Ryan will be here soon and she'll help decorate.'

Charlie hesitates. 'When Mum heard about the party she said she'd like to pop in too. And she's invited Crystal and Phoebe. I hope you don't mind.'

I do mind. But what can I say when this is Charlie's house and Tasha and Ryan will be here? 'Not at all,' I lie.

Tasha is really impressed with Charlie's house, her eyes pop out as if they're on stalks. 'Oh my God, Sarah, it's like something out of *Homes & Gardens*,' she gasps as she steps out of the car and looks around. She's even more impressed when she sees the inside. 'I can't believe it's this posh.'

'It is pretty amazing, isn't it? The kitchen here is bigger than the whole downstairs of my old house.'

'No wonder you decided to live here instead of sleeping on my sofa,' she says in awe. She gives me a quizzical look. 'Will you really move into that house by me and leave all this behind?'

'Yes, this is Charlie's home, me and Liam need our own place. I'm scared we might break something,' I admit.

'I would be too. And Alice is still Queen of the Domain, isn't she? You'll be much more comfortable in your own little house. It will be cosier and it will be yours to do what you want with. No Alice.'

She's right. Much as I love it here, I can't wait to have my own home again.

Liam tugs at my sleeve. 'Can we put the Hallowe'en decorations up now?'

I fetch them and we all spend the next couple of hours decorating the playroom door and walls with orange paper covered in black bats, spiders, witch shapes and other bits and bobs, then we cover the kitchen table with the Hallowe'en tablecloth I bought and lay out the food.

I make a jug of dark red witch punch and open the cupboard for a big glass dish to put it in. My eyes rest on a large pink glass bowl on the top shelf. I've never noticed that before but it will be perfect, and I carefully take it down. It's beautiful with a lighter pink around the edge of the bowl and darker burgundy colour at the bottom.

I pour the juice into it, adding blackberries for effect. 'Let's make it look spookier,' Tasha says. She wraps some of the orange paper decorated with black bats around it.

When Charlie comes home we're almost done.

He walks into the kitchen then mock-screams. 'Oh my goodness, there's witches and pumpkins and skeletons in my kitchen! I think they've kidnapped my family.'

Daisy giggles and takes her mask off. 'Silly Daddy, we're here.'

Charlie staggers back in mock-surprise and we all laugh.

'Look at all the scary food, Daddy,' Daisy says.

Charlie looks over at the table and his eyes swivel from the freaky biscuits to the bowl of witch punch. 'This looks really great. I'll go and get changed into my outfit then we can get the party started.'

He comes down a few minutes later in his cloak and wizard hat and I put on some Hallowe'en party music. Then suddenly the kitchen door opens and Alice arrives wearing a black cape as her token costume. Phoebe is a witch too, but Crystal has pulled out all the stops and looks incredibly sexy in a skintight red leather devil outfit with cute devil horns.

'She's always got to be the centre of attention, hasn't she?' Tasha whispers. 'Don't let her get to you.'

'I won't.' No one is going to spoil this party. The kids are having a great time and I can see that both Alice and Crystal are impressed by our decorations and spooky food. I go over to the bowl of witchy punch which is now half-empty. 'Want a glass?' I ask Tasha. 'It's non-alcoholic but it's really tasty.'

'As if I could ever forget your special punch,' Tasha says with a grin.

I pick up the ladle and a glass and start to spoon the punch in it.

Suddenly I'm knocked sideways, falling onto the table and into the bowl. I try to grab it but it's too late, it shoots off the side of the table and crashes onto the floor. I look down in dismay at the broken glass strewn across the room.

'I'm so sorry,' Tasha says, 'Crystal bumped into me.'

I raise my eyes to hers, and over her shoulder I swear Crystal is gloating.

'Isn't that your vintage cranberry glass bowl, Alice?'

Vintage?

Alice looks down to the floor and her eyes widen in horror. 'Yes it is! How dare you use that! It's very valuable, it was hand-made on Murano. It was a wedding present for Kenneth and I.'

'Oh no! I'm so sorry. It was in the top kitchen cupboard...' I feel terrible but why didn't she put the bowl away if it was so valuable?

'Nonsense! I always keep it in the display cabinet in the front lounge.'

'It was definitely in the cupboard,' I protest.

'I would never keep it there. Apart from its sentimental value, it's a very rare piece of cut crystal.' Alice's face is stony. 'I can't believe that you used my expensive glassware without my permission and covered it with that stupid decoration so that I wouldn't recognise it.'

I'm fuming. 'I'm sorry that it got broken but I can assure you...' I start to say then I see Crystal smirking in satisfaction and there's no doubt in my mind who's behind this.

NOVEMBER

48

'It's brilliant, Mum! Can we move here? Please!'

It's two days after our Hallowe'en party and the girls are with Alice while me and Liam are taking a look at the house by Tasha's. Tasha and Ryan have accompanied us, of course, and we're all impressed. It's very similar to Tasha's, small and compact and pleasantly decorated. The two bedrooms are a decent size and so is the back garden. Our furniture will fit in it nicely, and it will be good to have our own place again, although it's going to be at least a month. The rent won't be a problem as I'll have been paid by then. I'll talk to Maddie and Tom on Monday, see if they can give me an advance on my wages for my deposit. And I'll ask my bank if I can increase my overdraft too. I can do this.

'If you're interested, I can pass your number on to my land-lord,' Stacey, the current tenant, says. 'It's a private rental and hasn't been advertised anywhere yet so you're in with a good chance.'

'I am interested, so yes please,' I reply.

Tasha is delighted. 'We can share the school runs, and

babysitting,' she says, her face alight with excitement. 'And have lots of girly evenings together. It's going to be fantastic.'

'Maybe we can all go out as a foursome for a meal or something too,' I suggest. 'I haven't met Caleb yet and am eager to meet this guy who's got my best friend so smitten.'

'How was it after we left yesterday?' Tasha asks when we're back in her house. She insisted we come back for lunch. 'I could see that Alice was furious about that bowl and I reckon Crystal shoved me on purpose so it would get broken.'

I have to admit that I thought the same. Charlie swooped to the rescue and helped me clear up the broken glass and we continued with the party but I felt sick inside and I could see that he was annoyed. No wonder, I'd broken his parents' gorgeous wedding present. 'I wouldn't put it past her,' I agree as I nibble on cream crackers and cheese. 'I don't know how it got in that cupboard though.'

'Alice probably put it there hoping you'd use it and break it so you'd look bad to Charlie. Honestly, Sarah, I don't know how you cope living there. It's still very much Alice's home, isn't it?' Tasha unwraps a cheese triangle and takes a bite out of it.

'I know, I feel like I'm walking on eggshells when Alice is around,' I confess. 'And stupid things keep happening, like Charlie left a pile of marked assignments on the table the other day but when he went to get them they were gone. He eventually found them on the sofa in the family lounge, and then he was late for college. And I swear I put Liam's football kit in his bag but he said I didn't and he couldn't play football. The autumn display Daisy made at nursery was broken. No one knows how any of these things have happened, of course, but the blame always seems to point to Liam. He insists it isn't him but maybe he's acting up because he's unhappy at Charlie's.'

'How is Charlie taking it?' Tasha asks.

'He tries to be patient but I can tell that he's getting fed up.'

'Well, at least you'll have your own house soon, and if it gets too much before then you know where I am. Any time, day or night.' Tasha raises her eyes to mine. 'You've got my key. Let yourself in if I'm out.'

Me and Tasha gave each other our spare house keys a couple of years ago in case we ever got locked out. We've never used them and always knock when we visit each other, not simply walk in, as Alice does.

'Thank you. I really appreciate it,' I tell her.

'That's what friends are for.' She wipes her hands on a napkin. 'Fancy a drink before you go?'

'Sorry but I need to get back. There's a couple of jobs I want to get on with while the girls are out.' I push my chair back and stand up. 'Thanks for lunch. I'll give Liam a call.' The boys had disappeared to Ryan's bedroom as soon as they'd finished eating.

'What did you think of the house?' Charlie asks me later that afternoon as we all sit around the kitchen table drinking hot chocolate with marshmallows.

'It's good!' Liam says. 'I'll be able to play with Ryan every day.'

'We'll miss you,' Daisy says sadly.

'We won't be moving for a while. Someone else is living in the house at the moment,' I tell her.

'And we'll still all see each other lots,' Charlie adds.

I look at him, wondering if he's pleased we're going. It has been one thing after another since we moved in. He will probably be glad to get rid of us. Maybe I should take up Tasha's offer of living with her until the house becomes available.

Later, though, we all sit and watch a film together, eating popcorn. The children are giggling sitting side by side on the sofa, a throw over them, while me and Charlie are sitting together on the other sofa, his arm around my shoulder, and I can't help thinking how much I'll miss them all when we leave.

49

Two Weeks Later

I've had the day off today to do Christmas shopping. I was hoping that we'd be in our own house for Christmas but Stacey phoned last week to say that her partner, Lee, isn't starting his new job until January now so they are staying where they are until then. She said she's given my name to the landlord, who has promised to give me first refusal. Charlie was pleased when I told him. 'We can spend Christmas together,' he said. Tasha was disappointed though, me and Liam have spent the last few Christmases with her and Ryan.

'It's okay, we'll be going to Mum's,' she said but I could tell she felt let down so promised her that we'd come around when she returned back home.

I am determined to make this a wonderful family Christmas. Charlie said they have a huge tree in the attic that they put up in the family lounge every year, so I decided to get another smaller tree for the playroom and ask the kids to help me decorate it.

I've bought a beautiful silver tree, and some blue, purple

and rainbow-coloured baubles – all the kids' favourite colours. I'll put it away until the first of December and then we'll decorate it. It's only a couple weeks away. I've bought a few stocking fillers too. I'll talk to Charlie about ideas for bigger presents tonight.

As I drive down the lane towards Charlie's house I see a white Corsa parked on the kerb beside the gates. When I pull up a woman gets out, she must have been waiting for me. She's got shoulder-length, mousy-brown hair and is wearing jeans and a beige duffle coat. My hand goes over my mouth as I realise that it's the same woman who was staring at Daisy and Mia at the Autumn Fayre.

I wind down the window. 'Are you looking for someone?' I ask her as she walks over to me.

Her eyes, dark and brooding, meet mine. 'Yes. I'm looking for my sister, Lynn.' She says it so matter-of-fact. As if Lynn has been living here all this time and just popped out for a few minutes. 'I'm Claire,' she adds.

Neither Charlie nor Alice ever talks about Lynn, or her family.

'And who are you?' Claire has her arms folded now, head tilted to one side.

'I'm Sarah. I live with Charlie.' I narrow my eyes at her. 'Charlie and Lynn aren't together anymore.' I regard her suspiciously, wondering if she's lying. If she really is Lynn's sister, surely she would know what happened between Lynn and Charlie.

Claire doesn't look as surprised by this as I'd have expected. 'Alice finally got to her then. Where is Lynn living now? Do you have an address for her?'

I shake my head. 'Charlie told me that Lynn left a note one day saying she'd met someone and gone off with them. He doesn't know where she's gone. She doesn't even bother to see the girls,' I add.

The look on Claire's face has now been replaced by shock. 'You're saying...' she stammers, gathers her breath and continues, 'You're saying that Lynn has gone off and left her daughters?'

'Lynn walked out about eighteen months ago and left the girls with Charlie, that was before I knew him. He hasn't seen her since.' I frown. 'Surely you know all of this?' Then I remember my brother, Leo, and how we barely have contact with each other.

The colour has drained from Claire's face, she looks horrified. 'He's lying!' she shrieks. 'Lynn adores those little girls. She would die for them. Charlie is bloody lying!' She holds a shaking hand to her mouth and backs away from me. 'There is no way my sister would ever leave her daughters.' Her eyes darken, the white a luminous circle around the blue, her pupils like big black stones. 'What the hell have Charlie and his freaky mother done to my sister?'

50

I let out a gasp at this, my chest tightening. She can't mean that, it's the shock at hearing what her sister did.

I push the heinous thought from my mind and look worriedly at Claire, she is visibly distraught, her body shaking, her face blanched. The news that her sister has left her husband and children and gone off with someone else has really distressed her. It's understandable, it is a lot to take in. I make a snap decision. Charlie won't be home for some time yet and I can't leave Claire like this.

'You look really shaken up, I can see that you had no idea that Lynn and Charlie had split up. Why don't you come in for a coffee and we can talk a bit more?' I suggest. 'I don't have to collect the children from school for another couple of hours.'

She swallows. 'Thank you.'

I remotely open the gates, and Claire gets back in her car and follows me through. They automatically close behind us.

'Well, Charlie's moved up in the world,' she says bitterly as we both get out of our cars and walk over to the front door. 'He and Lynn lived in a much smaller place than this when I last saw them.'

'This is Charlie's family home. Alice handed it over to Charlie and now lives in an apartment,' I explain.

As I open the front door and lead the way into the kitchen, Claire follows me, her gaze sweeping everywhere, taking everything in. I switch the coffee machine on. 'Black, white, decaf or something fancy?'

'White, normal please.' She pulls out a chair and perches on the end of the seat as if she might take flight any minute, her eyes darting nervously about the room.

I give her time to compose herself, making the coffee, putting her mug on the kitchen table in front of her and sitting down nursing mine before I begin gently. 'Lynn's been gone for over a year and a half. Why haven't you looked for her before?' I don't ask the question that's burning inside me: why she thinks that Charlie or Alice have something to do with Lynn being gone.

She twists her hands in her lap, gazing down at them. 'We fell out and I lost touch with her. Didn't Charlie tell you?'

There's a lot Charlie hasn't told me.

But then there's a lot he doesn't know about my past, too.

'When did you last see her?'

'Just over two years ago.' She stares pensively into her cup. 'I shouldn't have left it so long, I know that. I was so angry and hurt.' She chews her bottom lip. 'There's a lot of things I shouldn't have done. I wasn't there for Lynn when she needed me, but I didn't realise how bad things were.'

'What do you mean? Charlie said Lynn was having an affair, that she left Charlie for another man. She went off to make a new life for herself.'

'That's bullshit! Lynn adored Charlie and she would never leave those girls,' Claire shouts slamming her mug down on the table. Coffee spills out and forms a dark pool.

I should wipe it up but I'm riveted to my chair, my eyes fixed on Claire. She looks scared – and furious. 'I should never have walked away from Lynn, I should have known she didn't mean what she said. She wasn't herself.' She closes her eyes briefly then snaps them open again. 'I should have been here for her. I should never have left her alone with them when she was so vulnerable.'

I lick my lips, a cold hollowness settling in my stomach. 'What do you mean? What was wrong with Lynn?'

Claire swallows. 'Lynn had postnatal depression after she had Daisy. It was such a difficult birth. She was getting better, feeling stronger, but she was so insecure. She was jealous of everyone Charlie talked to, totally obsessed with the thought that he was going to leave her.' She pushes her chair back and gets to her feet, pacing around, then turning back to me. 'She accused me of having an affair with Charlie and we fell out. I was so upset and angry with her that I never tried to get in touch. I waited for her to apologise and when she didn't I got even angrier.' She runs her hands through her fringe, pushing it back from her forehead. 'All I'd ever done was try to support her and Charlie, it was such a difficult time for them both, and bloody Alice made things worse.'

I put down my cup, my hand shaking slightly. 'How?'

Claire flicks a contemptuous glance at me. 'She undermined Lynn all the time, she was always there, taking charge of the girls, making Lynn feel that she was incapable. Lynn was sure that Alice was deliberately hiding things and doing things to make it seem like Lynn was losing her mind. Charlie didn't believe it, of course. His darling mother can't do any wrong in his eyes.'

My mind is buzzing. This is exactly what Alice is doing now. She wants to drive us away. But why did Lynn leave her girls? Another thing puzzles me too.

'Why did Lynn think you were having an affair with Charlie?'

Claire's eyes darken and a steely look comes over her face.

'Because Alice manipulated it. Lynn and Charlie weren't getting on and then Lynn found my earring in their bedroom, under the bed. I lost it the week before when I visited – Alice must have found it and put it there to set me up. Lynn jumped to conclusions and accused us of having an affair. I was so furious I stormed out.' She glances into the distance, her eyes glistening with unshed tears. 'The times I wished I hadn't.' She swallows. 'Last week a memory of us flashed up on my phone – it was my birthday and we were having a drink together, laughing, looking so happy. I felt sad remembering how close we were and how we're now estranged. I should have tried harder to convince Lynn it wasn't true but instead I walked away. Deserted her.' She reaches for a hankie out of her pocket and dabs her eyes.

Lynn remained with Charlie though, didn't she? He must have convinced her of his innocence. Is that why she had an affair, as payback?

Why didn't she take the girls though? None of it makes sense.

Claire has composed herself now and continues, her eyes fixed on the wall, as if she can't look at me. 'I decided that it was up to me to make the first move. Lynn had been depressed and vulnerable, I should have reassured her not stormed out. So I went to the house but obviously they don't live there anymore and they had no forwarding address. I didn't think that Charlie would move far from his mother, and I knew that Mia would have started school, so I went around the schools in the area, hoping to catch a glimpse of her. I saw Alice collecting her one day, along with a little boy, and I saw Mia and Daisy playing in the park at a pub but there was no sign of Lynn. Then I saw the Autumn Fayre advertised and decided to go there, hoping to bump into Lynn. Instead I saw you and Charlie.' Her eyes flick to me. 'I followed you home, watched the house for a bit, trying to pluck up the courage to knock on the door. I wanted to talk to Lynn on her own. I thought maybe she and Charlie had split up and were co-parenting.' She shakes her head. 'Lynn would never go away and leave those girls. They were her life.' She raises her eyes to mine. 'Now I'm worried that she might have done something to herself. If she has, they drove her to it.'

'Killed herself?' The words burst out of me. 'Surely her body would have been found?' My heart is racing, I'm struggling to take all this in.

'Where is she then? I know that she wouldn't leave the girls. I know it!' Lynn paces around restlessly. 'Does Charlie ever talk about her?' she demands.

'No. He says it's too painful.'

'Well, he's not too upset to take up with someone else and move you in, is he?' she says accusingly.

She walks out of the kitchen and into the family room, and I follow her, not sure what to do.

'Why are there no photos of my sister?' she demands as she surveys the room. 'Look at all these photos of Charlie and the girls, Alice and the girls. Not one single one of Lynn, their mother. Don't you think that's odd?'

'Charlie said he doesn't want the girls to keep waiting for her to come home, it's best to have a clean start,' I stammer, my stomach churning because Claire is voicing the same doubts that I've been having.

'Why hasn't he looked for her? Reported her as a missing person to the police?' Claire sounds almost hysterical. 'He knows Lynn wouldn't leave those girls behind. Why is he so certain that she won't come back?' She walks along the corridor into the front lounge, scrutinising the room, scanning the walls and shelves. Then her eyes widen as they rest on something. She dashes over to the wall unit and picks up a tiny silver box.

'Claire would never leave this behind. She cherished it.' She opens it up to reveal a pendant. 'We've both got one of these, they hold our mother's ashes. We swore that we would never take them off.'

She opens her jacket and reveals that she's wearing an identical pendant. Her eyes are like dark moons as they rest on mine. 'Something awful has happened to her. I know it has.'

51

I sit at the table after Claire has gone, my mind going over and over her words. I tried to convince her, convince myself, that there is another logical reason that Lynn disappeared.

I pointed out that Claire said Lynn had postnatal depression, so she might not have been thinking straight – in her depressed state she might have thought the girls would be better off without her. Then as the days and weeks went by it would be harder for her to come back. She knew that Charlie would look after them, he's a fantastic father, and that Alice would always be there as back-up.

Claire wouldn't hear of it. 'I know my sister. She idolised those girls. Idolised. She would never willingly leave them.' She'd almost spat the words out. 'Charlie or Alice have done something terrible to her and I'm not going to rest until I find out what they've done.'

Instinctively I feel that Claire is right about Alice being instrumental in driving Lynn away. I can well believe that she would plant the earring to cause trouble between them. She is obsessed with Charlie and the girls and seems determined that no one is going to replace her in looking after them. But accusing them of murder is too extreme: surely neither of them is capable of that. Claire's alternative explanation, that Lynn killed herself, doesn't bear thinking about either.

After Claire left, I think about her threat that she is going to report Lynn missing to the police. I'm certain that she will do it and I have to warn Charlie. The past couple of years must have been traumatic enough for him without having it all brought up again. I don't want to tell him over the phone but I'm scared to leave it too long, the police might decide to come and question Charlie as soon as Claire reports her suspicions.

I won't be able to talk to Charlie properly with the kids around, and I certainly don't want them here when the police arrive to question him, so I message Tasha and ask if Liam can stay overnight – thank goodness it's a Friday – and she replies right away.

Of course. He's always welcome here.

Thanks, I owe you one. I'll bring his things to the school.

Then I text Charlie and tell him we need to talk and could he ask Alice to have the girls overnight, explaining that Liam is going to Tasha's and I'll meet Alice at school with the girls' things. He texts back:

I hope it isn't as serious as it sounds.

I'm wound up like a tight spring by the time Charlie walks in. 'What's the matter?' he asks, obviously noticing my anxiety. 'I've been worried all day.' He goes to wrap his arms around me but I step back. He frowns, puzzled. 'What's up?'

'A woman turned up, she said she's Lynn's sister...' I relate the events to him and what Claire said. 'I know it sounds nuts, of course it is nuts, but she's convinced that Lynn is dead and...' I can't bring myself to say the rest.

To my surprise Charlie rolls his eyes. 'Don't tell me, my mum and I are the culprits.'

I nod. He seems to be taking this a lot better than I thought he would. I still keep my distance from him though and watch him warily.

He runs his hands through his hair. 'God, that woman is a nightmare! She did nothing but meddle when Lynn and I were together. She's mentally unstable.'

'She said that Lynn had postnatal depression after Daisy's birth.'

'Yes, she did unfortunately. It was a difficult birth and Daisy didn't sleep well as a baby. Claire just made the situation worse though.'

'She said you should have reported Lynn as a missing person and that she's going to call the police.' I look at him anxiously. 'As Lynn was suffering from postnatal depression, didn't you worry that something might have happened to her when you didn't hear from her for a while? Weren't you concerned when she didn't come to see the children?'

He sits down, elbows on the table, hands steepled, and lets out a big sigh. 'I didn't see any reason to involve the police. Lynn left me a note saying she'd been seeing someone else, Sarah, and that she was going off with him to start a new life. That she couldn't cope with the girls. How do you think I felt about that? I'd done my best to support her and help her. She withdrew a big chunk of money from our joint bank account too. I had to open a new account and transfer the remaining funds to that before she wiped it all.'

'Do you still have the note?' I ask him.

'Yes, thank goodness. I kept it for the girls when they were older. She left them notes too, telling them to remember that she always loved them and always will.' His eyes harden. 'Yeah, she loves them so much she walks out and never sees them again!' He stands up. 'I'd better go and get them as the police will want to see them too.'

He goes upstairs and comes back down a few minutes later with a small red box and opens it up. It's full of photos of a pretty, fair-haired woman with a baby and a young girl – Mia and Daisy. Those photos must be of Lynn. So he did keep photos of her and put them away for the girls when they're older. He takes out three letters in white envelopes and hands them to me. 'Read them.'

I shake my head. 'They're private.'

He sits back, folds his arms and gives me a hard stare. 'I'm pretty sure that Claire's words have made you suspicious, and probably anxious for your own safety, so I'd like you to read them. It's a horrible thing to be accused of.'

I tentatively open the first envelope, the one with Charlie's name written on the front, and am surprised to see the neat handwriting. This note has been written with care.

Dear Charlie,

I'm sorry, I've really tried but I can't do it anymore. I can't stay here in this home. I feel like I'm being suffocated. I've met someone else and I'm going away to start a new life. I know you'll look after the girls, you have your mother to help. Tell them I love them and please give them both these notes when they're older. I won't be in touch again.

Lynn

I look up at Charlie: there's a range of emotions flitting over his face. 'I'm so sorry,' I whisper.

He inclines his head briefly. 'Read the girls' letters. I want you to.'

I open Mia's letter first.

My darling Mia,

I love you so much and I'm sorry that I can't look after you. When you're older I hope that you'll understand. I know that Daddy will look after you, and make sure you are happy. Remember that I love you and always will.

Love and hugs,

Mummy

Daisy's letter says the same. I can feel the love in the words. These are letters from a mother who adores her children. So she did go off with someone else then. But even if her other man didn't want children, or Lynn felt that she couldn't cope with them, why has she never even come back to see how they are?

52

'Does that put your fears at rest?' Charlie says when I've read the letters. 'If Claire comes back, I'll show them to her too.' He looks frustrated. 'I wish she'd have waited to talk to me and then I could have explained things to her.'

'I'm sorry for doubting you. It's just that Claire was so distressed.'

'Probably guilt that she ran out on her sister when she needed her most,' Charlie says grimly. 'She knew that Lynn was mentally unstable, paranoid. I know she said some horrible things but it was her illness talking.'

He is such a wonderful man. After everything Lynn did, he is making excuses for her. And I've never heard him badmouth her, either to Alice or the children, I realise.

'Are we good then?' he asks. 'You believe me?'

I nod. 'Absolutely.'

He walks over to me and pulls me into a hug.

'I'm sorry.' I nestle my head against his shoulder.

'So am I. I should have talked to you about it more, but it's still a bit raw.'

I glance up at him, his jaw is set and his face grim.

'I find it difficult to believe that Lynn could be so heartless as to leave the girls,' he mumbles.

'I think that's what Claire is struggling with,' I tell him.

As we have the house to ourselves Charlie orders a take-away and opens a bottle of wine, and we settle down to watch a box set together. We cuddle up together on the sofa but neither of us can relax properly.

The loud ring of the bell on the gate interrupts us. Charlie glances at the camera on his phone. 'It's the police!' he exclaims and I'm sure I can hear panic in his voice.

So Claire was serious about reporting Lynn's disappearance.

'I'd better let them in,' Charlie says grimly as he presses the button to open the gates and walks off along the hall to open the front door.

I want to hear what the police say but guess that Charlie will want to be questioned alone, so I hover in the hallway waiting for them to approach the front door. There are two of them: a tall, lanky one with short dark hair who looks as if he should still be at college, and a short, rounder, bald one. It's the bald one who speaks.

'Evening, Mr Harris. We've been alerted to a potentially missing person and we have a duty to investigate it. I believe the missing person, Lynn Harris, is your wife.'

Charlie lets out a sigh and rakes his right hand through his hair. 'Estranged wife, she left me eighteen months ago. I presume her sister, Claire, reported her missing.'

The policeman glances down at his notebook. 'Yes, she said that they fell out over two years ago, which is why she wasn't aware her sister had disappeared until recently. Could we come in and ask you a few questions, sir?'

'Of course.' Charlie steps aside and the two officers enter, the taller one bending his head so that he doesn't bump it on the doorframe.

The officers glance at me. 'Would you like to talk somewhere private, sir?' the tall one asks.

Charlie shakes his head and winds his arm around my waist, pulling me closer. 'No, this is my partner, Sarah. She knows all about it.'

I don't, I want to say, *I only found out this afternoon*, but I keep quiet because I want to hear what the police have to say.

We go into the family living room. I haven't had time to tidy up and there are still toys scattered around – although the kids are supposed to keep their things in the playroom, they always spill into the other rooms too.

'I understand you have two children,' the older PC says. 'Are they here?'

'My two girls are with their grandmother and Sarah's son is staying over at his friend's house so you can speak freely,' Charlie says. He indicates the two chairs. 'Please sit down.' Then he sits down on the sofa and I take the space beside him.

The police are here for a good half an hour, asking Charlie about his marriage, the state of Lynn's mind, her relationship with the children. He replies in a clear, concise, nothing-to-hide voice. When he shows them the letters Lynn left, the two policemen exchange a sympathetic glance.

'Does Mrs Phelps know about these letters?' the taller PC asks, referring to Claire.

'Highly unlikely... As I said, I haven't seen her for over two years, after she had a fallout with Lynn. If she'd bothered to visit and ask me, instead of hounding and harassing my partner earlier, then I would have shown them to her.'

'Thank you, sir, you've been very helpful.' They both get up. 'Due to the state of your wife's mental health, we'll have to put an alert out and see if we can trace her. Also' – he waves the letters – 'we'll need a photocopy of these and a bank statement showing she withdrew a large amount of cash from your joint bank account the day she left.'

'No problem. I have a photocopier in my office, I'll make copies now and give them to you. These letters are personal and I want to keep them to show my daughters when they're older.'

'Of course. We'll come with you.' The two officers bid goodbye to me and follow Charlie out of the room.

I sit there for a few minutes, my mind buzzing, then I get the bottle of whisky out of the drinks cupboard and pour it into two glass tumblers, handing one to Charlie as he comes back in. 'I thought you could do with this, I know I could.'

'Thanks.' He sinks down into the sofa, the tumbler of whisky in his hand. 'I can't believe that Claire has done this.' His expression darkens. 'She hasn't bothered about Lynn – or the girls – all this time, how dare she come along now and try to make out that I'm somehow responsible for Lynn's disappearance?' He tips the whisky back, swallowing a large mouthful.

I've never seen Charlie look so angry, although he has every right to be.

My hands feel cold and clammy and my pulse is racing.

'Do you think that something's happened to Lynn?' I venture, trying to keep the tremor out of my voice.

'Not in the way Claire is suggesting. When I saw the police to the door, they said that Claire has actually accused me or my mum of killing her!' His hand is shaking and he takes another gulp of whisky. I'm not sure if it's from shock, fear or anger. 'The police want to investigate due to her suffering from post-natal depression. They think...' He gulps. 'That she might have killed herself.' He turns to me then, and I can see the total devastation on his face. 'I never even thought of that, Sarah. The letters, I believed what they said. It never occurred to me that she might be suicidal.'

He puts the whisky down and holds his head in his hands.

'Oh God, what if something's happened to her? How will I tell Mia and Daisy?'

My fear slips away to be replaced by compassion. No one could pretend to be this upset. I can see the distress in the very core of his body. Of course he would believe what was in the notes, and be angry that Lynn not only cheated on him but walked away from her beautiful daughters. I wrap my arms around him and hold him tight, hoping that we are all wrong and Lynn is safe.

53

'Liam!' I shout his name as loud as I can but he doesn't answer. I run along a corridor of closed doors, frantically turning the handles. Why are they locked? Which one is he in? I bang with my clenched fists on each door, calling Liam, but no one answers and the doors remain locked.

Then I hear someone coming. Slowly I turn around. Charlie and Alice are striding towards me. Charlie is frowning but Alice has a big, triumphant grin on her face.

'Where is he?' I demand, my voice trembling. 'What have you done with my son?'

'I've got him!' I swing around at the sound of Dylan's voice.

'Don't hurt him!' I scream.

Then I bolt upright, woken from my nightmare.

I'm trembling. I blink and try to focus. It takes me a moment or two to remember that I'm in Charlie's bedroom. I can hear him snoring softly beside me. I swivel my eyes and look at the small clock on the chest of drawers beside my bed. Three thirty. I doubt if I can go back to sleep now so I carefully slide out of bed so as to not disturb Charlie and go downstairs to make myself a warm drink.

I shiver as I pad down the stairs in my bare feet and thin pyjamas. I should have stopped to put on my dressing gown and slippers. I make myself a chamomile tea and take it up to my own bedroom, wanting to sip it slowly and quieten my thoughts. I used to regularly have nightmares of losing Liam, or him calling me and my being unable to get to him. I knew it was only natural after what had happened on Arran but nevertheless, they had unnerved me, causing me to wake up shaking in the night, like now. I hadn't had one of the dreams for over a year now though.

I sip the hot calming drink and feel myself relaxing a bit. Claire's visit, followed by the one from the police, alarmed me and that's what caused the nightmare. Charlie was restless at first when we went to bed, tossing and turning, and who could blame him? It's a horrible thing to be accused of harming your wife. Or to have to consider that she might have taken her own life. It is all such a mess, and those poor little girls.

Finally, I feel sleepiness coming over me so I put the cup down and snuggle up in bed.

'Morning!' I feel the mattress dip as Charlie sits on the edge of the bed, and I open my eyes drowsily as he leans over and kisses me. 'Was I snoring last night?' he asks, clearly wondering why I went back to my own room when there were no kids in the house.

'No, I couldn't settle and didn't want to disturb you.' I yawn and sit up.

His gaze rests on the empty mug on the table. 'Chamomile?' he asks. He knows it's my go-to drink when I can't sleep.

I nod and he pulls back the duvet and slides in bed beside me, wrapping me in a hug. I breathe in the warmth of him and feel the tension fading away.

'I'm sorry, all this with Claire has been stressful for you,' he murmurs, stroking my hair softly.

'For both of us,' I concede.

'Yes, but it's my mess, not yours.' He holds me tight and for a couple of minutes we cuddle the stress away. I feel so much better, ready to face the day again.

'How about we go out for lunch? Make the most of having no kids,' Charlie suggests a little later.

'Sounds good to me,' I agree. Some alone time is exactly what we need after everything that's happened.

We both get showered and dressed but neither of us wants breakfast. Charlie has dark bags under his eyes and is very subdued. I know I look the same. Hopefully a brisk walk and lunch at a country pub will put some colour in our cheeks. I'm glad that none of the kids are coming back until tea time, it gives us a few hours to get ourselves together.

Charlie phones Alice to check on the girls and I phone Liam, who's just woken up and sounds very happy. I'm so pleased that he wasn't here yesterday. Or the girls.

Then we get into Charlie's car and set off, just as we drive out of the gates a white Corsa drives in. Claire.

She stops the car halfway across the entrance so that Charlie can't close the gates, gets out and leans on the bonnet, arms folded.

'What the hell does she think she's playing at now!' Charlie fumes, sliding out of his seat and marching towards her. I follow him.

'What do you think you're doing, Claire?' Charlie demands.

She fixes him a cold stare. 'I want to see my nieces. You've no right to stop me.'

'You could ring the gate bell and ask like normal people do.'

She cocks her head to one side. 'Like you'd let me in.'

He stands in front of her, his body taut, his clenched fists stiff by his sides. 'Can you blame me after the stunt you pulled yesterday? My daughters have suffered enough. I'm not letting you upset them further with your wild accusations and lies.'

Neither of them glances at me or acknowledges me in any way so I stand back and listen to the angry exchange.

'Lynn is my sister, I have a right to ask about her and to see her children.'

'The girls are with their grandmother, thank goodness, as I would hate them to witness this. But if you love your sister so much, where were you when she needed you, Claire? Don't pretend you care about her when it's taken you over two years to show up. Just go away and leave my family alone.'

'I'll find out what's happened to Lynn, Charlie. I won't leave any stone unturned until I expose you for the bully you are. And if you've hurt her' – she steps forward, her face etched in anger – 'you'll regret it.' Then she turns back. 'And you won't keep me away from my nieces. I owe it to my sister to look out for them.'

She yanks open the door of her car, climbs inside, then winds the window down. 'Watch your back, Sarah. You and your son might be in danger too.'

54

Claire clears Charlie's car, swings around to drive forward and speeds off. Charlie glares after her, his face blanched, a deep furrow between his brows.

Thank goodness none of the children are home.

Charlie wipes his hand over his face and turns to me. 'Sorry, Sarah, this must be awful for you. I wish Claire had simply come and asked me about Lynn, instead of all this. There's no need for it. I've nothing to hide, and when the police find Lynn everyone will know that.'

We carry on out for our meal but the day is ruined for me. I think it is for Charlie too. He's very subdued. I can't get Claire's words out of my mind. Or the way Charlie's face paled, the corner of his mouth twitching, when she accused him of hurting Lynn.

Tasha phones as we're on our way to the pub, asking if Liam could stop over another night. 'He's having a great time and it's much easier to look after two boys than one. They keep each other occupied,' she says. Then Liam comes on the phone and begs me to let him stay so I agree. Me and Charlie could do with a day to get our heads around this.

Charlie must be thinking the same because he glances at me when I've finished the call. 'Mum suggested keeping the girls an extra night when I told her about the police coming around. I think it's a good idea. I need to think what to say to them if Claire comes back shouting the odds again. I'll phone and let her know.'

I need to explain this to Liam too, I realise, although my instinct is to keep it from him. I could do with a day to myself to get my head straight and figure things out so am pleased that I've booked a couple of days' holiday next week. Charlie is back at college Monday, which will give me a chance to have a bit of a look around.

I don't know what I'm looking for but something about Lynn's disappearance isn't right. And I'm going to find out what it is.

55

ALICE

So Claire's back and interfering once again. I'm so angry when Charlie tells me she turned up at the house today, filling Sarah's head with lies and reporting Charlie to the police. Obviously they will take it no further once they see Lynn's letters, and learn that she emptied the bank account.

It's a good job I told Charlie to keep that bank statement. I knew this day would come. People accept a man walking out on his wife and children, but they find it more difficult to believe it of a woman. I don't know why: women don't have the monopoly on loving their children and being good people. Kenneth was a wonderful father, and Charlie is too.

That Claire has been trouble from the start. When she and Lynn fell out I hoped that we were finally rid of her but here she is, only back in our lives for five minutes and already stirring things up.

She's partly to blame for her sister going missing. If she'd have kept out of it, things wouldn't have got so bad. Well, I'll be watching her and will deal with her if she becomes too much of a nuisance. Nothing is going to come between me, my son and my grandchildren.

Charlie said that the police are satisfied Lynn went away of her own accord but they are going to try and trace her as she'd been suffering from mental health issues at the time of her disappearance. Still, I could hear the anxiety in his voice.

Damn Claire. Everything had been going along just fine until she burst back into our lives. The only good thing to come out of this is that Sarah seems unsettled and might take her son and leave.

I hope she does... It will save me a lot of bother.

56

SARAH

As soon as I return from dropping the kids off at school on Monday morning, I set about my search for something that will tell me more about Lynn's disappearance.

I start in the family lounge, checking all the drawers and cupboards, then the dining room and finally the posh front lounge. Nothing. Next I go upstairs and check the wardrobes and drawers in Charlie's bedroom – I still think of it as that even though I sleep in there too now.

I'd hate anyone to mooch through my private things, but Claire's accusations spur me on. There's nothing that could belong to Lynn. Maybe she took everything with her.

Then, underneath a pile of tee shirts in a drawer at the bottom of the wardrobe I find a photo frame, placed face down. I turn it over and see that it's a wedding photo of Charlie and a woman, who must be Lynn. although the frame is broken and the woman's face is scribbled over in blue ballpoint pen with so much force that it's made a hole in the photo. A shudder runs through me. It's such a sinister thing to do.

Did Charlie do this? Angry that Lynn had left him for another man?

What else did he do? Could he have followed Lynn, furious at her betrayal and things had got a bit out of hand?

Charlie isn't like that. He's kind and calm, I've never seen him angry.

I'd never seen Dylan angry until that night at the party I remind myself.

I don't really know Charlie, do I?

I put the photo back, exactly how I found it, then go downstairs and make myself a hot drink to try and calm myself down. The damaged photo has unnerved me. I'm sure something sinister has happened to Lynn. I need to keep searching, there must be other clues here but where would they be? Then it hits me – the study. It's Charlie's private workspace and he keeps it locked, to stop the kids messing he said as a lot of his dad's things are still in there. It would be an ideal place to hide something. And I know where he keeps the key.

I live here, this is my home too. Surely I'm allowed to look around, I tell myself as I get the key from the top drawer of Charlie's bedside cabinet, where he keeps it tucked at the back, and go downstairs, guilt shadowing me at every step. Taking a deep breath I unlock the study door and enter gingerly. I've never been in here before. Charlie often shuts himself away for an hour in the evenings to mark assignments but I don't disturb him when he's working.

It's a traditional study, furnished in dark mahogany. A huge desk with a green leather top dominates the room, the back walls are lined with bookcases, a big ornate globe stands on a polished wooden stand in one corner of the room and a tall filing cabinet looms in the other. On the wall is a Constable print of a landscape, and a square of burgundy Axminster carpet covers the middle of the floor, exposing wooden floorboards around the edge. I can almost imagine Charlie's dad sitting at the desk, working away, and Alice hovering in the doorway, offering him a cup of tea. I bet nothing has changed in here since he died.

I walk over to the desk, feeling like I'm committing a sacrilege. *Charlie's out, he won't know you've been in here, just put everything back where you find it*, I tell myself but my hands are shaking. What am I scared of? Of Charlie coming home early and discovering me snooping? Or of what I'll find?

I start with the desk drawers, going through them one by one. Nothing unusual there: pens, pencils, stationery, spare ink cartridges. There are two keys hidden away in a small tin in the top drawer. I take them out, guessing that one of them is for the huge filing cabinet.

The first key doesn't fit but, to my relief, the second one does. There are five drawers. The top four are full of files and a glance at a couple of them shows me that they're related to Charlie's father's work.

I guess Alice never got round to getting rid of them and now that job will be Charlie's. His father has only been dead a few years though, I remember, and I think business files need to be kept for six years, maybe more.

I pull out the bottom drawer expecting to find more files and am surprised to see nothing but a shiny black handbag lying on its side. I take it out – Saint Laurent, I notice – and it doesn't look fake so it's got to be worth a few grand. I open it up. There's some jewellery inside and that looks expensive too.

I pull the jewellery out one by one: a thick gold rope chain and a matching bracelet, a blue velvet box containing a pair of pearl and sapphire drop earrings, a sapphire ring. Right at the bottom of the handbag is a silk scarf, and underneath that a gold pen and a small black notebook. Did these all belong to Lynn? Why were they hidden there? I hold the notebook: it's thin, like a pocket diary, and has a velvet cover.

'Well, you're a nosy little madam, aren't you?' Alice's voice startles me so much I drop the bag. Quickly I slide the notebook into the back pocket of my jeans, pulling my jumper over it as I turn to face her.

'What are you doing here? I stammer.

'I came to collect some of my things, I still have lots of stuff here. And a good job I did too, I've caught you red-handed. I'll take that.' She stoops down and picks up the handbag. 'And I'll be letting Charlie know that you've been snooping.' She gives me a scathing look. 'Now get yourself out of here, lock the door and give me the key. Just because you're temporarily lodging here, that doesn't give you the right to snoop.'

I keep my hands behind my back. 'I wasn't snooping, I was looking for some printing paper.'

'Which, as you can see, is over there on the table. Not in the filing cabinet.' She holds out her hand. 'Key. Then get out!'

I shake my head. 'You're the one who shouldn't be here. This isn't your home any longer.'

She puts her face close to mine, close enough for me to see the whites of her eyes, smell the peppermint on her breath, recoil from the rasp in her voice as she replies. 'But it is. Didn't Charlie tell you? I still own this house, Charlie simply lives in it. And this study is full of my husband's private things, so I'll tell you once again. Give me that key and get out of my husband's study!'

I back away, dropping the key onto the floor.

She picks up the key and smirks in satisfaction. 'Now if I were you I'd start packing because when my Charlie hears about this latest stunt he'll be giving you your marching orders.'

'I don't think he'll be happy to hear that you've been snooping on me either,' I retort, marching out of the study, but I'm shaking.

She follows me out, locking the door behind her and putting the key in her pocket. 'I will be collecting my granddaughters from school this afternoon and I'll be texting my son to let him know why.

So you had better get your excuses prepared, young lady, because Charlie won't be impressed with your behaviour.' She throws me a triumphant look then walks out, taking the handbag with her.

I'm shaking so much that I have to make myself a calming tea, sitting at the kitchen table to sip it, my mind a whirl. Alice is probably on the phone to Charlie right now. I know it looks bad, I shouldn't have taken Charlie's keys and gone snooping in his study. It isn't like me at all, but Claire's words had me spooked. Surely he'll understand when I tell him? Maybe I should phone or message him first.

I take out my phone and make a few attempts at typing a message but nothing I say sounds right.

I can't get Lynn's notebook out of my mind. Why was it hidden away like that? I can only guess that Charlie and Alice didn't discover it – otherwise, surely, if Lynn had written anything incriminating, they would have destroyed it. I have to read it and find out what Lynn has written. So I take it out of my pocket and open it up. .

It's like a journal, I notice, with dates written at the top of each entry. It starts just after Daisy is born. The writing is difficult to read, as if it's written in a rush. I squint as I try to decipher the scrawl.

Daisy isn't sleeping well and Lynn is struggling to feed her. She sounds tired and at her wits' end. I feel for her. Liam was a difficult baby and I was on my own with him a lot, I don't know how I'd have coped without Tasha.

I can almost feel the despair in Lynn's voice as I read her words. Alice is practically living there, helping to look after the girls, but Lynn feels that she's pushing her out, taking over the care of her daughters, making Lynn feel that she isn't needed. Charlie's getting impatient with her and Crystal keeps coming round, immaculately dressed, flirting with Charlie, chatting with Alice. Poor Lynn can barely summon up the strength to shower some days. She feels ugly, useless, unloved and unwanted.

As I read the entries I can feel Lynn's frustration and desperation. She is clearly struggling to cope. I turn over the page, engrossed in what I'm reading. In my mind I can see Lynn having a hard time adjusting to life with a toddler and a newborn, being constantly criticised by Alice.

Tired, worn out, depressed, feeling like a shadow compared to glamourous Crystal. She feels that she has no one to turn to, not even Charlie. She writes of Claire being supportive at first then trying to get her to 'snap out of it'.

Then one entry catches my eye. It's one line written clearer than the others.

I'm destroyed. My sister and my husband. The two people I lean on and trust most in the world. How could they do this to me?

Her despair oozes out of the page.

So this is when Lynn and Claire had the big argument. And a few months later Lynn left, to make a new life with another man.

Or did she?

Charlie messages me to say that he has to go to the police station after college so will be a bit late home. So they want to question him further. Does that mean they're suspicious about his part in Lynn's disappearance? He adds that his mum's told him that she's keeping the girls overnight again and she needs to talk to him.

I don't know what's going on but I'll drop in and see Mum before I come home so it might be late.

I know what's going on but I can't tell him via text. I know that Alice will try to poison him against me, but right now that's the least of my worries. Why does a detective want to question him? This sounds serious to me.

Then I notice the time. I've been so engrossed in reading Lynn's notebook that the afternoon has sped by and now I have to go and pick up Liam. Luckily it's raining so none of the mums are hanging about. Heavy storm clouds are building and everyone's heads are down, brollies up, collecting their kids and getting into their cars as quickly as they can.

Alice gives me a steely look as she passes me, hurrying the girls along. I don't even look at her, but I give the girls a hug when they run over to me. 'Have a lovely night at Nanny's, see you both tomorrow,' I say.

Back at Charlie's, I make a sandwich for me and Liam.

'I'm tired, can I lie down on the sofa with a blanket?' Liam asks when we're done eating. 'I don't want to be upstairs on my own.' The rain is lashing down now, and the wind is blowing fiercely. It looks like there's a storm brewing. Liam hates storms. So do I.

'Sure you can,' I tell him. I know tomorrow is a school day but I want to keep Liam close to me until I know how this will pan out with Charlie.

I fetch him a blanket and a pillow and make him comfy on the sofa in the family room. 'You can sleep in my bed tonight, if you want.'

He nods sleepily. 'Yes please.'

He yawns and closes his eyes. He really is shattered, he always is for a couple of days when he's had a sleepover with Ryan. I bet they chatter half the night. I kiss him on the fore-head and sit next to him so that I can carry on reading Lynn's journal.

The entries get less frequent and shorter as I work through, each one laced with despair. Lynn is struggling and can't cope with Alice's constant criticism, she feels she's a bad mum and the girls would be better without her. That Charlie would be better without her, that's why he turned to Claire.

Tears fill my eyes as I read them. Didn't Charlie see how she was struggling?

There is no mention at all of another man.

Yet the letters she left clearly state that she went off with someone. It doesn't make sense.

A text from Charlie interrupts me.

Still at the police station.

I feel a chill run through me as I read it. Why are they still questioning him?

I go back to the notebook. I've nearly finished now and there is nothing to suggest that Lynn has gone off with another man, but plenty to suggest that she might have killed herself. The poor woman sounds desperate.

I turn to the last entry and fingers of ice run down my spine as I read it.

> *I have to get away before Charlie comes home. I can't stay here*
> *any longer. It's not safe. Alice will look after the girls, it's what*
> *she's always wanted.*

The words jump off of the page and almost suffocate me with the fear behind them.

Lynn was terrified.

She left because she was too scared to stay.

She was sure the girls were safe though. It doesn't make sense.

I get up and pace the room. What do I do? Lynn sounds petrified in her journal entries. Terrified enough to run away and leave her own children and home behind.

And I'm not convinced that there was another man.

But what about the letters she wrote to her daughters?

My mind is in a whirl and my gut is telling me to run. If Lynn was in danger, then maybe we are too, and I can't risk anything happening to Liam. I vowed that I'd protect him and never put him in danger again. Tasha is out now but I have a spare key to her house, I can go there and wait for her. She won't mind, she's told us to come to her any time day or night. She's a good friend. The only one I can trust.

Another message comes in from Charlie.

Out at last. On my way to Mum's. See you in a bit.

Oh God, Alice will tell him that she found me snooping and he will be furious wondering what secrets I've discovered. I have to get out of here now! Quickly, I text Tasha to tell her that I'm coming to hers but not to rush back. Then, fear giving wings to my feet, I bound up the stairs, two steps at a time, and throw some of mine and Liam's clothes into a suitcase and put it in the boot of the car. The rain has got heavier now, there's definitely a storm coming.

It's only twenty minutes' drive to Tasha's. We'll be fine. I worry that Liam will freak out if he sees that we're going out in this rain but luckily he is still asleep so I carry him out to the car. He mumbles as I strap him in then drifts back off.

I climb into the driver's seat, place my handbag on the front passenger seat and grab my keys. My hands are trembling as I try to insert them into the ignition, fumbling and dropping them. Cursing I bend down, scoop them up and try again. *Keep calm, keep calm*, I tell myself as this time I manage to start the car.

58

Now

My head is throbbing, my shoulder hurts. For a moment I'm confused, wondering where I am and what's happened. All I can see is darkness enveloping me like a thick blanket and all I can hear is rain rat-a-tatting down above me. Then it comes back to me, I'm in my car. I was fleeing, running away to Tasha's with Liam, and I careered off the road.

Oh God! Liam!

I lift my head from the steering wheel, which it must have hit when I crashed. No wonder it's throbbing.

'Liam! Liam, are you okay?' I ask as I unfasten my seatbelt, wincing as pain shoots down my arm, stabbing like a knife. I turn to look in the back, mentally bracing myself for the worst. My young son is lying slumped in his seat, his chin on his chest, his eyes closed. I can't see any obvious injuries but he's not making a sound.

'Liam!' I open the driver's door and get out, every sinew and muscle in my body aching. I look around, my eyes getting used to the darkness now, and can make out that we've crashed into a fence. We're lucky it wasn't another car.

I jerk open the passenger door and lean over to check on my son still strapped in the back. He's on a booster seat and I suddenly remember that he unbuckled his seatbelt just before I crashed and I yelled at him to fasten it back up again.

Thank goodness he obeyed me or he would probably have shot through the windscreen. He might have been killed. I close my eyes and shudder, then I open them again and concentrate on my son.

'Liam. Can you speak to me, darling, and let me know you're okay?'

I put my finger under his chin and gently lift it. There's a bruise on his forehead where he must have hit my seat in front. Normally Liam likes to sit in the middle so he can see my face in the mirror but because he was so sleepy I put him behind me. If I hadn't done that, he would probably have been killed as the whole left side of the car is caved in where I hit the fence.

Nausea swirls in the pit of my stomach as the involuntary image of my young son crushed flashes across my mind. I swipe it away. I have to hold it together, I can't break down now. I have to save Liam.

I hold his wrist to feel his pulse: it's strong. He's alive.

I choke back the sobs that are threatening to burst out. *Stay calm, stay focused, get help.* Much as I want to take Liam out of the seat and cradle him in my arms, I know that I can't because you're not supposed to move anyone after an accident like this. He could have internal injuries.

I have to get my phone and call for help.

'Don't worry, darling, you're going to be all right. Mummy is going to get help,' I say, hoping that Liam can hear me. I go back to my seat and look for my handbag. There's no sign of it. Maybe it slipped into the footwell. The passenger seat is so crushed all I can do is bend down and feel for it while trying to avoid the broken glass that's scattered everywhere. Then my fingers close on the handle and I pull my handbag out through the gap. I open it up and search inside for my phone.

It isn't there.

Oh God! Despair overwhelms me. It must have fallen out in the car, which is now a mangled mess so I've got no chance of finding it. Damn! What do I do now?

Outside the storm is still raging. Thunder crashes and a bolt of lightning zigzags across the black sky.

I check on Liam again, relieved to see that he's still breathing. I've got to get help for him fast. I can't bear it if he dies.

A huge sob wells up in my throat and bursts out my mouth. I'm trembling with fear. I pull myself together. I need to get help.

The only thing I can do is walk back to the main road and flag down a car. I'm aware of the dangers, I've read the newspaper stories of men who've pretended to stop to help but instead have attacked their victims. I've got to chance it though. I must save my son.

'I'm going to the road for help, Liam. I'll be back soon, darling,' I say, trying to keep my voice steady and calm. I put the hazard lights on so that I can easily find the car on my return and make my way up the muddy embankment.

Slipping and slithering, I finally get to the top and relief floods through me as I see the headlights of a car coming towards me. I step out into the road, wave my arms and shout 'Help!' as loud as I can. I desperately wish that I had my phone or a torch with me, but at least my jacket is red so hopefully the driver will see me in the dark. I pray that it's a woman.

The car pulls up.

Tentatively I look at the driver's face then cry out in alarm.

It's Charlie.

59

He's found us.

I back away in horror, my eyes frantically searching the road, hoping to see the headlights of another car, but it's completely clear. Sobbing with fear, I turn and run, scrambling back down to my crashed car, wanting to get to Liam, to lock us both in, keep us safe.

My breath is coming out in gasps, hurting my throat as I stagger and slide down the muddy bank, praying that another vehicle will come along and see Charlie's car parked at the side of the road. Then, if they look down they will see my hazard lights and hopefully stop and help. That's the only thing that can save us now.

'Sarah! Wait!' The wind carries Charlie's voice and I know he's closing in on me. I'm so battered and weak I don't see how I can fight him off, but I have to find the strength for Liam's sake. I will do anything to save my son. I stumble and trip over a broken branch of a tree, managing to right myself before I hit the ground.

'Sarah! Please don't run from me! I won't hurt you!' Charlie shouts.

No you bloody won't! Not if I can help it! I reach down and pick up the branch, turning around to face Charlie, brandishing it in front of me.

'Get away from me!' I shriek.

He stops and holds his hands up, palms facing outwards. 'Sarah, I would never hurt you. I've been worried sick about you.' Then he looks beyond me to the car. 'Oh shit, is that your car? Is Liam in there? We've got to get him out quickly!'

He races past me down to Liam, pulling his phone out of his pocket at the same time. 'Ambulance, it's an emergency!'

I follow him, still holding the branch, unsure whether to trust him, but Liam needs help and Charlie is calling an ambulance. He reaches the car seconds before me and pulls the back door open. I see that Liam is stirring in his seat now, his eyes flicker open. 'Mum?' His eyes widen and he shouts, 'Mum! Mum!'

'I'm here, darling.' I drop the branch and push in front of Charlie, kneeling down by Liam, holding his small hand in mine. 'We had an accident. The ambulance is on its way.'

'Listen, Liam, it's really important that you keep still until the ambulance gets here.' Charlie's tone is calm, soothing.

Sheer panic envelops Liam's face and his eyes shoot to mine. 'Mum!'

'It's okay, darling. I'm here. I'm going to stay with you.' I gently squeeze his hand to reassure him. 'Everything's going to be all right but Charlie is right, you need to keep still. Try not to move, darling. The ambulance will be here soon.'

I pray it is. It has to be. I can't bear to lose my darling son.

A few long minutes later sirens announce the arrival of the ambulance, and, I think, the police, but I'm so shaken up, so worried about Liam, that I can't pick up the sounds clearly.

'I'll go and let them know where we are.' Charlie stands up, ready to climb the muddy bank again, when a torch shines down and a woman's voice shouts, 'Everyone all right down there?'

Charlie waves. 'My partner's car went off the road. Her son is injured but conscious, and she's badly bruised.'

My partner.

Charlie is so calm, so confident, as he takes control, comforting Liam, comforting me. I wonder if I've judged him wrong, if my imagination has got the better of me. He didn't come after us to kill us, he came after us to help us.

Was Claire wrong?

Have we all misjudged Charlie, when the simple truth is that Lynn left because she wanted a new life, one not encumbered by children? Did she write those terrified words in her journal because of her mental state?

'You go in the ambulance with Liam and I'll follow,' Charlie says. He puts his hand in his pocket and hands me my phone. 'I found this on the kitchen floor. When I realised you'd gone and didn't have your phone on you, it scared the hell out of me, especially on a night like this.' His eyes meet mine as I take the phone from him. It must have fallen out of my handbag. I'd texted Tasha to tell her I was going to hers, then slipped the phone back in my handbag, which I hadn't stopped to fasten because I was in such a panic to leave before Charlie returned. Did Charlie read my text to Tasha? Is that how he found me so quickly?

'I don't know what it is that made you decide you had to run away, Sarah, but I love you. I love Liam too. I would never harm either of you. Now isn't the time to talk about this but maybe later, when we know for certain that Liam is going to be okay and you've had time to rest, we can talk things over?'

I nod and swallow. I owe him that much. Then I get into the ambulance and sit by Liam, who is fixed up to all sorts of machines and has now drifted into unconsciousness again. The doors close and we set off.

'He's got a strong pulse, love, and he's been talking, I'm sure he'll be fine,' the paramedic reassures me as she monitors the screens.

I hope he will. I'll never forgive myself if he dies. It was stupid to drive off like that on such a stormy night, I should have waited until morning. I was so scared, so desperate to get away from Charlie, that I almost killed us both.

No. What almost killed us was the brakes not working.

Someone tampered with my car. Someone wanted to kill us.

Then another thought slams into my mind. My car was fine when I collected Liam from school. So it must have been tampered with when we returned. But Charlie was at the police station and Alice had the girls, so it couldn't have been one of them.

I only have Charlie's word for it that he was at the police station – he could have gone to see Alice earlier, so knowing that I was on to him he came home and messed with my brakes. He's a trained mechanic, he'd know how to do it.

Why would he come after us and rescue us though?

I don't know. I have no answers but every nerve in my body is shouting that we're in danger and I'm not ignoring it.

60

At the hospital the doctors check us both over and to my relief assure me that apart from cuts and bruises and a huge bump on his head, Liam is fine. I've got a bad headache and am battered and bruised too so the doctor wants us both to stay in overnight for observation. I hug Liam and hold him close before they take him to his ward. I can't believe that we both escaped without serious injury. And that I'd been so reckless to risk our lives like that.

Liam could have been killed. I could have lost him. Or I could have died and left him motherless. Or killed us both.

What had I been thinking of to take off like that?

I'd been terrified, sure that we were in terrible danger. Did I get everything wrong? My head is pounding and I can't make sense of it all.

My phone rings, it's Tasha. I answer it, my hand shaking. 'Where are you? I expected you here by now. Is everything okay?' she asks.

I feel bad that she's cut her evening with Caleb short to be with us. Haltingly, I tell her what happened and explain that I'm in the hospital.

'Thank God you're both okay.' I can hear the relief in her voice. 'Shall I come and get you?'

'I don't know when we can go home yet,' I say. 'We have to at least stay in overnight.'

'You're coming to me then, aren't you? You're not going back to Charlie's surely?'

I don't answer because my mind is in a whirl. Too much has happened for me to take in.

'Sarah, please tell me that you're not going back to Charlie's. Not after everything.'

'I don't know. He saved us both, Tasha. That doesn't sound like the actions of a man who murdered his wife and believes that I have proof of that.'

'But your brakes, you said that they didn't work. That someone meddled with them.'

'Maybe I'm wrong. Maybe water got into them and the road was so wet that I lost control of the car.'

I think back to the few seconds before the accident. I can recall stepping on the brakes, trying to stop the car but it kept on veering towards the tree. Was it the rain? Am I overreacting to all this?

'You need to tell the police, Sarah. They can investigate and find out for certain whether your brakes were messed with. You have to find out for sure.'

She's right, I have to tell the police. I can't risk Liam being injured. I have to keep my son safe.

'Your partner would like to see you now, if you feel up to it,' the doctor says.

'I've got to go, Tash. I'll talk to you later,' I promise and end the call.

I don't know whether I trust Charlie or not, if I've judged him wrong. But I do know that he saved my son's life so I should at least thank him. I nod.

A few moments later Charlie comes in. He looks pale and shaken.

He takes my hand, his eyes holding mine. 'Sarah, why did you run off like that? Was it because Mum found you snooping? She told me about you finding Lynn's handbag. You don't have to worry about that, I understand why you felt the need to try and find answers, especially after what Claire said and the police questioning me. I would too. I promise that I'm not a threat to you, Sarah. I love you. I would never harm you. You and Liam, you've become part of our family now.' His voice breaks. 'I was so distraught when I found you'd run away. It was like Lynn all over again. I thought I'd never trust anyone after that, never let anyone close enough to hurt me or the girls again, but as soon as I laid eyes on you, you blew me away.' He runs his other hand through his hair, making it stand up like a quiff. 'I don't want to have to tell the girls that you've left too. They've had so much loss and devastation in their young lives. Please tell me what I can do to put this right.'

He looks so devastated and sounds so genuine. I think of Mia and Daisy losing another mummy. Liam and me have only been in their lives a couple of months but we have gelled so well and I adore those little girls. I really don't know what to do. *Just be honest with him, give him a chance to explain.*

'I found Lynn's journal. She left because she was terrified,' I tell him. 'Why was she scared, Charlie? And why did the police question you for so long?'

He licks his lips. 'Because they've found Lynn.'

61

Charlie's words stun me. I scan my eyes over his face: he seems to have aged ten years in the past few hours, his skin is sallow, there are dark bags under his eyes and creases furrowed across his forehead. Is Lynn dead? And if she is, was it murder? Or suicide? I squeeze my eyes shut.

'She's alive. They found her working in a B&B in Lincoln.' I can hear the sheer relief in Charlie's voice.

I snap my eyes open. 'What?'

'Lynn's alive,' Charlie repeats. 'She'd walked out to start a new life, as her letter said.'

I'm stunned. So I got it all wrong. Charlie is innocent. He didn't harm Lynn. A mixture of relief and guilt at judging him wrong floods through me.

'Look, you're exhausted. None of this is what you think. The police wanted to question me about Lynn's state of mind, that's all. Rest and get a good night's sleep. I'll come back and see you tomorrow and maybe we can talk then?'

I nod. I feel so weak and exhausted that I can barely keep my eyes open.

'Could I...' Charlie hesitates as if he's not sure whether to ask the question. He swallows and continues. 'Could I check on Liam? I want to see for myself that he's okay. The girls are asking about you both.'

What can I say when he helped rescue us? 'Of course, but don't be long, please. Liam needs to rest too.'

'I'll only be a few minutes.' He leans over and kisses me on the cheek. 'Have a good rest. I'll be back tomorrow.'

I'm so weary that my eyes close before he even leaves the room.

I sleep all night, waking up to the sound of the nurses changing shifts early the next morning. I pick up my phone and glance at the time on the screen: six thirty. I wonder if Liam is awake yet. If he's slept all night too.

There are message notifications on my phone but I don't feel up to answering them yet so I push back the covers and swing my legs out of bed, looking around for my clothes and shoes. A blinding pain shoots across my forehead and I sit on the edge of the bed and close my eyes. I don't feel like I can walk yet, but I need to know how Liam is.

'How are you feeling, love?' a nurse asks, glancing up at me.

'I've got a bad headache. Where are my clothes? I want to see my son.'

'All your things are in a bag in the bedside cabinet,' the nurse tells me. 'Let me go and check on your son for you. We'd prefer you not to get out of bed yet, you had a nasty bump on your head and have mild concussion.'

'I want to see my son,' I say again. I gingerly slide off the bed and open the cupboard of the bedside cabinet, taking out the bag of clothes, and am slipping my shoes on my feet when the nurse comes back.

'Liam is still fast asleep but he's absolutely fine. We've had no problems in the night. The doctor will come round to check on you both later this morning. He may want to keep you both in an extra day before you can go home.'

Home. But where is our home now?

'Thanks.' I stand up. 'Can I see Liam?'

'Of course. Let me get you a wheelchair, we don't want you collapsing.'

I still feel so weak that I don't protest. I sit on the edge of my bed and wait until she returns a few minutes later with a wheelchair, helps me into it, then pushes me to the children's ward. Liam is sleeping peacefully in a bed in the corner.

'I'll leave you with him a few minutes,' the nurse says.

I sit by the side of the hospital bed, reach out, clasp his hand in mine and watch my son sleeping. What shall I do? Lynn has been found, and is safe. I still don't understand why she hasn't been home to see her children, but I judged Charlie wrong. I ran away and put Liam and myself in danger instead of trusting Charlie.

'Mummy.' Liam's eyes are open and he is looking at me.

'Hello, darling. How are you feeling?' I lean over and kiss him on the cheek. 'Can you remember what happened?'

'We crashed. I was so scared.' His voice is wobbly and his lip trembling. 'I thought we were going to die, Mum.'

'I'm so sorry. I tried to stop but the brakes didn't work.' A shudder runs through me as I realise again how close I came to losing him. I shuffle out of the wheelchair, sit on the bed beside Liam and put my arm around his shoulder, pulling him close. Guilt is eating into me. I promised to keep Liam safe, I swore that I would never put him in danger again.

'It's okay, Mum. It's not your fault. It was the storm.' He leans his head against my shoulder. 'I was so scared,' he repeats.

An image of the storm, the thunder and the rain lashing down onto the windscreen slides across my mind. Liam was frightened. I was too. But I drove slowly, carefully, until the storm hit the tree, breaking it, sending it into the road. Even then I didn't panic. I held my nerve and braked. Only my brakes didn't work so I had to swerve the car off the road.

Had my brakes really been tampered with? If so, who could have done it? Only me, Charlie and Alice have a key fob to the gates.

Unless...

Dylan is out now. My fear of him finding me and getting his revenge, as he'd promised, had subsided over the past few weeks but now it has surfaced again. He could have found out where I live. And I'm pretty sure that picking a lock and tampering with the brakes of a car is within his capabilities. Would he do something so terrible in revenge for me getting him put away?

Tasha is right: I have to tell the police.

62

Charlie comes to see me again later that morning. He sits by the side of the bed, reaches for my hand and holds it tight. 'I have to tell you something.' He swallows and I can see that this is difficult for him. 'I want you to come back home, for us to start again, but I can't do that if I'm not completely honest with you.'

I suck in my breath, my eyes resting on his face, wondering what he's about to confess. He looks worried, and ashamed.

'The things that have been happening... the drink spilt over Mum's phone, Daisy's painting being ruined, my paperwork being messed up' – he swallows – 'I'm afraid that it was all Mia. I'm truly sorry, I had no idea. She confessed when she heard that you'd had a crash and Liam was badly hurt in hospital.'

I'm stunned. 'Mia? I don't understand. Why would she do those things?'

Charlie rubs his chin. 'She wants her mother to come back and thought that Lynn wouldn't return if she knew that you were living with us. So she decided to drive you both away. I really am sorry and so is Mia, she's very upset and ashamed now. She thinks that you left because of her behaviour and that you and Liam almost got killed. She blames herself.'

This is a lot to take in. Mia seemed such a sweet girl and I thought she was happy for me and Liam to be there. I shake my head in disbelief. 'Did she open Thumper's cage too?' I ask.

'No, unfortunately that was Daisy. She admitted that she sneaked out to give Thumper a carrot. She thought she'd locked the cage, but it's so stiff she obviously didn't fasten it properly.' His eyes cloud over. 'They are both very sorry and want you and Liam to come back. Do you think that you can forgive them and give us all another chance?'

I fix my eyes on Charlie' s face. I want to see his expression when I tell him what I discovered. 'I found a broken photo frame in your drawer. It was of your wedding and Lynn's face was scribbled over with blue biro.'

'God! And you thought I did that!' Charlie leans forward, and squeezes my hand. 'It was Mia, Sarah. I kept that photo on the sideboard in our former home but Mia was so upset and angry about her mother leaving her that she smashed it and scribbled out Lynn's face. I kept it because when... if... Lynn came back I wanted to show her how much she had hurt the girls. And that's why I decided it was best to put all the photos of Lynn away.'

'And what about the handbag hidden in the drawer?'

He runs his hand over his face. 'Mum said that Lynn left that handbag on the hall table when she left. It was her favourite bag. I think she meant to take it with her but then something made her forget it. So Mum took it home with her and put it in the filing cabinet, in case Lynn came back. She explained that she didn't tell me about it because I was devastated about Lynn going.'

I steel myself. 'Lynn's journal was in the handbag. And she'd written in it that she left because she was scared of you.'

'What?' He jumps up, his eyes wide. 'Why would she write such a thing?'

'I was scared too, that's why I left...' I rest my eyes on his face. I don't want to say it but I have to. I can't possibly go back to Charlie's unless I'm absolutely sure that it's safe. Even though Lynn has been found, there are still questions to be asked, such as why she's kept away and not tried to see her daughters all this time. 'I was scared that you or Alice might have killed Lynn.'

'Christ, Sarah, what do you take me for? How can you think I'm capable of murder? And the mother of my children at that!'

'I don't know what you're capable of, do I? We barely know each other. If it wasn't for my bathroom flooding, we probably would never have moved in together.'

I see the sadness in his eyes, I've hurt him. But I'm hurt too and I don't know who I can trust. And there is no mistaking Lynn's terror, it's there in her journal for anyone to read.

'There's more.' If we're getting everything out in the open, I can't hold this back. 'I'm sure that someone tampered with the brakes of my car, that's why I crashed. I've told the police and they're investigating.'

'And you think it was me?' He stands up, thrusts his hands through his hair, paces around the room. Then he turns back to me. 'What the hell, Sarah! What sort of monster do you think I am?'

Then he leaves without kissing me goodbye.

63

Later that afternoon I get another visitor. A fair-haired woman dressed in a navy coat and black leggings, a light blue scarf around her neck. She stands at the foot of my bed, looking at me hesitantly, and I frown.

There is something familiar about her but I can't place where I've seen her. She steps forward, twisting the scarf with her fingers. She looks anxious and immediately I start to feel nervous too. Who is she? What does she want?

'Can I speak to you for a few minutes?' Her voice is so quiet I can barely hear her, and there are dark shadows under her eyes. She bites her lip like Mia does and in that moment I know who she is.

'Lynn.'

'You know about me then?'

I nod. 'You're Mia and Daisy's mum and you walked out almost two years ago and never came back.'

She casts her eyes down to the floor, staring at her feet, which are encased in black ankle boots. 'I was made to leave,' she mumbles. 'You have no idea what my life was like.'

'I think I do. A bit anyway. I read your journal,' I confess.

She lifts her head but doesn't meet my eyes. She twists her scarf into a knot around her hands. 'Can I sit down?'

I nod. I want to hear what she has to say. She sits herself on the chair beside the bed. 'I read about your accident and I had to come and see you.' Lynn swallows hard. 'Exactly the same thing happened to me. My brakes failed. I crashed.'

'What? Someone tampered with the brakes of your car too?' I can hardly take this in.

Someone tried to kill both of us.

She fiddles with her scarf. 'I can't prove it, of course. But I tried to brake and I couldn't.'

I ponder over this. 'It couldn't be Charlie, he came after me and saved Liam's life,' I tell her.

'I don't think it was Charlie either. He was angry with me but he never threatened me. I think it was Alice. I wouldn't put anything past her, she's obsessive. She wants Charlie and the girls to herself and never thought I was good enough for him.'

Lynn sinks her head into her hands. 'I was lucky and escaped with a few bruises, like you.'

'Where have you been all this time?' I ask her.

'Working in a B&B in Lincolnshire.' She fiddles with the hem of her coat. 'I was too scared to come back. Then the police found me.'

'Why did you leave Mia and Daisy behind?' I ask. 'Didn't you think that they might be in danger too?'

She shook her head. 'Not at the time, Charlie and Alice both adore those girls. The only danger they were in was from me. I wasn't fit to take care of them. I almost killed them, Sarah. Alice came home just in time to save them.' She swallows and, stunned, I wait for her to continue. 'It was an accident. I would never willingly harm my beautiful girls but Alice was furious. She forced me to go away. She said that she didn't trust me around Mia and Daisy, and she was right not to. I didn't trust myself either. Alice promised that she wouldn't tell Charlie what I'd done if I left and never came back. I felt so bad, so wretched, that I agreed.'

Tears are streaming down Lynn's face, and she wipes them away with the sleeve of her coat. 'It broke my heart to leave them. I've ached for them every single day.'

I don't know what this poor woman did but I believe her that it was an accident. She's obviously been torturing herself ever since.

I feel so sorry for her. I place my hand on hers and squeeze it reassuringly. 'I'm sure you didn't mean to hurt them,' I say softly. 'You obviously love them very much.'

She pulls a tissue from her sleeve and wipes her eyes then blows her nose. 'I love those girls more than life itself. I would never hurt them willingly. But...' She shakes her head.

'What happened?' I keep my voice soft, gentle.

She twists the tissue around her finger and stares down at it.

'Daisy's birth was so traumatic, we both nearly died.' She takes a deep breath and gulps. 'Charlie had recently started a new job as a skills tutor, and he took a couple of weeks off to look after us all, but he couldn't afford to take more, so Alice said she'd come and look after me.'

'How did you feel about that?'

'I was pleased at first. I was so weak, I could barely walk. I tried to breastfeed Daisy but I couldn't and she was crying all the time. Alice took charge of her, and Mia. She made sure I had food and drink but she never let me have the girls, said I needed to rest. Insisted that I was left to rest in my own room.' I can imagine Alice being like that. And the despair that Lynn felt at not being allowed to hold her baby or look after Mia. She trembles and takes a deep breath. I wait for her to compose herself and continue.

'Charlie came to see me every morning and evening but we became like strangers. By the time I felt stronger, Daisy had bonded with Alice, she never knew me as her mother. Mia went to Alice too. I felt like I'd lost my daughters. And my husband.' Tears well up in her eyes again. 'I had postnatal depression, really bad. It seemed pointless getting out of bed, no one needed me, the girls had bonded with Alice, Charlie shut himself in his study every evening.'

There's a faraway look in Lynn's eyes now and I can see that she's reliving it all. 'Claire tried to talk to me, she persuaded me to fight for my family, but I was no match for Alice, who was practically living with us by that time. She kept inviting Crystal over too, whenever Brandon was away. Charlie and Crystal were engaged once, you know, before Charlie met me.' She leans forward and sinks her head into her hands as if the memories are too much for her.

'It must have been a really bad time for you.' I place my hand on her shoulder sympathetically.

She lifts her head, her eyes are red. 'It was horrendous. I felt useless. Unloved. In the way. Then I found Claire's earring under our bed. I was devastated. I didn't know what to do. I had a massive row with Claire and told her that I didn't want to see her again. She denied it, of course, so did Charlie, said he had no idea how the earring got there.'

She gulps then looks at the jug of water on the locker beside my bed. There are two clean plastic beakers beside it. 'Do you mind if I have a glass of water?'

'Please do.'

She gets up from her chair and pours herself a drink, swallowing almost the entire beakerful in one go. I wait again for her to compose herself and continue.

'I was so confused and upset that I had a glass of wine, trying to numb the pain. It was only the one but I was on tranquillisers, and it completely knocked me out. The girls were in bed, Charlie was at a meeting. Alice came and found me passed out on the sofa and Mia trying to heat up some milk on the stove for Daisy. She'd been crying and Mia couldn't wake me.' She paces around, still holding the almost empty plastic cup.

She puts it on the windowsill then turns to me, her eyes full of sorrow and pain. 'It was a gas oven, Sarah. If Alice hadn't arrived just as Mia was about to light the hob, my little girls could have been burnt alive.'

64

'I know it's terrible,' Lynn continues. 'I hate myself for it. The place could have gone up in flames, my darling daughters...' Her voice trails off and tears flood her eyes. She struggles to compose herself then continues. 'I understand why Alice was mad at me. I begged her not to tell Charlie, and she said that she wouldn't if I promised to leave and not come back.'

She goes over to the window and stares down into the hospital car park. 'I wasn't thinking straight. I realise now that I was suffering from depression. I wrote in my journal that I had to get out before Charlie came home because I knew he would be angry at me when Alice told him what I'd done. And rightly so. I hated myself so much. I felt worthless. I couldn't deal with Charlie's anger on top of my guilt.'

'Was he abusive to you?' I ask gently.

She shakes her head. 'Never but I could tell that he was tired of me being so useless, lying in bed all the time. I knew that this would have been the last straw. Charlie tried to be patient at first but he didn't understand what was happening to me and why I couldn't seem to bond with Daisy. I didn't understand it either. And Alice was always whispering in his ear, making out that I was an unfit mum. Which I was.' A sob breaks her voice and my heart goes out to her.

'You were ill. It wasn't your fault.'

Even with everything I've witnessed from Alice, I can hardly believe that she could be so cruel, forcing Lynn to leave her own children. I know what Lynn did was wrong, but she was obviously in a bad place mentally. She needed help, not to be banished from her daughters' lives forever.

'There is no excuse. It was unforgivable.'

'It was a terrible mistake and I get that you feel really bad about it. But you were ill,' I repeat. 'Surely if you'd explained to Charlie, promised not to drink wine when you were on tranquillisers again, he would have understood.'

Lynn stares down at her fingers as she twists then untwists the scarf. 'There was nothing left of me and Charlie by then. He went to work, came home and played with the kids for a bit then shut himself in his study. Alice had managed to convince him that I was "unstable". If she had told him about this, he would never have let me near the girls again.' She bites her lip, keeping her eyes cast down. 'Alice threatened to report me for neglect, she said that if social services heard what had happened, the girls could be taken into care. I couldn't bear that.'

She picks up the beaker of water, her hand trembling, and takes a sip out of it before continuing. 'I realise now that this wouldn't have happened as they had Charlie to look after them but Alice got into my head, convinced me that I was a danger to my daughters, that I had to leave for everyone's good. I know how that sounds, but I was suffering from depression, I felt inadequate.' She goes back over to the chair and sits down. 'I thought that I wasn't a good enough mum or a good enough wife, that everyone would be better off without me. So I did as Alice said. I was all for getting my things and leaving right there and then but Alice said it wouldn't be fair for everyone to wonder what had happened to me. She told me to take some money from the joint bank account so that I could pay for somewhere to live and feed myself, and to leave letters for Charlie and the girls so that there would be closure. She actually sat by me and dictated what I was to write.'

Her words shock me to the core. 'So you didn't really have an affair?'

'No. I would never do that to Charlie. It was all Alice's idea. She said that if I wrote that I was going off with someone else, then Charlie wouldn't come looking for me. That it was kinder for him and the girls than if I just disappeared.'

How cruel! And Alice has kept her terrible secret all this time, has watched her son and granddaughters grieve and not said a word to put them out of their misery.

'I packed some clothes, got into the car and drove,' Lynn says. 'I had no idea where I was going. I was devastated, a mess. I drove for miles then my brakes suddenly failed. I almost crashed. Luckily the road wasn't busy and I managed to pull over safely but it shook me up. I called out my breakdown cover and they took the car to be repaired. I stayed in a small hotel for a couple of days while that was done, wondering what to do. Then I saw an advert for staff in a B&B in Lincoln and applied, it would give me a job and an income. When my car was fixed I drove there. Sadie, the owner, was really nice to me, gave me the job, took me under her wing. I've been there ever since.'

She takes a gulp of the water. 'Gradually I got better, recovered from the depression. I wanted to come back but I didn't know how or whether I'd be welcome, and the longer I was away, the harder it was to come back. How could I explain why I'd left my dear girls? I adore them and have missed them so much.' I wait for her to compose herself. 'When the police tracked me down, I confessed everything to Sadie, and she said that Alice had no right driving me away and that I should go back and try to connect with my girls again. And tell Charlie what really happened.'

She leans forward, clasping her hands and resting her elbows on her knees. 'I was on my way back when I picked up a local newspaper and saw the details about your crash. It said that you were Charlie's partner.' She raises her eyes to mine. 'I wondered what you and your lad were doing driving down that dark lane in that storm. And why Charlie had come after you and found you. It made me wonder if Alice had driven you away like she did me.' She pauses. 'It seemed too much of a coincidence. We're both with the same man, we leave in a hurry, we have an accident. It made me wonder if someone had messed with both of our brakes.' I can see the pain in her eyes. 'You took your child with you though, and I left my children behind. I thought they were safe but if someone tried to kill me, and you, then they could be in terrible danger.'

'What about your handbag? I found it in the filing cabinet drawer in Charlie's study. It had some jewellery in it, a scarf and your journal.'

'I was taking it with me but Alice snatched it off me. She said that I wasn't entitled to the expensive bag and jewellery because Charlie bought them for me. She must have taken them back home with her – it was her house then. Claire told me that Charlie's living there now. She must have locked them away. I guess she didn't bother to move the scarf so didn't see the journal.'

Lynn swallows, takes a tissue from her pocket and dabs her eyes with it. 'You must think I'm terrible.'

'Of course I don't.' I put my hand reassuringly on hers, trying to take in her words. Alice was behind all this. She even told her to take some money from the bank account. How devious that woman is.

'You made a terrible mistake. We all make mistakes,' I say to comfort her.

I should know. I made one of the worst mistakes ever and it almost cost me my son.

And although it now seems that Dylan wasn't responsible for my brakes failing he could still be a danger to us. I have to keep my wits about me.

65

I tell Lynn what happened on Arran, everything. It's the first time I've ever told the whole story to anyone and it's a relief to talk about it. Lynn listens to my story sympathetically. 'So you see, I've made a bad mistake too. But that doesn't mean I'm not fit to be a mother and should have my son taken from me.' A lump forms in my throat, those words still hurt me. 'And neither are you.'

'I can understand that you're upset but I bet your mum is sorry she said that now. It was probably the shock of seeing the bruise on your arm and knowing the little lad witnessed such a horrible assault. None of that was your fault though and when she had time to think about it I'm sure your mum regretted it,' Lynn says gently. 'Hasn't she been in touch with you since?'

'No. Although to be fair she doesn't know where I live. I took off without leaving a forwarding address and I changed my phone number because I didn't want Dylan to be able to contact me. I never go on social media either because of him. She has no way of getting in touch with me.'

'What about your friend, Tasha, can she contact you through her? Or your brother?'

'She doesn't know Tasha. And I haven't seen my brother for years, we've drifted apart.' I lean forward. 'Never mind my mum, I told you this so that you'd understand that sometimes we mess up. It doesn't make us bad people. It was wicked of Alice to play on your depression and insecurities and drive you away from your own children.'

'The thing is, I want my family back.' Lynn shoots me a reassuring look. 'Not Charlie, there's no need for you to worry on that score, but I want to be in my girls' lives and I don't know how to go about it. I'm scared that they hate me for leaving them and won't want anything to do with me.' She twists a lock of her hair around her finger. 'And Charlie won't believe me about Alice. He'll think I'm making it up.'

'You've got a right to see your daughters, and they're both desperate to see you again. They miss you so much,' I tell her. 'I think Charlie should know the real reason why you left. Although Alice will probably deny her part in it.'

'I know.' She sighs. 'Thank you so much for listening to me and for sharing your story too. That means a lot.'

'You're welcome.' Then something occurs to me. 'Why did you leave your pendant behind?' I ask. 'Claire was worried that something had happened to you because she said you always had it on you.'

'I left it because I wanted to think that my mum was looking after Mia and Daisy. And because I hoped I could come back one day.' Lynn pushes back her chair and stands up. 'For what it's worth, I think you should give your mum another chance. I'm sure she regrets her words now.'

When she's gone, I think about the things Lynn has told me, and everything that happened to me and Liam while we were at Charlie's. Mia has admitted to some of them and Daisy was the one who left Thumper's cage open, but what about the brakes on my car?

Lynn's right, it seems too much of a coincidence that the same thing happened to us both.

I wake to my phone ringing – I must have drifted off after Lynn left. It's the police who are investigating whether my crash was just an accident or something more sinister, I'd told them my fear that it might be Dylan. I listen as they tell me that when Dylan was released he went back to live in Australia. There is no way he could be responsible for tampering with my brakes, or anything else that has happened.

My relief at this news is dampened by the knowledge that someone else is still out to get me.

Then I remember Lynn said she had been driving for a while when her brakes failed. So someone could have tampered with my car that afternoon. Alice had come to the house and I have no idea how long she had been there before she walked into the study and found me with the handbag.

Or if she went straight home afterwards. I was so shaken up, I went to the kitchen for a calming drink.

Is Alice responsible? Did she panic that the truth might come out when she discovered that I had Lynn's handbag, and so she resorted to trying to kill me?

Another thought worms into my mind. Does Charlie know about it and is covering for her?

66

ALICE

So, Lynn's back. And I wonder what tale she's telling.

I've always acted out of love for my son and his girls, everything I've done has been to protect them. I knew that Lynn was struggling and tried to help her but she wouldn't even help herself. So yes, I encouraged her to go away. She was a danger to those precious girls.

All I could think of when I walked in that day and saw Mia trying to warm up milk for Daisy on the gas stove was that they could have all got killed. Lynn was completely out of it, she wouldn't have come round until it was too late, and my two darling granddaughters would have been burnt to death.

I was so angry. I knew she'd had a bad time when Daisy was born and I tried to help, I really did, but the more I did, the less Lynn did. I couldn't understand why she couldn't pull herself together and look after her children. A mother's love is supposed to overcome everything but she didn't love those little girls enough to look after them. She didn't even bother to get out of bed most days.

'She's not fit to be their mother, she'll have them taken off her at this rate,' Crystal said when I told her my concerns.

That's what made me decide I had to make Lynn leave, before my two beloved granddaughters were seriously injured, or killed.

I knew that if I simply forced Lynn to go, Charlie would search for her, bring her back, tell her everything would be okay. I couldn't risk it, so I told her what to write. And she did it without any protest. That shows how much she loved Charlie and her daughters, doesn't it? She did what I suggested then walked away and never came back. She never even bothered to fight for them.

I kept expecting her to return, but the weeks passed into months and there was no sign of Lynn. Not even a card on the girls' birthdays or at Christmas.

As time went on, it made sense for Charlie and the girls to move into my home, nearer to me, and Crystal promised to keep an eye on things, to let me know if Lynn ever came back.

She promised to keep an eye on things when Sarah and her son moved in too. She's the one who told me that Sarah had met Claire.

I knew I had to put a stop to Sarah's snooping. Then it all got out of hand.

SARAH

The police get in touch again later and tell me that the tests are inconclusive and they can't say for certain that the brakes of my car were tampered with. Maybe it was the rain, after all, but I know that I can't go back to Charlie's. There are too many unanswered questions and I don't feel that I can guarantee our safety. Plus, I think that I should give Lynn space to get to know her daughters again.

Stacey and Lee will be moving after Christmas and until then I'll ask Tasha if I can move in with her. I don't mind sleeping on the sofa for a few weeks. At least we'll be safe. I'll miss Charlie and the girls, although I'm pleased that Mia and Daisy will have their mother back in their lives.

'Of course you can!' Tasha sounds delighted. 'And for what it's worth, I think you're doing the right thing. Mia might have admitted to some of the things but what about the brakes on your car? Someone tried to kill you, Sarah.'

'We don't know that for sure,' I remind her. 'But I think it's best if we don't go back to Charlie's.'

I've already spoken to Liam and he's admitted that he doesn't want to go back to live in Charlie's house. 'I don't like it there anymore,' he says. 'Alice is always telling me off and saying that we'll have to leave if I'm naughty, and me and Mia are always arguing.'

So that's why he was always nervous around Alice.

I don't want to go away, like Lynn did, without saying goodbye. I phone Charlie to tell him about my decision, and ask him to bring the girls so I can talk to them too. We're being discharged today and I think it's best if we meet on neutral territory.

He doesn't argue with me, so I think he must agree that it's the right thing to do. Too much has happened. He looks solemn when he comes into Liam's room with Daisy and Mia. I want me and Liam to be together when we say goodbye.

'Your mummy is back now and it's best if you all spend a bit of time together,' I tell the girls. 'We'll all still be friends but me and Liam are going to move into our own house soon. Until then we'll stay with a friend.'

Mia and Daisy hug me tight. Then they hug Liam. 'Sorry, Liam,' Mia mumbles.

'It's okay, I get it,' he replies. He's such an understanding little boy.

Charlie calls me to one side, out of the kids' earshot. He looks sadly at me. 'I wish you wouldn't go. I don't want to be with Lynn. I'm glad that she's back for the girls' sake, and I'm furious with Mum for what she did, but I don't love Lynn, I love you.' He reaches out and takes my hand. 'I was looking forward to us all spending Christmas together. Please tell me that we can still see each other.'

I shake my head. 'I'm sorry, Charlie, but I think it's for the best if we don't. It was all too quick. I need to concentrate on Liam, and you need to rebuild your family.' I lean forward and kiss him on the cheek. 'Thank you for everything. For taking us in when our house was flooded, and for coming after us, for saving Liam's life, but now isn't the right time for us. Maybe some time in the future, if we still want to.'

'I'll be here waiting, hoping you change your mind,' he says.

I look at him. I still love him but all this is too much of a mess for me. 'It's nearly Christmas. You all need time to come together again as a family – even if you and Lynn don't want to be together, the girls need their mother,' I tell him. 'And me and Liam need time to settle into our new home.'

He holds out his arms and we hug. It's a hard decision but I know that I'm doing the right thing.

The doctor gives both me and Liam the all clear to go home that afternoon, and Tasha and Ryan come to pick us up.

I don't have a car now. I don't have a car, and I don't have a home either.

We survived, we're alive, I remind myself. The insurance company have promised to provide me with a courtesy car by the weekend. I've told Todd what's happened and he's promised to help me with the deposit money so that we can secure the house. It will all work out.

We have a great weekend, the boys play games, me and Tasha watch rom-coms, drinking wine, catching up. It's like old times, when we used to get together when Todd was working away. My courtesy car arrives on Saturday morning, a white Ford Fiesta. It feels good to be mobile again.

Maddie and Tom insist that I take some time off after the accident, with full pay. 'Don't come back until the new year,' Tom orders me with a smile. 'You and that lad of yours have had a nasty experience. You need time to recover.'

It's so kind of them, and I'm grateful because I feel so

battered by everything that's happened that I really do need time to rest and recover.

Liam wants to go back to school though, he'd be bored at home and doesn't want to miss the Christmas plays or party. Guessing that I don't want to face the Mum Gang, or Alice, Tasha offers to take him there and back. 'No need for both of us to go, and I have to drop off and pick up Ryan anyway,' she says.

I'm so grateful to her. She's always been such a good friend.

I make myself a brew when they've all left on Monday morning, and sit nursing it as I think about the craziness of the past few weeks.

A clatter from the letterbox announces the arrival of the post. I go to get it. There's a few Christmas cards and a couple of bills. I pick them up and carry them into the kitchen to put them on the side for Tasha when I notice that one of the Christmas cards is addressed to me. I stare at it, puzzled. No one knows I'm here. Unless it's from Charlie?

I look more closely at the envelope and my heart jumps into my mouth as I recognise the writing. Mum. I sit down at the kitchen table, holding the card, my heart thudding. It's been three years and I haven't heard a peep from my mum. Why is she writing to me now?

And why has she sent it to Tasha's? How would she know where I am?

I have to find out. I get a knife out of the drawer and slide it underneath the envelope flap, then I ease out the card. A festive one showing baubles hanging on a Christmas tree. 'Merry Christmas, daughter' is written across the front in gold letters. There's another card in the envelope too. This one says 'Merry Christmas to our special grandson'. A lump forms in my throat as I realise how much I miss my mum. How much I love her.

I open my card. There's a long message written on the inside. I mentally brace myself as I start to read it.

Darling Sarah,

I don't know how many times I have to say sorry before you forgive me, love, but I'll keep saying it. I'll keep trying, however long it takes, to convince you that I mean it. You have no idea how much I regret my harsh words and how much I miss you and little Liam. I don't know if you're getting my cards and letters because you never reply. I don't know how to contact you except here. I know you and Tasha were such good friends, but maybe Tasha has moved, or you've both fallen out and my cards and letters have never reached you. Or maybe you just rip them up. I hope that you and Liam are both well and happy, and that one day you will forgive me and call me. There is always a home for you and Liam with me and Bill.

Lots of love,

Mum xxx

Mum has been sending me letters and cards to Tasha's, and Tasha has never told me.

Tasha is my best friend. I can't believe that she's kept this from me. Has she destroyed all the letters or hidden them?

She knows how hurt I was about our argument, and about the fact that Mum has never tried to get in touch with me, yet she's never said a word. How many letters has Mum sent? When did she send the first one?

And what sort of friend is Tasha to keep this from me?

68

I search the house, determined to find the rest of the letters, if Tasha hasn't destroyed them, that is. I'm guessing that she would hide them out of reach, not wanting Ryan to get his hands on them, so I start with the kitchen cupboards that run along the top of the main wall. I can see several boxes piled up there, so I stand on a chair and look through those.

There's lots of bills – to my surprise Tasha seems to be having money problems – letters from the school, photos and leaflets. Nothing addressed to me. Nothing from my mum. Surely she hasn't destroyed them? She couldn't. Wouldn't. She has no right, they're my property. Anger is welling inside me at the thought of Mum reaching out, trying to get in touch with me, saying she's sorry, and getting no reply because of Tasha's deceit. How could my best friend keep this from me?

I work my way through all the cupboards and drawers. Nothing. I go into the lounge next, search through the drawers of the dresser. Nothing. Then I go upstairs into Tasha's bedroom. I feel a bit guilty as I start going through her chest of drawers, then her bedside cabinet, then move on to her wardrobe. I push the guilt away. I've got a right to find my letters.

There are several shoes piled along the bottom of the wardrobe, mainly trainers, which are Tasha's favourite footwear. She has pairs in various designs and colours. I stand on tiptoe to reach the wardrobe shelf, knocking a couple of shoes onto the floor. I pick them up, notice one of them has a discoloured patch on the front – it's a wonder Tasha hasn't thrown it out, she's really fussy about her trainers.

I put them back and search all along the shelf. Nothing. I sit down on the floor. Tasha must have destroyed them. I'll never know what my mum wrote. And I'll never forgive Tasha for this.

I hadn't faced up to how much I missed my mum until now, now I realise that she's been trying to get in touch.

From my vantage point on the floor, I spot a big drawer in the base of Tasha's bed. I pull it open and see that it's full of underwear. A quick mooch through doesn't reveal any letters. I go round to the other side of the bed, there's a drawer there too, and this is full of jumpers, all neatly folded. Tasha likes to be organised. As I shut the drawer back up I see a brown envelope peeping out from underneath it.

Puzzled, I pull it out. It's a Jiffy bag. My hand is shaking as I reach inside and pull out several letters and cards in my mum's handwriting. Christmas cards, birthday cards, all addressed to me or Liam. I sit there reading through the messages of love, asking for forgiveness. Then I come to the very first one, sent a couple of weeks after we'd left Arran. My eyes fill with tears as I read the words.

My dear Sarah,

I'm so, so sorry, darling. Of course I didn't mean what I said. You're a wonderful mother and I would never take Liam from

*you. I regretted my words the very next day and was distraught
when we got up and I read your letter. Bill drove me to the ferry
so that I could tell you how sorry I was and beg you not to go
but it was too late, the ferry had already set off.*

*I should never have said those terrible things but please
understand that it was the shock of seeing Liam so traumatised,
the bruise on your wrist. Worrying what could have happened
to you both. You both could have been killed, darling, you read
about these awful incidents all the time. I'm not saying this to
make you feel guilty, I know that you adore Liam and are
already punishing yourself enough. I'm saying it so that you
understand why I was so cruel. It was the shock. Please forgive
me and let me know that you are both okay. I love you so much.*

Mum xxx

Tears spill down my cheeks as I finish reading the letter,
and the memories of that day come flooding back. Mum was
right, I was a bad mother. I knew that Dylan was violent and
still took Liam with me to meet him. I should have walked away,
kept my son safe. Dylan could have turned on me in front of my
son, and as it was Liam had nightmares for weeks. I've never
forgiven myself and have done my very best to keep him safe
ever since.

Until now.

Suddenly I recall how upset Tasha had been when I left for
Arran with Liam, she'd seemed furious that I was leaving her.

She's always been a bit obsessive. She's a good friend but
sometimes she's a bit too consuming. Did she hide the letters
because she didn't want me to go back and live on Arran?

I take the envelope downstairs, wondering what to do.
Tasha won't be home for a few hours yet, and she'll have the
boys with her. I don't want to stay here with her after this, and I

can't go back to Charlie's. I make myself a strong cup of coffee and sit down to think.

When I go to get my phone out of my handbag, I spot the badge that my landlord had found in the bathroom. I don't know why I kept it, but it had seemed important. It's quite a distinctive badge. You would think that if anyone lost it, they would search for it, because the trainers wouldn't have been cheap and they wouldn't be able to wear them with one badge missing.

An image of Tasha's trainer with the discoloured patch on the front pops into my mind.

I push my chair back and dash up the stairs to Tasha's bedroom, pulling the trainers out of the wardrobe one by one. And there it is.

I put the badge on the discoloured patch. It fits perfectly. I rummage through all the other trainers and find the matching one, which still has the badge fixed firmly in place.

Tasha had been in my bathroom lots of times, I remind myself. She is my best friend.

These are expensive trainers though, and Tasha would have told me that she'd lost the badge. She would have made me search everywhere for it.

The only reason she wouldn't tell me is if she didn't want me to know.

And she must have lost it recently otherwise I would have found it when I was cleaning the bathroom.

It was Tasha, my best friend, who flooded out the bathroom.

69

ALICE

I let myself into the house. I have it all to myself, Charlie is at work and the girls are at nursery and school. It's so good to have things back to normal. I know that Charlie misses Sarah, and her son, but that woman was trouble, I could see that from the beginning. And now, thanks to her, Lynn has come back and is stirring up even more trouble, along with Claire.

All I want is to look after my son and my granddaughters without everyone else interfering. Is that too much to ask?

I wish that Charlie and Crystal had stayed together, they were such a well-suited couple. Crystal was so unhappy with Brandon, and Charlie was on his own when Lynn left, and I kept hoping they would get back together. Then just as Crystal and Brandon finally split up, Charlie moved Sarah in. Sarah isn't good enough for my Charlie, whereas Crystal is like a daughter to me.

I go into the kitchen and put my bag down. There's something I need to do today. Something Charlie should have done but he believes Sarah, still loves her. Well, I wasn't taken in by her. I didn't trust her with my special girls and today I'm going to find proof that I was right. Sarah was a danger to them, just like Lynn was.

I go into the study and switch on the desktop still standing on Kenneth's desk. Charlie never uses it, he prefers his laptop, but Kenneth always used it. The screen springs into life and I scan the icons on the screen. There it is. I click onto the CCTV that Kenneth installed a few years ago, worried about a spate of burglaries in the area. It only shows the front and back of the house, but maybe that will be enough to prove that Sarah left the children in the garden unsupervised, or something else that will prove to Charlie what she isn't worth him moping over her.

I trawl through the images: Sarah bringing the children home from school, the children playing in the garden, and my heart shoots into my throat as Daisy almost falls off the top of the slide. She could have hurt herself then and Sarah is nowhere in sight. Just as I suspected she sent them out to play and left them, so that she could have a bit of peace and quiet.

I flick through the images of the following days, stopping at a night-time one. A shadowy figure bending down by Sarah's car. I check the date on the screen. The date Sarah left. The night she crashed. The night she said someone had tampered with her brakes.

I zoom in on the face. It's blurry but there's no mistaking who it is. And they have a key fob for the electric gates. I gave it to them myself when I lived here.

If this comes out, they will go to prison. I can't let that happen. I click onto the image and the cursor hovers over the delete button.

70

SARAH

I pack our things. I can't stay here any longer. I trusted Tasha, thought she was my best friend, but she's let me down, lied to me, and I'm pretty sure it was to keep me close to her. I recall the times I found her friendship overpowering, stifling.

Why would she flood our bathroom though? I remember how angry she was that I'd gone to live with Charlie, saying I should have come to her. Is that why she did it?

What else has she done? My mind goes back to Alice's expensive Murano bowl. Had Tasha moved that, hoping it would be broken and Charlie would be so furious that me and Liam would have to leave? She kept telling me to come to her if anything went wrong. Another thought flashes into my mind. Was it Tasha who wrote 'TRAMP' on the boot of my car? Had she been plotting to drive me away from Charlie so that I would live with her?

I shake my head. That's insane.

Someone tried to kill us, they interfered with the brakes of my car. I know I can't prove it but I'm certain of it. Surely that wasn't Tasha? How could it be, the car was parked on Charlie's drive and no one can get in through those gates without the fob. It couldn't have been Charlie, he came after us, he saved Liam's life. He wanted us back.

So I'm back to Alice. She wanted Lynn gone, and she wanted me gone too. She's the obvious suspect but will I ever be able to prove it?

My head is aching with it all. I need to get away, give myself space to think. Part of me wants to stay until Tasha comes home and confront her, but then Liam will be here and I don't want to do this in front of him. He's been through enough. He and Ryan are like brothers, and now he's going to lose him too.

I pack everything in the boot of the hire car the insurance company provided for me, intending to pick Liam up from school then drive away from all this madness. I go into the house to get the last case and come out to find Tasha parked in the driveway.

'Where are you going?'

I stare at her. 'What are you doing home from work early?'

'I saw you on the doorbell camera.' She shows me her phone. 'Why are you sneaking off without telling me?'

I glare at her. 'A Christmas card came for me this morning. From my mum.'

The colour drains from Tasha's face.

'Mum said that she's sorry and that she's sent me lots of other letters and cards. She wanted to know why I haven't replied.'

'I can explain. Please can we go inside and talk?'

I pause. I have an hour before I need to pick up Liam and I really want to know why she kept my mum's letters from me. And what the badge from her trainer was doing in our bathroom.

'Okay, but whatever you say, I'm still leaving,' I tell her.

She flinches at this then nods resignedly. We go into the

house and I close the front door but something urges me not to click the latch.

'I didn't tell you because I wanted to protect you. Have you forgotten how horrible your mum was to you?' We're in the kitchen now and Tasha is standing with her back against the work surface. I'm standing near the door, a few feet away from her.

'Protect me from my own mum? I found the letters, all of them, Tasha. She wrote to me straight away, she was so sorry about what she said. She was begging me to forgive her. You opened and read them all but didn't show them to me. How could you be so cruel?'

Anger flares in Tasha's eyes. 'You've been snooping in my bedroom. How bloody dare you!'

'How bloody dare you conceal my mum's letters?'

Tears suddenly brim in Tasha's eyes. 'I did it for us, for our friendship. I didn't want to lose you, Sarah, like I did before. I thought if you knew your mum had contacted you, you might go off to Arran again.'

'And is that why you broke into my house and turned on the taps to flood out the bathroom? And don't deny it! I saw your trainer with the missing badge. I know it was you.'

Tasha bursts into tears. 'Okay, yes, it was me. We promised to always be there for each other, to put our friendship before men. And then you started mooning over Charlie. I was scared you were going to ditch me for him.'

'But you have Caleb!' I point out. 'And it was the flood in the bathroom that made me move into Charlie's so that doesn't make sense.'

'You were supposed to move in with me!' she shouts, pointing at me now. 'I told you that you could come to me. That's why I did it, so we could live together and then you'd forget all about Charlie. Then you went and ruined it all. You moved in with him and you hardly knew him.'

I stare at her, speechless, barely able to take in her words. She's ugly crying now, tears down her face, snot everywhere. She takes a tissue out of her pocket and wipes her nose. 'I've always been there for you. Always. But you always put me second. When you split up with Todd, you went to stay with your mum instead of coming to me. And when you came back I said you could stay here as long as you wanted but you couldn't get your own place quick enough. Then we got close again, until Charlie. We promised to never let a man come between us but you broke that promise.'

'You have Caleb,' I point out again. 'You were going away with him for the weekend.'

She shakes her head. 'I *had* Caleb. I was never really into him. That's why we finished. That's why I finished with Jay.' She takes a step towards me, her eyes imploring. 'It's only ever been you, Sarah. I've been waiting for you to feel the same way.'

I back away, stunned. 'What? But you're not...'

'I'm bi, Sarah.' She's walking nearer now and I'm still backing away. 'I've loved you since the moment I saw you, Sarah. I'd do anything for you.' She looks at me, love shining out of her eyes. 'We could be so good together. We could rent a bigger house and bring up Liam and Ryan together, they're already like brothers.'

'I don't... I'm not...' I stammer. What the hell is happening here? Tasha is my best friend, she's never shown any sign of looking at me as anything other than a friend. And I definitely don't look at her that way. I shake my head. I can't believe what she's saying.

She takes my hand and fixes her eyes on my face. 'It doesn't matter if you don't love me the same way. That's okay. We can still have a beautiful life living together as two single mums. We can help and support each other. We could all be so happy.'

I pull my hand away and gape at her as things start to slip into place. 'It was you who tampered with my car, wasn't it? You tried to kill me!' My voice rises to a screech. I turn to run out of the kitchen door but Tasha is before me. She slams it shut, her back against it.

My heart is racing in my chest as I face my former best friend and realise that I don't know her at all, and I'm genuinely scared of what she's capable of.

71

'Sarah! Are you in there?'

Charlie. Oh, thank goodness! 'Charlie! Help! I'm in the kitchen,' I shout. 'Help me!'

The handle turns but Tasha is still backed against the door. Charlie pushes harder and the door flies open with such force that Tasha is thrown out of the way.

He strides in and looks at Tasha sprawled out on the floor, then to me. 'What's going on?'

I run over to him, stand by him, pointing at Tasha, who is getting to her feet. 'It was Tasha. She sneaked into my house and caused the bathroom to flood,' I tell him. 'She's crazy. She thinks she's in love with me.' Charlie looks incredulous as I continue. 'I think she was the one who messed with my brakes too. She tried to kill me and Liam.' I put my hand up to my mouth, choking back the sobs as I glare at Tasha. 'I can't believe it! I thought you were my friend.'

'I didn't touch your brakes!' Tasha protests. She scrambles to her knees and looks at me imploringly. 'I would never hurt you, Sarah. Why would I? I told you, I love you. Besides you were both coming to me.'

'Who knows why? You're crazy! I've no idea what you're capable of,' I snap, my voice shaking.

'She's telling the truth, love. That's why I came to see you.' Charlie puts his arm around my shoulders, pulling me into him. His voice is thick, heavy. 'You were right, someone did tamper with your brakes, and I know who it was now. So do the police. They're questioning her now.'

'Her?' My eyes fix on his ashen face. 'It was Alice? Your mum?'

He looks shocked. 'Hell no! I know my mum is possessive and it's her fault Lynn left, but she wouldn't do anything like that. She wouldn't try to kill someone.'

'Who then?'

His eyes meet mine. 'It was Crystal.'

72

Tasha scrambles to her feet. 'I told you that it wasn't me. I would never hurt you, Sarah. All I've ever wanted is to keep you safe.'

I glare at her coldly. 'No, you want to control my life and you'll do anything to stop me getting close to anyone else.' I look up at Charlie, who still has his arm around me. 'Can we go outside and talk? I have to pick up Liam soon.'

'Don't go. Please hear me out!' Tasha shouts. 'If you just listen to me, then you'll understand.'

'I never want to speak to you again,' I tell her as I walk out with Charlie.

We stand by my courtesy car and I listen as Charlie tells me how Alice was still certain I was up to no good so had checked the CCTV cameras. 'Dad put one at the front and back but I'd forgotten all about them. I use the doorbell camera on my phone. The cameras are linked to the desktop computer, which I never use,' he explains. 'Mum saw Crystal bending down by the front of your car the night you ran away. It's dark and the image is a bit blurred but it looks like she is tampering with the car.' He shakes his head ruefully. 'Mum gave Crystal keys to the gate and house when she lived here – she and Crystal used to pop into each other's houses all the time.' He wipes the back of his hand across his forehead. 'I told you they were close.'

I feel sick. I reach out and put my hand on the bonnet of the Fiesta to steady myself. 'Crystal tried to kill us? Why would she do such a terrible thing?'

'To get back with me. Apparently she's still in love with me.' He runs his hand down the side of his neck. 'When Lynn left we got close again. I've only ever looked on Crystal as a friend, but it seems she still carried a torch for me. And she recently split up with Brandon so she was hoping she could get back together with me.' He reaches out and touches my arm. 'I'm so sorry, Sarah. I can't forgive myself for not seeing what was going on. You and Liam could have been killed.' His shoulders slump. 'And there was all the trouble my own daughter and mother were causing for you. How could I have been so blind? Mum drove Lynn away, and she tried to do the same to you.' I can hear the anguish in his voice.

'It must have been a shock for Alice, seeing Crystal tamper with my car.' I'm actually surprised that Alice told him, she adores Crystal, but I don't say that.

'It was. She admitted that her first instinct was to destroy the evidence – you and Liam had recovered and she didn't want Crystal to go to jail. Then she thought about it and realised that Crystal is unhinged, that Lynn had sworn her car was tampered with too and that could have been Crystal's doing as well. She was scared what Crystal would do now that Lynn was back so she showed the police the CCTV footage. When the police questioned Crystal, she admitted that she'd also tampered with the brakes on Lynn's car.' He looks so grim. 'She's obsessed with me.'

Like Tasha is with me. She hasn't tried to kill me though, has she? Although one of us could have been badly hurt when the kitchen ceiling collapsed.

A couple of things are still bugging me. 'Was it Alice or Crystal who took the cranberry crystal bowl out of the cabinet and put it in the kitchen cupboard, do you think, hoping to get me in more trouble? And who wrote that horrible word on my car?'

He looks at me steadily. 'Both of them were Crystal. She's confessed to everything. She wrote on your car boot when you were parked at the school. And she sneaked in the house when you were out buying stuff for the Hallowe'en party and moved the bowl. She was hoping you would use it, and that Mum would be mad. She didn't push Tasha though. She said that Tasha pretended to fall into you.'

'I didn't mean to break it, just knock it a little so that Alice and Charlie would be mad at you and you'd leave and live with me,' Tasha says plaintively. She followed us outside and has been standing behind me, listening to it all. 'I'm sorry, Sarah. Please forgive me. I did it for us, so we could be together.'

I'm reeling from all this. There's so much to take in. I can't believe that Tasha, my best friend, the person who was my rock for so long, has done all these things. Hidden the letters from my mum, destroyed our home, tried to drive me out of Charlie's home, all supposedly in the name of love. I'm so angry and hurt. On top of everything else that's happened I've lost my best friend.

'There's no us. I was never interested in you in that way. And I never want to see you again,' I tell her. 'You were supposed to be my best friend and all you've done is cause trouble for me.'

Tasha lets out a huge sob and drops to her knees, putting her head in her hands, wailing loudly. I turn away, I can't bear to look at her after everything she's done.

'Where are you going now?' Charlie asks. 'Your house isn't ready to move into yet, is it?'

'I've cancelled it. I phoned the landlord after I found the

letters and told him that I've changed my mind. Thankfully no money has exchanged hands yet.' I don't trust Tasha and don't want to live anywhere near her. 'I'm going to stay with my mum and stepdad over Christmas and decide what to do. The insurance company said I can take the car until my claim is sorted out.'

Tasha lets out a big sob then gets up, runs inside and slams the door shut. I'm fighting back the tears too. I've lost my best friend, Charlie and his two adorable daughters as well as my home.

I tell Charlie how I phoned my mum when I finished reading the letters and explained what had happened. 'She was so pleased to hear from me. She said that she'd found Tasha's address on the back of a birthday card envelope she'd sent to Liam, which is why she'd contacted her as she thought she might know where we'd gone and could pass her letters on to me. We talked and talked, then she asked me to come over for Christmas so I agreed.' Tears spring to my eyes as I recall our conversation and how happy my mum was to hear from me. 'Mum can't wait to see us again, and I know that Liam will be excited to see her and Bill. He's missed them so much.'

'Will you be coming back here?' Charlie asks me softly.

I shake my head. 'Too much has happened. I think me and Liam need a fresh start.' I look at him steadily. I know none of this is his fault and I love him and the girls, but I can't be with Charlie, I can't risk anything else happening. We've been through enough. 'We might even stay there permanently,' I tell him. 'I've given notice at work although Maddie and Tom are keeping my job open for a couple of months to give me time to make up my mind as to what I want to do.'

'I'm sorry it didn't work out between us. I'll miss you,' Charlie says.

'I'm sorry too,' I tell him. At the end of the day, he's just as much a victim in all this as I am. I'm sad at losing him and the girls, they'd become such a big part of my life. And Liam's. I have to break all this to him when I pick him up from school and I know he'll be upset, but what choice do I have? I can't stay here after everything that's happened. I need to get away, get my head straight, come to terms with it all. And Liam will be happy to see his nan and grandad again. Mia and Daisy have their mum back too. It will all work out.

Me and Charlie hug then I break away, open my car door and get in. I don't look back, I daren't. I have to be strong. I'm going to pick up Liam then we're going to see his nan and grandad. I don't know what I'll do after that, but I do know that whatever happens, my son will always come first.

A LETTER FROM KAREN

Dear Reader,

Thank you so much for choosing to read *Don't Trust Him*. If you enjoyed it and want to keep up to date with all my latest releases, just sign up at the following link. Your email address will never be shared and you can unsubscribe at any time.

www.bookouture.com/karen-king

I always think of my psychological suspense books as being the dark side of relationships, where instead of a happy ever after, things go wrong. It's exciting when you meet someone that you click with and it's easy to get carried away with those heady feelings, especially if they profess to feel the same way. But how do you know that you can trust them, that they don't have a dark secret? I believe that you don't really know someone until you live with them, but even then they could hide something from you.

The idea for this plot came from a scene in my head of a group of mums in the school playground, all vying with each other to get the attention of a hot single dad. He so clearly adores his two daughters, and everyone thinks that he must be kind and caring to look after them on his own since his wife left. But what if his wife didn't simply walk out to be with someone else, as he says, what if she was driven out? What if she doesn't come back to see her daughters because she can't? How do you know if someone is telling you the truth, or if you can really trust them? Sometimes you only find out when it's too late.

I hope you loved *Don't Trust Him*, and if you did, I would be very grateful if you could write a review. I'd love to hear what you think, and it makes such a difference helping new readers to discover one of my books for the first time.

I love hearing from my readers – you can get in touch through social media, or my website.

Thanks,

Karen

www.karenkingauthor.com

 facebook.com/KarenKingAuthor
 x.com/karen_king

ACKNOWLEDGEMENTS

There are a lot of things that go on in the background when writing a book, and a lot of people who help with the process. I would like to thank all the Bookouture editing team for their expertise and support, and particular thanks to my amazing editor, Rhianna Louise, for her invaluable input and constructive advice. A special thanks to Lisa Horton for creating such a stunning cover. And to the fabulous social media team of Kim Nash, Noelle Holten, Sarah Hardy and Jess Readett, who go above and beyond in supporting and promoting our work and making the Bookouture Author Lounge such an enjoyable place to be. You guys are amazing! Also to the other Bookouture authors who are always willing to offer support, encouragement and advice. I'm so grateful to be part of such a lovely, supportive team. Thanks also to the Facebook groups of The Savvy Writers' Snug and Trauma Fiction for answering my research questions.

I'm indebted to all the bloggers and authors who support me, review my books and give me space on their blog tours. I am lucky to know so many incredible people in the book world and appreciate you all.

Massive thanks to my lovely husband, Dave, for all the love and laughter you bring to my life, answering my numerous questions and reading through my final manuscript to help me catch those troublesome typos. And to my family and friends who all support me so much. Special thanks to my brother

Gary, who lives on the beautiful Isle of Arran, for the chats to help refresh my memory as it's been many years since I visited.

Finally, a heartfelt thanks to you, my readers, for buying and reviewing my books, and for your wonderful messages telling me how much you've enjoyed reading them. Without your support there would be no more books. Thank you. Xx

PUBLISHING TEAM

Turning a manuscript into a book requires the efforts of many people. The publishing team at Bookouture would like to acknowledge everyone who contributed to this publication.

Audio
Alba Proko
Melissa Tran
Sinead O'Connor

Commercial
Lauren Morrissette
Hannah Richmond
Imogen Allport

Data and analysis
Mark Alder
Mohamed Bussuri

Editorial
Rhianna Louise
Melissa Tran

Copyeditor
DeAndra Lupu

www.ingramcontent.com/pod-product-compliance
Ingram Content Group UK Ltd.
Pitfield, Milton Keynes, MK11 3LW, UK
UKHW040955250325
456693UK00002B/114